What other wri

In a time-travel
himself, Craven and
history, geography, a
use, crafting a fast-paced and thematically rich narrative that will stay with you long after you turn the last page. —David Bowles, author of *The Smoking Mirror*

With a suspense-packed time travel plot, toggling between Russia's 1990 invasion of Azerbaijan and the 1221 Mongolian invasion led by Genghis Khan, *Parallel Hours* will be good reading for those who like science fiction as well as readers of both historical novels and mainstream fiction. —Dede Fox, author of *Postcards Home*

If you were to go back in time eight centuries, you couldn't imagine all the troubles you'd face. But you wouldn't have to because Jerry Craven and Andrew Geyer have imagined them for you. The adventures in *Parallel Hours* are so breathtaking that you won't have time to realize how much you miss the future.
—Jerry Bradley, author of *South of the Boredom*

In this mesmerizing mixture of historical and science fiction, Craven and Geyer have created a world where a window connects the years 1221 and 1990. Through its compelling storytelling and harmonious blending of two accomplished writers' talents, *Parallel Hours* is an experience you should not miss. —Gretchen Johnson, author of *Single in Southeast Texas*

An ill-matched trio find themselves transported to 1221, where their encounters with political turmoil in thirteenth-century Baku, Genghis Kahn, and the dangers of travel along the Silk Road to Constantinople will keep the reader both amused and on edge. —Richard Moseley, fiction editor for *Amarillo Bay*

In the grand tradition of *The Time Bandits* and *Back to the Future*, Craven and Geyer offer up a fast-paced time-bender through the near east. A fun read. —Melvin Sterne, author of *The Shoeshine Boy*

The Maiden's tower in Baku before Genghus Khan and
his golden horde destroyed most of the city

Parallel Hours

Parallel Hours

Jerry Craven and Andrew Geyer

ANGELINA RIVER PRESS

Copyright © 2017 Jerry Craven and Andrew Geyer
all rights reserved
Angelina River Press
Fort Worth, Texas
This is a work of fiction that contains fictionalized presentations of historical as well as totally imaginary people who lived and traveled along the Silk Road in both the 13th and 20th centuries.

ISBN: 978-0-9987364-2-6
Library of Congress Control Number: 2017950204

For those who ponder history
and wonder
what it would be like to travel back

History belongs to those who make it.
—Chuck Greenberg

Part One: Into the Past

Chapter 1

When the troops landed down the beach and began firing weapons, Tejmur's first response was to curse them for coming on the day he had perfected his time window. He raised the flask he had been cradling in his lap and tilted it up, holding it against the silver disk of the full moon. The moon had emerged golden from the Caspian fogbank while the sun settled behind him. And he had sat on his park bench sipping vodka in celebration of his great discovery while imagining the moon zipping across the sky beyond Armenia, beyond the Black Sea. The Soviet invasion had interrupted his solitary moment of triumph. "Shoot me, hah," he said, and gave the bottle a shake. I should run, he thought, not sit here pretending to be brave. Such bravery, Tejmur knew, had to be born of vodka; though he had little enough of it inside him at the moment—bravery, that is. He had, he discovered as he took the last swallow, the dregs of a small bottle of vodka in his belly and his blood. The flask had held only two small drinks, he thought: not enough to get him through the night. No matter. He had another flask of vodka in his jacket pocket. With an indifferent grimace, he tossed the empty bottle into the water's edge, then put a hand into his pants pocket to feel for the coins that the time window had allowed him to take—with the help of the gypsy woman, Papusza—from the distant past.

The roar of engines from the approaching landing craft seemed to fracture the water. Vibrations rolled onto the land to bounce against buildings behind him, shaking the park bench where he had made up his mind to spend the night. Time to go, he decided; but he remained seated and kept fingering the coins. So lovely, he thought, these silver disks, many with two heads on one side and Zoroastrian fire worshipers on the other. A fistful of the ancient silver was worth a small fortune. The coins were much like the one he had once dug from a dacha garden outside the city. Those ones in his pocket looked new, but they had been made centuries ago.

"So I die rich, and a nobody," he muttered with a chuckle, and envisioned it: the landing craft crashing against the shore, the front of the boat falling open and Soviet troops running out. One would fire a handgun at him, maybe a rifle, to make him crumple in a bloody heap on the park bench. And the time window? he asked himself. Its metal sides, disconnected and telescoped down, rested inside a case designed for holding a camera tripod. The control box for the time window was in there as well, along with an even smaller black box that allowed Tejmur to open a sort of peephole onto the same parallel hour that the larger time window was set for. The carrying case sat on the bench beside him. Maybe the soldiers would shoot the case, and that would be the end of so much possibility.

The soldier who shoots me, Tejmur thought, will be a boy with blue eyes and golden hair; and I will die, killed by one of Gorbachev's troops.

The park bench vibrated with a still and subtle sound, and shapes appeared in the moonlight between Tejmur and the fogbank, shapes that assembled themselves into huge floating boxes. Tejmur stood, picked up the carrying case, and told himself he would hate to die from a bullet fired by a Soviet soldier. Death should come in another form, later. Or maybe, earlier.

He paused to run a loving hand over the carrying case that held the time window. The idea of putting off death until earlier amused him, so he started up the hill toward the garden that the gypsy woman, Papusza, had told him was one of the places she sometimes hid to spend the night.

Behind him came the clank of more landing craft, sounds that set him running. From farther around the shore of Baku, just beyond the Maiden's Tower, came the biting claps of pistol shots. They are shooting the people they catch in the street, Tejmur thought—gypsies like Papusza, and others who wandered into the city to sleep in the doorways and alleys, bums and the unemployed, maybe even an engineer or two . . . like me. And why not? Hadn't Tejmur himself been on the water's edge just minutes before? Others like him could be on such benches beside the sea. He considered taking the cap from the other vodka bottle in his pocket for a quick drink. Something just to warm and settle me, he told himself. But fear overruled the impulse, and he continued up the hill.

Would Papusza be back there, Tejmur wondered, on the Caspian's shore and in danger? Not likely, for she was a survivor who had walked many kilometers to Baku from Karabakh so she could escape the civil strife—and resulting ethnic cleansing—stirred up by the ethnic Russians in that region. She could fend for herself. Besides, she was a woman, a pretty one. And she had some of the ancient coins. A three-time winner, Tejmur told himself, that's what she was: pretty, female, and rich.

While clutching the places where his ribs protested into cramps, he ran past the huge mosaic of Lenin that was without a face because a mob had chipped it away to leave the mosaic on the cement building wounded, a gray mass where the communist mastermind had looked down upon citizens of Baku for close to a hundred years of Soviet rule. Tejmur ran with protesting lungs past the mansion of the oil mogul who had lived ninety years before and then died at the hands of the Bolsheviks. Run, run, he thought, to the garden in the old school for girls where Papusza had told him that she hid at night from Azerbaijani police.

But Tejmur slowed, then stopped, gasping for air.

A glance down the hill confirmed what he feared: military craft spitting into the shallow Caspian their loads of Gorbachev's soldiers sent to slap the city, to make the Azerbaijanis pay for rejecting Mother Russia. In that moment Tejmur hated the Russians with their fair skins and light eyes and terrible sense of justice that demanded vengeance upon break-away peoples with dark skins and black eyes. People like me, he thought. And if I should bleed my life away from a Russian bullet, where would my treasures be then, those ancient coins snatched through my time window from a long-ago merchant of the Asperon Peninsula? Stolen, that's where, pillaged by a soldier. And worse, the science that allowed me to build the window would be gone, lost to the world forever.

From down the hill came the sounds of men slogging ashore and the sound of boots on cement—perhaps, Tejmur thought, pounding the very place he had decided to spend the night in solitary celebration with his two bottles of vodka. Bent almost double from pain caused by unaccustomed running, he limped crab-like up the hill.

The soldiers will run faster, he thought. Looking back he saw dark shapes popping fire from their hands to terrify, and to exact a terrible price for disloyalty in bleeding flesh. They syncopated death with the rhythm of their running boots. Cries of the street people reached him, the poor and beggars and drunks who knew nothing of Gorbachev or the Soviets. By the time he reached the gate to what once was a girl's school, army boots pounded in the shadows behind him. They had reached the home of the dead oil mogul.

A shiver of fear shot through Tejmur when the garden gate wouldn't open. He pulled again on the wrought iron handle. But the great wrought iron gate stood locked and stubborn and too high to climb. He yanked desperately at a huge Soviet lock snapped into a hasp. So this is where I die, he thought, and slumped in despair against the gate.

To his surprise, the gate pushed open. He almost laughed in knowing the Soviet lock was a hoax, a show. It locked out nothing—that is, nothing that knew to push instead of pull on the handle.

Cacophonous sounds came from behind, just around a corner. "Boots," he whispered, "and pistol shots." But where to hide in the courtyard, a garden where moonlight illuminated statues that were heads only and huge, all three of them cast from brass. One was Narimanov, the friend of Stalin whom the dictator had sent to the island of execution in Baku Bay to stand him unblindfolded before a firing squad. Narimanov's face in brass stood as tall as Tejmur, taller right then because of Tejmur's need to bend over and clutch ribs unused to running. The other faces loomed silver-brass in the moonlight, one a woman poet who spoke magic words in her poetry, the other a playwright turned into a silent two-meter brass head glinting metallic in the Baku night while soldiers approached the gate.

The old school for girls wore a quarried limestone facade and held glass windows reaching up three stories to make two walls of the garden. A third wall ran three meters up to the street above and a handrail, where in happier times people might look into the garden of the heads. They could see Narimanov and the poet and the playwright as celebrities turned into sculptured art. Beside the fourth wall grew a fig tree, and rose bushes that still held their late summer green. Tejmur ran to the fig tree and crawled underneath it to the wall, only to find moonlight flickering over him instead of shadows. Anyone entering the garden would see him for sure.

In a panic, he crept between the wall and the roses where thorns snagged his jacket and pants, and scratched his hands. He could see through the leaves and the nubby remains of roses, and he thought of the Azeri name for rose hips: *it burun*. Dog noses. In the dark they did resemble dog noses, Tejmur thought. He liked it that he could be thus amused in the face of death.

Shadow soldiers ran by the gate. Two of them pushed through the gate and into the garden even as Tejmur dug deeper into the roses. One thing Tejmur had to admit about the Russians—they always seemed to know when to push and when to pull.

Then, to Tejmur's horror, a cat he hadn't seen suddenly yowled at his presence.

One of the soldiers, barely inside the gate, lifted an arm and fired with spurts of light leaping from the barrel of his weapon.

Chapter 2

Bullets slapped the wall close to Tejmur's head, and tiny fragments of rock peppered his face. The cat ran from the bushes. It screeched and rolled as bullets jerked it this way and that, and the soldier laughed. "There's a dead Azerbaijani rebel," one said in Russian. "Though it happens to be only a cat."

"It was a cat," another laughed. "Now it's a lump of hot, red fur."

"Look," the first soldier said. "Statues of the Turkish pigs," and both soldiers fired again, pinging the statues and sending sparks flying into the night. As if their weapons could kill brass heads, Tejmur thought with contempt. Then the soldiers were gone in a clanging of the gate.

"They'll be back," a voice whispered, a familiar one.

"Papusza?" Tejmur looked around, seeing no one. But her voice was close.

"I watched you fumble with the gate," Papusza said. "And I whispered for you to push it, but my voice was lost in the sound of gunfire."

Amazing, Tejmur thought. The gypsy woman was hiding right beside me, and I didn't see her. Or maybe not so amazing. His entire attention had been focused on the men with the guns. But now he turned and looked for Papusza. Just hours before, she had climbed through his time window into the past to fetch the coins that now rode heavy in his pocket. And here she was again, trying to help him escape the Soviet scourge that was even now bloodying Baku.

Thinking of all the help Papusza had given him, Tejmur remembered the first time he had seen her. It had been in the park beside the Caspian Sea. He had recognized her as a gypsy by the bright reds and greens of her rural gypsy garb. Over the last few days he had talked to her several times on the park bench by the water, bought bread for her, and peanut butter—something she had never tasted. She'd clearly thought he courted her for sex, and she played coy with flirtatious smiles that amused him. On his fourth day of meeting with her, he had brought her bread and tea. She sat on the bench, broke a piece of the bread, and took a bite. "What is it," she'd asked, "that you want of me?"

The question was timed well, for just the day before Tejmur had used the peephole—opened with an eyepiece on the smaller control box—to look across the centuries and watch a long-dead dealer in carpets count his money and then hide it. Tejmur sat beside the gypsy woman, looking out to sea, pretending he had not already decided to trust her with the secret of his invention. He needed money to continue his research. To live, even. His government pay had stopped with the country's break from the Soviets, even though he still had access to his office at the power plant where the much bulkier and more powerful master chronoton was located. The master chronoton was the time manipulation machine that the smaller portable time window, and the

15

even smaller peephole, ran as adjuncts to.

"I have a window," he said, "that can carry you across centuries to a place where a man dead for almost eight hundred years has stashed some silver coins. I want you to retrieve the money."

She nodded. "You think I'm a thief because I'm a gypsy."

"I think you're clever enough to help us both. We'll divide the silver. You'll be pleased."

"I take eighty percent, you twenty."

"Split. You get half, and half for me. Or no deal."

She munched the bread, broke some to throw to the pigeons at her feet, and nodded.

It had been fortunate that the place they needed to open the window was nearby, in a narrow and ancient street that had long ago fallen out of general use. He led her there, took the carrying case from inside his jacket, opened it, and pulled out the four sides of the time window. These he telescoped to their full length and snapped them into a rectangle, then he leaned the frame against a brick wall in the alley. He plugged the larger black power box into his window and turned to her.

"There's a drop of half a meter, for the city has built up over the years. As you go through, grab this handle on the side of the window and pull it through with you. In case you forget, I'll tie a chord to your wrist and to the handle. You must take the window with you, along with that black box beside the handle."

"Take a window with me as I climb through it? This is impossible."

"The window opens only one way, and it stays open only until it sees you have climbed through."

"You mock me, expecting me to believe such nonsense as there being a window through time that watches me go through it."

"This is not mockery, and I know it sounds crazy. But this is science, a new kind of technology that only I—and now you—have access to. You must reset the window on the other side, for it opens only one direction for anything more massive than light to pass through. Once on the other side you cannot climb back, for the window will be closed to you. Reverse the time frame by flipping this switch, and the window will open to let you return. Bring the time window with you, when you come through again. But before returning, pick up the bag of silver coins."

"The act of thievery, yes. We have come back to that. But I don't steal."

"Again, the owner of those coins has been dead for centuries on this side of the window. So taking the coins will not make you a thief, unless you believe that taking money from a dead man is stealing."

"Then he is alive on the other side, and he will shoot me down like a dog for taking his money."

"There are no guns on the other side of the window. Besides, there is a slight lag in time—just a few hours—between the time of day the window opens in the present and the time of day it opens in the past. The reason for this does not concern you. All that matters is that it will be quite early in the morning beyond the window, and the owner will be asleep. Barely on the other side of the window you'll find a table, and under it a crate. Inside the crate is a bag made of carpet. Move it aside and take the leather pouch it hides. Then get back through my window. And do it fast, for the owner of the coins will take it amiss if he finds you with the pouch."

"But I thought you said that the man, who is dead now, will be asleep in the past."

"I know for certain that he is dead, now. But beyond this window, he's still alive, and I only believe that he is asleep. Knowing and believing are not the same thing. But it is a good bet that, in the past, he is a vicious man when it comes to guarding his wealth. Take the money and get back. Fast. Bring the window with you. It will close, locking him in the past and you in the present. You will be safe, and rich."

"You're either crazy, or you're kidding. And as much as I have enjoyed your company and your food, I think it is time for me to find another way to fill my belly."

Tejmur flipped the switch on the larger black box, and lights flickered on the sides of his metal window. He muttered a curse at the cheap Soviet battery the box contained and gave the box a shake. The tiny red LED lights came back on and glowed. The bricks in the metal frame of his window suddenly seemed to melt away. In their place, a small room appeared. In the room, a lamp burned low on a wooden table surrounded by rolls of carpet.

"You see?" Tejmur asked. "It is just as I told you. Now do you want to be rich, or not?"

Papusza climbed through the window, and it vanished as she snatched it with her. Tejmur activated a tiny window in the smaller black box at his side. The opening was indeed a peephole, but the eyepiece he looked through allowed him to see Papusza locate the sack of money. Just as she picked it up, a man shouted. The carpet dealer, Tejmur thought in a panic. He watched Papusza swing the sack of silver coins and strike the man's face, just below what Tejmur assumed to be a knife scar. The merchant stumbled back, and Papusza fingered the box on the side of the window. It opened, and Tejmur saw himself appear in the window's metal frame. It was an eerie feeling, seeing himself projected in the past and feeling himself physically inhabiting the present moment. Then Papusza scrambled through the window, appearing beside him as though she had stepped out of thin air. She dropped the telescoping sides of the closed time window and glared at Tejmur.

"He was neither dead nor asleep," Papusza said, "and he certainly didn't appreciate me taking his money. I barely escaped with my life."

"Now he is dead. I had the window set for a link I discovered for the year 1221."

"That makes no sense to me."

"It makes sense to me, though finding a parallel hour when the window will function is hard work."

"A parallel hour? How can hours be parallel? Time moves in a straight line. Even a child knows that."

"Time does no such thing. Its movements are circuitous, and complicated by many things: mass, velocity, gravity, the master chronoton machine that sits in my office . . . but again, such things are not your concern. The only thing that matters at this moment is that the money will not be missed. I read my history with care and chose a parallel hour right before the army of Genghis Khan sacked Baku, killing ninety percent of the population. So we took money from a man about to be murdered. That way, our impact on the flow of time would be minimal."

"That makes even less sense. And the idea that I have taken money from a man killed by Genghis Khan is absurd. What I do understand is that now I'm a thief, just as everyone believes me to be because I'm a gypsy. Yesterday I was not a thief. This morning when I awoke I was not a thief, though I was a gypsy. Now, thanks to you, I have become what everyone always says I am. A gypsy and a thief."

"Those who pick up items from the long dead are not thieves."

"You toy with words." She watched Tejmur dismantle the window and asked, "Is this magic?"

"Technology sufficiently advanced is indistinguishable from magic," he said.

"You're so prim. Comical." And she had laughed without genuine humor.

And now, lying against the wall of the girl's school, among *it burun* and rose thorns, Tejmur himself laughed without humor. It was almost inconceivable to Tejmur that so many things, of so much consequence, had happened in a single day: the final test of his time window, his sudden wealth as a result, and now the invasion of Azerbaijan by the Soviets. At least he knew that all his work on making tunnels through time was not for nothing. No one else who had ever lived could say the same.

"Papusza!" he whispered. "I can't see you. Where are you, Papusza?"

"Behind you. I see you too well, and I fear the soldiers will also. They'll find you, then me. When they come again into the garden, we'll both die unless . . ." her voice trailed off.

"Unless?" Tejmur prompted.

"You can open that magic window for us. We can run away into the fairy world of silver coins. Then you can open the window again in another place, somewhere far from Baku, and we can come back. Safe."

Such a stunningly simple plan, Tejmur thought. He remembered thinking of her as a survivor. Perhaps if he hadn't drained the last of that flask of vodka, he told himself, he would have thought up such an escape plan on his own. He sighed. Perhaps not. "It isn't a magic fairy world. It's the past, our past."

"When?"

She cuts to the core of the matter, Tejmur thought. Clever. "As I told you before. Almost eight hundred years ago."

Pistol shots rang out in the street on the hill above them, and from a distance came the chatter of automatic rifle fire.

"There," Papusza said, "beyond the fountain. A doorway where you can open your window for our escape. We must move fast. But—wait a moment!" The sound of running feet echoed in the night, and more gunfire. "Now."

Rose thorns snagged Tejmur's sleeves as he struggled from his hiding place. He took the carrying case, hunkered down, and followed the shadow that was the gypsy woman. In the doorway he fumbled for the metal rods and the larger black box.

"Hurry," she said.

"It's dark. The time frame for the window isn't something I can reset without being in my lab, so it will open into the year 1221. Remember: the time window is locked to a parallel hour in the past that's much earlier in the day than it is here and now. So when the window opens, it will still be daylight, and the Russians will see. They'll shoot."

"Stop whining. Open the window."

If the run up the hill didn't sober me up, Tejmur thought, this accursed fumbling in the dark will—especially with Russian weapons firing all over the city. He snapped together the sides of his window and leaned it against the wall.

"Someone is at the gate," Papusza hissed.

"When I flip this switch," Tejmur whispered, "those Russian soldiers will see a blast of light. So we must move quickly. Remember that there will be a drop, for Baku has built up over the centuries, and we are outside the ancient city." He gave the reluctant battery a shake, then fingered the switch on the box.

Afternoon light from the window filled the courtyard in the garden of the heads. Someone at the gate shouted in Russian. Bullets smacked into the wall close to Tejmur, and Papusza scrambled into the window.

Tejmur squeezed into the window after her. He heard running footsteps behind him as he grabbed the handle on the frame. Then he felt the soldier's body slam into him, pushing him through into the sunlight, and he fell less than a meter.

The soldier also fell, landing with a surprised grunt on top of Tejmur.

Chapter 3

Tejmur struggled to push the soldier from his chest.

The man squinted in the suddeness of the full sun. He leaped to his feet and swung his rifle around, pointing at nothing in particular. "What a fantastic trick, and so skillful," the man said in Russian that carried a heavy foreign accent. "How did you do it?"

"Tejmur is a powerful wizard," Papusza said. She sat on the hillside several meters away. To Tejmur, she looked quite unruffled. The ground around her was pebbled and devoid of vegetation, and not far from her stood some huge and jagged rocks. The hill fell away toward a walled fortress on the edge of what had to be the Caspian Sea, judging from the stiff breeze so typical of Baku. "Listen," Papusza said. "I hear voices nearby, whispering voices."

"I hear only the wind." Tejmur sat up.

"Tejmur, is it?" the soldier said. "And a wizard? That, of course is a gypsy lie, but a good one. I'm Masud and a soldier, not a wizard. How did you do this trick?"

"Trick?" Tejmur glanced above him, hoping to see the blackness of the twentieth-century Baku night through his window. But he saw only the blue sky of the distant past.

"Trick, yes," Masud said. "Making the night seem to be day, making me believe the buildings of your city have vanished. I once saw a magician make an entire elephant seem to disappear. But hiding streets and buildings? That's truly astonishing. And look. The sun. It's a bright light, right? Not the sun at all."

"It's no trick," Papusza said.

"Real magic, eh gypsy woman?" Masud eyed her colorful dress and frowned.

"Papusza, look." Tejmur spoke in despair. "We lost the window." He did a fast mental inventory of the parts needed to build another, took a look east at the medieval walled city just down the hill, and felt despair.

The year 1221 couldn't possibly supply him with the modern materials necessary for making another time window. He examined the huge wooden gate on the city wall and looked at the crude stone road running from the gate up the hill. The Maiden's Tower on the edge of the sea was more beautiful than he remembered, as if it were made from fresh-quarried rock. In his own time, Tejmur disliked the tower for its sooty walls, blackened by the air pollution from Soviet industries.

Tejmur looked west. From the history books he had examined in looking for the best time to take coins from the past, he knew the road split into three dirt trails at the summit of the hill, all rutted from caravans. One ran west toward the Black Sea; another led south across a desert into the heart of Persia; and the third, no doubt less used, ran north into some mountains and ultimately to what was known in Tejmur's day as the Soviet state of Georgia. It was the road to Georgia he and Papusza would have to travel, and travel quickly—for the historians said Baku would be sacked and burned, its population virtually wiped out, an event that would take place soon.

"You were shooting at us." Papusza narrowed her brows at Masud.

"What? No, no. It was that idiot Alexiev with his stupid pistol. He likes shooting at anything that moves, even cats and dogs."

"My window." Tejmur heard the hope die in his voice and spoke fast, trying to sound less like a terminal patient in a cancer ward. "I tried to grab the handle as I went through, but the Russian pig pushed me."

"A pig?" Masud sputtered. "And a Russian pig, at that?" He pointed the rifle at Tejmur. "I have half a notion to shoot you in the leg." He laughed. "Then you will be Tejmur the Lame. Tejmurlane the not-so-great. Ha."

"There," Papusza pointed. "On the ground, those metal sticks and the black box. Isn't that your window? The Russian probably grabbed it as he came through, clutching for something to keep from falling into the past."

"Yes, yes." Tejmur picked up window and turned off the switch, though the battery had been jarred loose and the window he held was dead. He snapped the sides apart, telescoped them down, and placed them alongside the peephole in the carrying case he had stuffed beneath his jacket in that future and dangerous Baku night. "It looks intact. We can get back as soon we let enough time pass for the cursed

21

Russians to leave Baku. I was afraid that we would be stuck here." Tejmur felt hope returning, and with it, resolve. "And you, soldier, point that rifle somewhere else."

"If you shoot the wizard," Papusza said, "you will never see Mother Russia again."

"I'm no Russian. I'm Masud the Cossack. See this moustache?"

Tejmur looked at Masud. He was light-skinned, though not so light as the Russians; and he did have a magnificent moustache, something not allowed in the Russian army—except for soldiers from around the Caspian and eastward. Such men, Tejmur knew, believed that they were not real men without a moustache. The man also had a nose that any desert Arab might envy, and eyes dark as marbles carved from jet. Stroking his own moustache, Tejmur affirmed that he kept his better-trimmed and no doubt cleaner than did the Cossack.

Masud looked at the nearby jagged rocks jutting from the hillside, then at the fortress below. "This is all too real to be a trick with mirrors and lights. That's an ancient city all right, judging from the low and tiled roofs. I've seen places like this in Afghanistan. Where are we?"

"Whatever shall we do with this fellow?" Tejmur asked. "We must make him go away. He's a buffoon."

"A Russian soldier of a buffoon with a rifle," Papusza said. "That has to be the worst sort. Though I doubt he's a wild Cossack, for he doesn't stink so much."

"I heard gypsy women aren't nice," Masud said, "especially pretty ones. I heard that they are good for only one thing, and that thing isn't telling truth."

"Maybe he is a Cossack," Papusza said.

"There," Masud pointed, "the walls of the fortress. They have teeth, just like the old wall around Baku. And there, that funny-looking tower. How very like the pictures of the Maiden's Tower I saw before coming to Baku."

"Teeth?" Tejmur said. "A wall with teeth?"

"For the archers," Papusza said. "What do you call that?"

"A crenellated wall. The stones do look like teeth." Tejmur waved toward the fortress. "That's Baku as it looked seven hundred and seventy years ago. Or I should say as it looks now, since we're here."

"We're in the past? I don't believe it."

"You can choose not to believe if you wish," Papusza said. "But you might be sorry."

"Only a fool would believe such a story," Masud said. "But the trick you have pulled is a clever one, and I intend to enjoy it for as long as the illusion lasts. My captain said to kill any Azerbaijanis we found on the streets of Baku. A lesson, he said, from the Soviets to anyone stupid enough to break away from Mother Russia. And since, trick or not, we are still in Baku . . ."

"Remember what I said. Kill us and you will never see Russia again."

"But I never want to see Russia again. Nor, truthfully, am I eager to kill anyone. Especially not for that tyrant Gorbachev. Perhaps I will only wound you."

"Wounding us isn't a good idea, either," Papusza said. "You would win no good will from us, nor inspire either of us to send you back to your own time."

"I'll be in trouble with the captain. But of course, I could tie you up. That might satisfy the black-hearted Russian." Masud produced a ball of stout nylon twine from a pocket and tossed it to Papusza. "Gypsy woman, tie Tejmur's hands behind him."

"She has a name," Tejmur said. "Papusza."

"Of course she would have such a name. It means *baby*, right?"

"No," Papusza said. "It means *doll*."

Masud pointed the rifle at her. "Baby Doll Papusza, tie up this Tejmur who for now is not lame."

"The voices again." Papusza pointed. "Beyond those large rocks. Someone whispering."

"Enough of your gypsy tricks. Tie him. Arms behind."

With a heavy sigh, Papusza approached Tejmur.

Tejmur turned, crossed his wrists, and glared at Masud. "I've come across your name before," Tejmur said, "in the tales of the *Arabian Nights*. The king Shahrayar returned early from a hunt and found his wife's handmaidens and men servants in the courtyard of the palace, having a sex orgy. Shahrayar watched his wife the queen go to a tree and call out for Masud."

"I've read the story. Do you think me an uneducated simpleton?"

"I haven't read it," Papusza said. "Tell me the story."

"Be quiet, and finish tying his hands."

It was easy for Tejmur to feel that Papusza had made the string loose enough for him to slip out of the knots she'd made.

"I tied them already."

"Then come here so I can tie yours."

"No." She backed away as he approached her.

When Masud raised his hand as if to strike her, Tejmur heard the twang of what could only be a bow—and saw an arrow strike Masud's leg.

Chapter 4

Masud didn't utter a sound. Tejmur expected the man to lift the rifle and deal death to the five men standing beside the rock outcropping. Instead, Masud stepped back, dropped the rifle, and held his hands out so the archers could see he was unarmed.

The only one of the newcomers not carrying a bow stepped forward, a man with a regal air about him. He wore tight leggings and a white silk shirt that gleamed in the sunshine. A long, curved sword was strapped to his side. The four archers, who also had curved swords, wore clothing made of coarse-spun wool, undyed and dirty.

"Kill no one unless I order it," the man said.

"He spoke Azeri," Papusza said, her voice filled with amazement. "Strange Azeri, and old-fashioned, but understandable enough."

"Silence, woman," the man in silk said.

Tejmur shook the string from his wrists, glanced at the twine, and stuffed it into a pocket. "I am Tejmur," he said.

"He is a great wizard," Papusza said.

"I said silence, woman. I am Rostam, surnamed The Great, Shah of Baku. What is your business here?"

"I'm no wizard," Tejmur said. "Papusza likes to exaggerate."

"Answer my question." Rostam put his hand on the hilt of his sword, and the four archers backed away from him.

"We are travelers," Tejmur said, "and we hoped to do some trading in your fortress."

"But you carry nothing to trade. And this one," Rostam gestured toward Masud, "had you bound, and he moved to strike the woman. So I asked my man here to kill him." He turned to one of the archers. "You will learn to use your weapon correctly, or I'll feed your body to the carrion birds."

"I would not have struck her," Masud said. "I wanted obedience from the gypsy woman."

"Did I address you?" Rostam's voice came out hard, threatening.

"Your leg," Papusza said in Russian. "It must hurt. I'll tend to the wound."

"My pain threshold is quite high," Masud said, looking surprised. "I'm a Cossack, remember. Yet I would be thankful for your help." He sat on the ground and Papusza knelt to look at the arrow.

"No more speaking in Greek," Rostam said. "I'll have my men put more arrows into you. All of you."

"If you must talk, do so only in Azeri," Tejmur said. "But it would be better if you didn't talk at all."

"Good advice," Rostam said. "Why are traders here without camels or horses or boats? What can you trade if you have no merchandise?"

"I have silver coins to trade," Tejmur said. "As does the woman, Papusza."

"A woman with silver? This is wise? I shall take it from her, of course."

"It's my silver, for this woman is merely a mule who carries what I require of her."

"Mule? A mule?" Papusza sputtered.

"Ah," Rostam said. "She's your slave, then. Of course, I will honor your property rights. My city lives on trade, and we treat merchants well. This slave is pretty enough. I might buy her from you, if you can train her not to talk."

"No man," Masud said, "can train a woman not to talk."

"Be careful with insults, or I'll not help with your wound," Papusza said.

"This man with the arrowed leg," Rostam said, "is he also your slave?"

"No. His name is Masud, and he is bound to me as an apprentice. One day when his training is complete, I will order him to travel without me. That day might come soon, for he sometimes practices disobedience."

"What is that ugly stick he carried?" Rostam pointed at the rifle.

"It's the magician's wand," Papusza said.

"You talk much," Rostam said. "Next time I'll allow apprentice Masud to strike you. I'll welcome you, Tejmur, to my home." He turned to one of his men. "You will help Apprentice Masud to our city."

"I'm a soldier," the archer said, "not a mule like that woman there."

"What?" Rostam's scimitar appeared as by magic in his hand, and he swung the blade into the man's side.

The archer looked in horror at the gash as he crumpled slowly to the ground. The man opened his mouth as if to speak; but instead of words, blood trickled out of his mouth. And despite the man's best efforts to close the gaping wound in his side with both hands, bright red blood poured onto the stones he lay among.

"I'll help Masud." Papusza's voice trembled.

"And I," Tejmur said.

"I can walk without help," Masud said.

The three remaining archers eyed each other and chuckled in nervous voices.

"What do you jackals find so funny?" Rostam demanded. His white silk shirt was speckled with blood.

"Not you," one archer said. "Akbar there, bleeding his life into the dry dirt, is the funny one. He called himself Akbar the Mighty, but now he is Akbar the Dead."

"He was a fool to question you, my Lord," another archer said, and the other two murmured in assent as they made obsequious gestures with their hands and bowed to Rostam.

Rostam wiped his sword on the clothing of Akbar the Dead. "Comical. Yes he was. You and you," Rostam pointed at two of the archers, "will help Masud down the hill."

"I'll carry your rifle," Tejmur said. "That is, unless you want it in your hands to use anytime soon." He nodded toward Rostam.

"No," Papusza said. "Two horrible wrongs make nothing right."

"I have no need of the rifle," Masud said.

"What is a rifle?" Rostam asked. "Is it a walking stick? Maybe also a crude weapon of some sort, perhaps like a club?" He picked up the rifle and inspected it with elaborate care. "Bah. This is trash. It's too heavy to use for anything. But perhaps the metal can be melted for something useful?"

"Yes," Tejmur said. "It's valuable only as scrap, and of course I'll carry it." He looked with alarm at the dead archer and at the grinning faces of the man's three companions. "I thought that the history books of this period," he said to Papusza, "had told me much about events and culture." He noted that Rostam listened, so Tejmur chose his words with care. "But none of the historians prepared me for such sudden and final discipline."

"Historians?" Rostam said. "Bah. I avoid them. So you can read, Merchant Tejmur. A useful skill, some say. But I think it is one better relegated to the holy men, the useless, the scholarly, and the idle. Discipline, you said. Yes, I deal in discipline, for I am Shah of Baku. I am Rostam the Great, so named because the world values a champion. In a kingdom such as mine, obedience is all. Without it, the people would have nothing. We wouldn't survive even a single day. There are men out there, and men among us even in Baku, who are waiting for a chance to tear down our walls, steal our hard-won possessions, make slaves of all who survive. Only my strong hand, my sword, and my decisive actions keep civilization alive and merchants such as yourself in business."

As Rostam and his party approached the fortress, the huge wooden gate swung open. A soldier met them in the entry.

"Captain Amin," Rostam said, "you look alarmed."

"A messenger has arrived," the captain said. "He rode his horse to death, and he brings frightening news."

"Not now," Rostam said

The captain started to protest. But then he looked at Rostam's bloody sword, and at the dark flecks on his shirt and face, and Amin fell silent.

With a smirk, Rostam turned to Tejmur. "You see? This is the captain of the palace guard. Discipline has earned me his silence when I command it. I'll not be bothered with messages of any sort until we sit together and have slaves serve us mulberries and curds."

It surprised Tejmur to find so many olive trees growing inside the city walls. They stood, dusty and drab, on the edges of the streets. Grapevines as big around as a man's arm grew up the sides of buildings, splitting into narrow ropy vines trained to run from balcony to balcony. An occasional mulberry tree grew beside houses that looked to be constructed from mud bricks made with straw. Ring-necked doves pecked in the dirt beneath balcony windows, and small flocks of pigeons flew from rooftop to rooftop. Just as in Tejmur's own day, the pigeons struggled with a steady and strong wind blowing in from the sea.

Tejmur expected Rostam to take them to the Baku palace. But he led them instead to a huge tent erected close to the crenellated walls beside the sea.

"You live in a tent?" Tejmur asked.

"I am a man of the desert," Rostam said. "Walls of cold stone that sweat and stink of mold and urine please me not."

The tent was like nothing Tejmur had ever seen. At least a dozen poles held it up, and the spacious interior was covered with Persian carpets that in later centuries would cost a small fortune. Rostam directed Masud and Papusza into a far corner of the tent, and he ordered a slave woman to bring food. The three archers stayed, but they moved back and stood at attention. Palace guards, Tejmur thought, and smiled at the term.

The slave woman brought bowls of mulberries and white cheese. Tejmur noticed she would not make eye contact with Rostam; but when she handed Tejmur a bowl, she gave him a quick, pleading look.

She was dressed in loose and flowing silk, clothing Tejmur imagined a Persian dancing girl might wear. Her eyes had a slight oriental shape to them and were as black as her hair. She had a fine, thin nose, wide-set eyes, and full lips. Tejmur looked at her from head to foot, finding her face and slim frame quite attractive.

"What is this woman's name?" he asked.

Rostam looked surprised. "The slave? Does it matter? I don't know. I call her Norin. Perhaps she has another name." He shrugged. "She's only a woman. A slave woman, though she cost me many pieces of silver."

Tejmur watched her go to the part of the tent where Papusza

tended Masud's arrow wound. Norin and Papusza, their voices low, seemed to be talking a great deal. Masud, his pant leg pulled up to expose the wound, sat on the carpet in stoic silence.

The captain who had met Rostam at the gate entered the tent, pulling with him a disheveled man who stank of sweat and horses. "This is the messenger," the captain said, and jerked the man onto his knees.

"Not there, fool," Rostam pointed. "He bespoils my favorite carpet. Tejmur, notice the brilliance of colors in that carpet, and notice the gold that sparkles in it. Those are golden threads woven by the cunning of the best artisan in all of Persia."

"I ask your pardon," the captain said. He dragged the messenger from the small carpet.

"You walk on dangerous ground, disturbing me thus," Rostam growled, then turned to the messenger. "So speak, man. Speak."

The man, his eyes full of terror, fell to his knees, clasped his hands, and poured out his message. "They come. The hordes, like locusts they blacken the land, the hooves of their horses throwing great clouds of dust into the air. They kill everyone. I've heard they live their entire lives on horseback, they fight on horseback, sleep on horseback, even breed their women on horseback. Everything falls before them. I saw them myself from a mountaintop, saw them thundering across the plains, saw the flashes of their swords and spears in the sun as they ran down women and children and murdered them."

"What nonsense is this?" Rostam demanded.

"They come this way, I tell you. I cannot say when they will sweep down upon Baku, but it will be soon. And your city will fall. Like locusts on leaves, they destroy everything in their path."

"You lie."

"I tell the truth, I swear. You must heed me, or you will surely die."

Rostam turned to his archers. "Dispose of this devil who calls himself a messenger."

"Wait," Tejmur said. But before he could say more, three arrows thudded into the man, one catching his throat.

"Wait for what?" Rostam turned to Tejmur.

"What he described sounds like the Mongol Horde." A wave of nausea swept over Tejmur at the sight and sounds of the messenger's sudden and bloody death. "I believe this man might well have seen them."

Chapter 5

The three archers elbowed one another and laughed. Pleased with their handiwork, they bowed to Rostam.

"Yes, yes." He waved his hand and nodded approval. "You did well. Captain Amin, take the false messenger out and throw him into the sea. Count yourself lucky that the rogue did not bleed on my small carpet there, the one with the golden threads woven into it." Rostam gestured at Norin. "You, slave, clean up that blood."

The soldiers dragged the body of the messenger from the tent, leaving Tejmur and his party alone with Rostam.

"So you see, merchant Tejmur," Rostam said, "the tasks that fall to me in the running of this little kingdom."

"But the Mongol Horde, if it is indeed on its way, is a force to be reckoned with." The thought of the Mongol horsemen reminded Tejmur of all that he had read about their brutal methods. "And their leader, Genghis Khan, is a man to be feared."

"Bah. I fear nothing. Tell me what you know of this horde you speak about."

"The Mongols take joy in killing."

"The wealthy can buy their freedom from any army," Rostam said.

"These Mongols especially enjoy killing those with wealth. The barbarians roll up the rich in their own expensive carpets, then ride over them with horses until the victims are dead."

"You've seen this?" Rostam demanded.

"No. I've read about it."

"Ah. From historians, no doubt. Never believe historians, for they are notorious liars. You see what reading gets you? Gullibility. Those scribbles on parchment seem to most to have the authority of all the sages of the past. But when men who scribble such nonsense stand before me, I detect their lying ways in the tremor of their voices and in the falseness of their eyes. Then I have them killed. But what can a mere reader do in the face of lies that come in a book? Books have no voices to betray lies and no eyes to shift about. Readers become victims of the historians, and so come to believe such nonsense as hordes of Mongols rolling up the wealthy in carpets to mash them to death with the hooves of horses. If you were wise, you would refuse to read books, and you would burn them. Baku once had a building full of books. What do you call such a building?"

"A library," Tejmur said.

"Yes, a library. The city once had one, but I gave the books to our slaves. They used the leaves of the books to wrap fish and butter, and to start cook fires. And so the lying books became useful, for as long as their pages lasted in the hands of the slaves. By my decree, Baku now has no books within its walls."

When Rostam dismissed Tejmur, claiming to have a city to run, the Shah told the merchant to take his slave girl and his apprentice with him. "Trade with honesty," Rostam said, "lest you end up like the liar I had thrown into the sea."

As he left the tent, Tejmur noted that Masud carried his rifle. "You have yet to fire that," Tejmur said.

Masud shrugged. "It's useless."

"Now I understand," Papusza said. "You have no bullets. You threatened us with an empty rifle."

"Sometimes a soldier must make do with what he has."

"As must I," Tejmur said. "Even without bullets, the rifle might yet be helpful somehow." He led Papusza and Masud into the narrow and labyrinthine streets, then along a massive wall on the edge of the sea. The streets had an odd familiarity about them. Then Temur remembered why. When he searched for silver coins, he had looked at the same streets through the peephole his smaller black box opened into the past.

The streets were almost empty. The few people Tejmur saw wore the coarse and patched clothing of peasants, and they stared openly at him and his companions.

"Where are we going?" Papusza asked.

"First we put a little distance between ourselves and that murderous tyrant," Tejmur said. "Then I open a peephole through to our own time and search for a place to use the window for escape."

"Can you take us anywhere?"

"You ask such stupid questions sometimes," Masud said. "You mean *anywhere*, not *anywhen*."

"I meant exactly what I said." Papusza curled her lip at Masud. "I would rather not go back to the night of the Russian troops shooting people in the streets."

"As I have said before, both the time window and the peephole are locked onto a parallel hour in our own time," Tejmur said. "To shift the time frame to another parallel hour requires much power, and I would have to make the adjustments on the master chronoton in my Baku lab."

"I don't understand," Papusza said.

"Of course you don't," Masud said, "for Tejmur speaks nonsense. If you have some trickster way for us to fool the locals into not seeing us as we escape, then do it. But stop all this ridiculous talk."

"This Cossack grows tiresome," Papusza said. "I say we open the window to that terrible night and shove him through."

"As for it still being night, I've already told you that in this particular time frame there is a difference of a few hours in the time of day between the centuries. Dawn should be breaking in our own Baku."

"It makes my head spin," Papusza said, "all this talk of moving back and forth through time."

"The head of a gypsy," Masud said, "and a woman. How difficult could it be to make such a head spin?"

Tejmur turned to face Papusza. "You treated his wound, and he speaks to you like this."

"The slave girl named Norin brought me water and soot from her cook fire while you talked with Rostam the Terrible. Norin and I together treated his wound." Papusza turned to Masud. "You need to get back to a doctor in our own time before an infection sets in."

Tejmur took the smaller black box out of his carrying case, flipped the switch, and looked into the eyepiece. "It is as I thought," he said. "Dawn is breaking in our own Baku. But it looks as though the streets are deserted. We should be able to slip back through undetected."

"What manner of camera is that?" Masud asked. "And why are you taking pictures at a time like this? That fool Rostam could come after us at any moment, and he's a proven killer."

Instead of answering, Tejmur turned off the power to the peephole and returned it to the carrying case. Then he removed and assembled the time window, attached the larger black box, and fingered the switch on the side. When the LED lights failed to come on, he shook the box and tried again.

"Damn!" he said.

"What is it?" Papusza asked.

"Maybe just the lights." Tejmur adjusted the connections to the battery in the box and looked carefully at the time window. Through the frame, he continued to see only the mud-brick wall that he had leaned the frame against. "Damn and damn and damn again. This is bad news."

"How bad?" Papusza asked.

"The worst. The larger battery is dead. The time window will not work in its present condition."

"Why not use the smaller battery?" Papusza asked.

"The smaller battery will power only the peephole. We can look into the present moment, but we cannot go through."

"Can you repair it?"

"I believe that I can make the repairs. But it will be complicated here in the thirteenth century, and I will have to do much improvising."

"All that talk about the Mongol Horde," Papusza said. "Did you mean it?"

"Yes. I spent a year poring over the history of this period when preparing to use the time window. I thought that using the window might disrupt the flow of time less—that is, lower the danger of our changing the course of historical events—if you and I took coins from people about to meet death at the hands of the Mongol horsemen. He's coming, I'm afraid."

"Who is coming?" Masud asked.

"Genghis Khan."

Masud laughed in genuine amusement.

"We must leave the city," Papusza said, and Tejmur could hear the fear in her voice.

"Yes," he said. "But we must risk staying long enough to repair the window. Among the supplies I'll need are paper and acid. Once out of the city, it will be difficult to find the proper materials."

"Paper should be easy to find," Papusza said. "In our time there is a library in the old part of the city. Perhaps it's here, also."

"Rostam destroyed all the books." Tejmur felt a stab of anger over the lost knowledge. "Maybe there's someone in the city who still has paper. But if not, I can make use of another material."

"Can you make the acid you need?" Papusza asked.

"Urine would be a good enough acid. Salt and water will also work. And I will need some coins."

"Urine?" Masud sputtered. "Again you play the trickster. You will use urine to repair a camera?"

"Urine contains acid. And again, it's not a camera."

"We have many coins." Papusza pulled a drawstring bag from a hidden pocket in her dress and jingled it.

"Of course, the silver," Tejmur said. "That's fortunate. But I also need copper coins. And I doubt there are any in this city, for the Persians used mostly silver and gold to make their money."

"How many copper coins?" Masud asked.

"A dozen or so."

"I don't know if I have that many." Masud dug into a pocket in his army pants. "But I have some."

Tejmur felt his spirits rise. "You might be good for something, after all," he said. "Let me see them."

Masud gave Tejmur a handful of change.

"Some of copper and nickel," Tejmur said. "And some only of copper. It might be enough. Now for the paper and urine."

"I would rather use salt water," Papusza said.

"You're serious? You would piss our way out of this city?" Masud asked. "The man is not a trickster. He's mad."

"Perhaps," Tejmur said. "But I'm also an engineer, maybe one of the greatest who ever lived. To prove that, I'll need to get back to the twentieth century. We need a quiet and private place for me to work on the repairs."

"An inn?" Masud suggested. "You said you have silver coins."

Tejmur stopped where the narrow streets branched in five directions. He watched a young woman approach them. Someone from the upper classes, he thought, given that she wore silk.

"Are there inns in the thirteenth century?" Papusza asked

"I think yes," Tejmur said, his eyes on the young woman who definitely seemed to be seeking them out.

"You two are so serious," Masud said, "that I'm in danger of believing you. Maybe that makes all three of us crazy."

"Papusza," the girl in silk said, and it was only then that Tejmur recognized her as the slave from Rostam's tent.

"Norin," Papusza said. "Did you run away from that terrible man?"

"No. He lets me come and go when he doesn't need me for something. Rostam knows I cannot get out of the city. If I did somehow manage, he knows I would not survive long in the desert. I came to warn you."

"Warn?" Papusza looked alarmed.

"Rostam wants the silver you and the merchant carry."

"He kills anyone he wants to kill," Tejmur said. "Why didn't he simply have his men murder us, then take our silver?"

Norin looked around the streets and lowered her voice. "Rules of hospitality. Rostam fears that merchants will stop coming to Baku if he kills any of them in that tent he calls a palace. So he orders his men to find and kill the merchants in the darkened city, and to bring their wealth to him."

"Now more than ever we need a place of safety," Tejmur said. "Perhaps you know of an inn?"

"Yes. A caravanserai on the edge of the city. That way, not far from the Maiden's Tower." Norin pointed. "It might provide some protection from Rostam's men."

"Do you have a home in the city?" Papusza asked.

"I have a hovel that I share with rats." Norin turned to Tejmur. "Is it true, what you said about the army of horsemen coming?"

"Yes."

"Then perhaps you will take me with you when you leave Baku. And you will leave soon, yes?"

"Perhaps," Tejmur said. "I will need some salt. Is it easy to find in Baku?"

"Salt?" Norin sounded amazed. "Men dig salt from the edge of the sea and bring large bags of it into Baku. Yes, salt is common here."

33

"What if Rostam catches you warning us or trying to escape with us?" Papusza asked.

"You know what he will do." Norin's voice trembled on the edge of tears. "His archers have probably seen me with you already."

"Your warning will save our lives," Papusza said. "The only decent thing to do is for us to take you along."

"Right," Masud said.

"Then it is decided," Tejmur said. "We'll leave soon. But for now, take us to the caravanserai. I have coins enough to buy lodging for all of us."

With a suddenness that startled Tejmur, Norin took his hand and brought it to her lips. Then she kissed his cheek and stepped back.

Tejmur felt his face burning, and tried to stop the blush he felt coming on.

As they approached the huge doors to the caravanserai, Papusza whispered to Tejmur, "You liked her kissing you, I could tell."

"Why shouldn't I? She's quite beautiful."

"Men," Papusza said with clenched teeth. "You think all women beautiful who show you any kindness."

Tejmur turned to Papusza, astonished by her anger, as Masud lifted the iron knocker on the gate to announce their arrival.

Chapter 6

The small door that opened was built into the huge main gate of the caravanserai, a gate that would open only for merchants with camels. Tejmur found himself staring at a ratty-looking little man whose abundance of gold rings and bracelets didn't match the poverty implied by his tattered pants and shirt. Behind him stood a huge Arab with a smooth-shaven, but blank-looking, face. He held a short spear in one hand and a club in the other.

"Strangers from afar," the ratty little man said. "I've heard Rostam favors you, though I see little reason for it. You're merchants, I heard, but seeing you makes me believe the reports exaggerated. What do you want with my caravanserai?"

"Lodging," Tejmur said.

"What? Dressed as rogues and in the company of one of Rostam's slave girls, you want me to believe you desire lodging? I think you came to rob true merchants, to cut their throats in their sleep."

"Watch your mouth, old man," Masud said.

"I'll pay in sliver," Tejmur said. "How much for one night?" He pulled a handful of coins from a pocket.

The innkeeper's tone softened. "I see you are truly a merchant, a dealer in coin. But of course you are welcome. Mine is a place fit for royalty. It will cost you all the coins in your hand."

"No," Norin said. "It will cost three of the coins. Only three."

"Three," Tejmur agreed.

"Seven," the innkeeper said.

"Four," Tejmur said.

"But you are young, vigorous men and have only two whores. Pay six, and I'll send more women to you."

"Whores?" Papusza curled her lip.

"Four," Tejmur said. "You provide us fresh straw, fresh water, and a cup of salt. We sleep in the same room. Four, and you keep your whores out of the room."

"Four it is, four." The innkeeper could barely contain his joy as Tejmur handed him the coins.

So I've been had, Tejmur told himself. "Remember. A cup of salt, right away, and a jar of fresh drinking water. Now."

"Of course, of course. The best." The innkeeper led them up some stairs and to a room with a window opening onto a courtyard large enough to accommodate trade caravans that traveled the Silk Road between Constantinople and the East.

"This room has no lock on the door," Tejmur said.

"Lock?" the innkeeper stared in astonishment. "If I were rich as a sultan, I would not have silver enough to buy locks for all doors in the caravanserai."

"Then take us to a room that has a lock," Tejmur said.

"None of the rooms have locks. What need do we have of them? The only door to the outside has iron bars holding it closed, as does the main gate. Merchants never steal from other merchants, at least not in my inn."

"No locks?" Tejmur wasn't surprised, though he spoke as if he were. "Such poor service. I suppose I'll settle for fresh straw."

"There is fresh straw already, against that wall. Beside the straw you will find a chamber pot. Do not empty it into the courtyard."

"The straw smells of camel dung," Norin said.

"You will bring fresh straw," Tejmur said, "or I'll discuss your poor hospitality with my new friend, Rostam."

"A joke," the innkeeper said. "I was making a joke. I will have this straw hauled away. In truth, though, the straw has hardly been used."

"Fresh straw," Masud said in a dangerous voice. "Fresh."

"But of course. I'll send a couple of stable boys to sweep up this almost fresh straw and bring some just cut in the fields beyond the city

35

walls."

When the innkeeper left, Masud asked, "Why do we want straw?"

Papusza laughed. "You helped us to convince the innkeeper to bring fresh straw, and yet you don't know the use of it."

"I could see the man was cheating us, and I'll not abide that. If you know so much about straw, Papusza, tell me why we want it, fresh or not?"

Papusza turned to Tejmur. "Tell us."

"You don't know either." Masud chuckled.

"For sleeping," Tejmur said. "Please remember we are in the thirteenth century. Many inns provide only straw for beds."

"I'd rather sleep on stone," Masud said.

Tejmur shrugged. "Suit yourself."

"When I walked from the Karabakh to Baku to escape the shelling in the Armenian war," Papusza said, "I slept on the hard earth. Straw sounds good by comparison."

"With luck," Tejmur said, "we won't need the straw. With luck, I can make the window work. If it does, we go into the courtyard, find a place to open the window, and return to our own time." He pulled his shirt tail from where it was tucked into his trousers and held the bottom of the shirt toward Masud.

"Use your small knife, Masud," Tejmur said. "Cut off this part of my shirt. Then cut small, round pieces this size." He took a coin from his pocket.

"Give me a reason for such madness." Masud opened his pocket knife.

"Just do it," Papusza said.

"Cloth should work as well as paper, which we do not have. I need electricity to make the time window work, and the Soviet battery in the larger black box that powers the window is dead. So I'm making a battery."

"Nobody can make a battery. Factories make them." Masud cut the tail off Tejmur's shirt, then sat on the floor busying himself with the task of slicing the cloth into tiny circles.

The stable boys arrived. One carried a great shock of hay in both arms. The other carried a cup of salt, an earthen jug of water, and a candle. "You get only one of these," the second boy said as he set the candle on the floor, "and one small striker that you must leave in the room." Then he helped the first boy gather and haul away the old straw.

"Empty some of the salt on the floor," Tejmur told Papusza. "Pour water into the cup, and stir the salt and water mixture to make a heavy brine."

"You order me around as if I were in fact your slave," Papusza said.

Tejmur scowled. "We must all work, if we are to escape. I meant no insult. Norin, please mix the brine water in the cup."

"You said please to her, and not to me," Papusza said.

Masud laughed. "Listen to yourself," he said. "Even as we face death in this strange country, you quibble and whine."

"I'll be your slave if she will not." Norin began mixing salt and water in the cup.

"You will not be anyone's slave," Papusza said. "Especially not his."

"Please," Tejmur said in an exasperated voice. "I'll be a slave to all the women in this room, then. But you must promise not to talk me half to death."

The others watched as Tejmur pulled two wires from the larger black box. He set one, its insulation removed at the tip, onto the floor and placed a copper coin atop the bare end of the wire. Then he moistened with salt water one of the pieces of his shirt Masud had cut, put it on the coin, and put a silver coin atop the wet piece of cloth.

"This," Tejmur said, "is the start of a crude Volta pile. Alesandro Volta made the first one sometime around the year 1800. We must build it as high as we can, and we must keep it from falling over. Masud, as I stack more coins and saltwater cloth, perhaps you can brace the stack. Not with your hands. Use something that won't conduct any electricity. Maybe your shoe?"

Alternating copper and silver coins stacked between layers of wet cloth, Tejmur made a tiny tower. "Here is the last one," Tejmur said, "for we are out of the coppers from Masud's pockets." He topped the stack with a silver coin, then placed the other wire on the top silver piece. "Papusza, please hold this wire in place while I try the window."

"Not with my finger, right?" She picked up several pieces of straw, bent them together, and pressed them against the wire.

"Clever," Tejmur said. He telescoped the metal pieces that made up the four sides of his window and flipped a switch on the larger black box. Nothing happened. With a sigh, he knelt and peeked into a tiny opening in the box.

"It didn't work." Papusza spoke with a despairing voice.

"Ah, but we are not done yet," Tejmur said. He took the smaller black box from his carrying case and flipped the switch. "I see what must be our own time in the eyepiece of the smaller black box. That means the smaller battery is working. Now I'll splice the wires from the smaller battery into the wires from the Volta pile. Perhaps, between the two of them, we can generate enough electricity to open the time window."

Tejmur pulled two wires from the smaller black box, removed the insulation from their tips, and spliced them into the wires from the Volta pile. Then he took a deep breath and flipped the switch on the time window. The LED lights flickered to life.

"It works!" Papusza said. "We can escape into our own time."

"No," Tejmur said. "Look more closely. There is power enough to run the lights, but the window itself is not functioning. See? Look through the frame. If the time window were working, you would see bright morning light over modern Baku."

"I do not understand," Norin said. "When I look through your metal square, all I see is the wall of our room."

"Precisely," Tejmur said. "We are not generating enough power to fire up the microlaser in the matrix of the window."

"What does that mean?" Masud demanded.

"It means we need to build a stronger battery," Tejmur said. "It means we use the fresh straw after all, for we must spend the night here. Then tomorrow we find materials for a different kind of battery. But the Volta pile gives me courage, for it proved that the window is still operative." Tejmur paused. "It will be operative, that is, once we find a way to generate sufficient power."

"What this means is risking our lives," Papusza said, "sleeping in a room with no lock on the door."

"It is not a matter of risk, but of certainty. Rostam's assassins will come to this room tonight," Norin said. "And they will slay all of us."

Chapter 7

"Have you forgotten what I do for a living?" Masud asked. "I'm a trained soldier, highly skilled in modern combat methods. I can stop Rostam's primitive killers."

"Some soldier," Papusza said. "You didn't even load your rifle. The damned thing is useless to us."

"I do have this." Masud reached under his jacket and pulled out a pistol.

Tejmur stared in astonishment. "You had that all along, and you never took it out, even when Rostam threatened us, and even after he had his man shoot an arrow into your leg. Why?"

"I already told you. I am not eager to kill anyone. Violence is an effective tool that can be used to accomplish many ends. But a trained soldier kills only when he must. Also those men pointed more arrows at us, and I had no desire to be stuck again."

"Are there bullets in the pistol?" Papusza asked.

"Of course."

"We need to think this through," Tejmur said. "Whatever we do back here in the past might well change our modern world. I spent a great deal of time and effort doing research on the history and culture of this period before Papusza and I stole the coins. Killing people, or even doing them permanent harm, might radically alter the timeline. For example, what if you killed one of your ancestors, Masud? Or one of Papusza's, or mine? If you shot one of Rostam's men, and the children of his children's children included you or Papusza or me, might we not cease to exist, perhaps the very moment when you pull the trigger? This is an altogether different thing from a little carefully orchestrated theft."

"Theft?" Papusza sounded outraged. "You told me we were not stealing because that carpet merchant was long dead. You tricked me into being a thief."

"Back in our century, you were not a thief. But I suppose that now, in the very city and at the very time when the merchant is alive, we are both thieves."

"I'll find him," Papusza said, "and give back his coins. All of them."

"Not a good plan," Tejmur said. "Besides, we have already spent some of them to rent this room."

"I am not a thief," Papusza said.

"There are other matters to consider," Tejmur said, "besides ourselves. What if we killed the ancestor of the poet Hafez, or the astronomer and mathematician Ulugh Beg, or Mohandas Gandhi? What would happen to world we know?"

"Taking the silver coins did nothing to our time," Masud said.

"So," Papusza said, "you now believe Tejmur's window dumped us into the thirteenth century?"

Masud shrugged. "I suppose that I must. But look. I'm real, a man of flesh and blood, no matter what I do here. I cannot simply disappear, even if I shoot the father of all Cossacks. Though as I said, I would prefer to kill no one."

"Let's see if we can find a compromise," Tejmur said. "Maybe we could damage these men of Rostam's some, and not kill them?"

"I understand little of this," Norin said. "But I do know you are considering not killing Rostam's assassins. It isn't wise even to discuss letting them live."

"Spoken like a true barbarian of the thirteenth century," Papusza said.

Norin stiffened. "I thought you were my friend."

"I am." Papusza softened her voice. "I am. But I so dislike violence. During the awful ethnic cleansing of the Nagorno-Karabakh War, I saw my entire family slaughtered. When you murder someone—a woman, say, you kill not just one person. You kill all the children sleeping in her eggs, along with all those who would be born of her children, and theirs, and so on for centuries. One murder means killing huge crowds of people."

"Eggs?" Norin looked puzzled. "Like chickens? You think women lay eggs?"

"Forget the word. I used a figure of speech."

"If a man came at me with a knife," Norin said, "and I had a bigger knife, I wouldn't think of eggs or anything else. I would kill him, if I could."

"Masud, could you disable men sneaking into this room in the dead of night?" Tejmur asked. "Put them out of action without killing them?"

"Of course. And if I failed, I could still shoot them."

"Will you try not killing before you use your pistol?" Papusza asked.

"Maybe I could shoot them in the knees?"

"Such a wound might well be a death sentence here in the germ-plagued past," Tejmur said. "A blow to the head, perhaps? Then tying them up? I have an idea." He took from a pocket the string Papusza had tied him with. "This is stout nylon, strong enough to bind the arms of the strongest man."

"I have more such twine," Masud said. "But how might we make the assassins cooperate while we bind their hands and feet?"

"I could trip one of them as he comes through the door," Norin said. "Then you bash his head in with your odd war club." She pointed at the rifle.

"Club him to death?" Papusza recoiled.

"It might work," Tejmur said. "But Masud could whack him around without killing him. Maybe a punch in the ribs and a tap on the head with the butt of his rifle? Then we could tie him up with the stout twine. It would be better than executing him with the pistol."

"But how would you trip the man?" Masud asked.

Papusza examined the wooden frame of the door. "Why not stretch tight a bit of the twine low across the threshold and let the assassin trip himself? Then Masud could do his work with the club of a rifle, and we could tie him up like a feral pig."

"An excellent plan," Tejmur said.

While Masud attached the trip twine to the door, Norin and Tejmur divided the straw four ways and spread it for sleeping. Norin pursed her lips as she watched Tejmur. "Allow me to help you," she said, as she rearranged what he had done with the straw.

Night fell, and the moon sent shafts of light through the window that opened to the courtyard. A crude shutter hung on the wooden window frame, a shutter that Tejmur assumed was used only in the winter and when it rained.

He struggled with the rusty hinge, bringing the shutter down, though it still allowed too much light into the room to suit him. He took off his jacket and hung it over one side of the window, but it was too short to cover the cracks.

"Use my dress," Norin said.

With a sudden motion that startled Tejmur, she removed the garment and handed it to him. As he switched the dress out for the jacket, he could see the outline of her breasts in the dim light that came in the window. In his surprise, he drew in a loud breath.

"Stop staring and cover the window." Papusza sounded angry.

"Maybe you should hand him your dress, too." Masud laughed.

Norin's dress covered the window well enough to cast the room into almost complete darkness. "When the assassin trips into the room," Tejmur said, "I'll take the cloth from the window so Masud can see to strike him. Papusza, please keep the candle close to you so you can light it after Masud hits the one who falls in the entry."

"We should sleep in shifts," Masud said. "Whoever is on watch will cough three times when there is any noise in the hall."

"Rostam's men will make no noise," Norin said.

"Men?" Tejmur said. "If there is more than one, we will have a real problem. I doubt we could handle more than one with our plan to trip and punch an intruder."

"Remember, please," Masud said, "that I'm an elite modern soldier. I can handle anyone who comes through that door. The Soviets might be pigs, but they train soldiers very well. I learned in hand-to-hand combat how to kick off a man's kneecaps, among other things. Few fighters without my kind of training know what to do about attacks below the belt."

"I hate that kind of talk," Papusza said.

"Two should stay awake at all times, perhaps," Norin said, "and I will be first. I see better in the dark than anyone else I know."

"No one sees well in the dark," Masud said.

"Some do," Tejmur said. "Good night vision is something you are born with or not, and has to do with the number of nerve endings inside your eye."

"I was born with those things in my eyes," Norin said. "What is dark for others is not so dark for me."

"Good," Tejmur said. "You and Masud stay awake first. Maybe for two hours."

"We have no clock," Papusza said.

"What is a clock?" Norin asked.

"I have a watch, but it's too dark to see the hands on the dial. We can just guess at the time," Tejmur said.

Sleeping on the straw proved easier than Tejmur had imagined. He pushed together enough to serve as a pillow, and slipped almost immediately into a dreamless sleep.

A tiny voice puffing into his ear awakened him: "I'm cold." Norin snuggled close to him, and he remembered with a start that she wore nothing.

"Take my jacket," he whispered, then sat up and removed it.

As Norin covered herself with the jacket, Masud coughed three times.

Chapter 8

Tejmur smelled the man before he heard him, an oily reek of unwashed hair and stale sweat. The assassin rushed into the room, tripped, and fell heavily. It seemed to Tejmur that another man entered the room, and maybe a third, for there seemed to be much chaos defined only with grunts and sounds he imagined to be the stock of the rifle striking flesh.

Someone cried out in pain—a man's voice, Tejmur thought. He plastered himself against the wall and imagined Masud whirling about in the room, wielding the rifle like a lethal club and kicking the kneecaps from the men who had come to kill them. Someone yelped and ran from the room. Tejmur heard footsteps pounding away down the hall. Then the room fell into silence.

"Masud?" Tejmur whispered. There was no answer.

"Are they gone?" Papusza asked.

"Only one ran away," Norin said. "The other two are here."

"Papusza," Tejmur said, "the candle."

As Papusza struck the flint and iron to light the candle, Tejmur took Norin's dress from the window and pushed open the shutter.

In the light from the moon and the flickering candlelight, Tejmur saw Norin standing with her back against a wall, nude and bloody, a dagger in her hand. Three figures lay on the floor. One of them was Masud.

Masud groaned when Tejmur turned him over. Papusza held the candle close to him.

"His head." Papusza put a finger on Masud's forehead. "One of the assassins hit him here. Hard."

"Check the others," Tejmur said.

"Dead, I think," Papusza said.

"Yes," Norin said. She remained standing, unmoving against the wall, holding up the dagger. Tejmur thought that in the light of the candle she looked like an avenging goddess, horrible and beautiful at the same time with blood smeared upon the lush curves of her body.

"The dress." He handed it to her and took the dagger from her trembling hand.

"Wait," Papusza said. "Tejmur, hold the candle." She thrust it into his hand, then picked up some straw.

Tejmur watched in fascinated horror as Papusza used straw to wipe blood from Norin's body.

"She isn't bleeding," he said. "No wounds."

"No," Papusza said. "The blood came from those two men. And maybe from the third who fled the room."

Norin remained still, her arm out as if she still held the knife, while Papusza rubbed her with the straw, then dressed her. "She's like a little child," Papusza said. "She trembles, and tears flow across her cheeks."

"She's in shock," Tejmur said. He tilted the candle to dribble wax on the window sill, then stood the candle in the hot wax. After putting on his jacket, he pulled Masud to the wall and pushed him into a sitting position. Tejmur felt the pistol, still jammed into the back of the man's belt. He took the weapon and tucked it into his own belt. With some gentle slaps to Masud's cheeks, Tejmur said, "Masud, Masud. Come on now. You cannot sleep."

A fast check of the other two men confirmed for Tejmur that they were truly dead. He dragged them into the hall, leaving dark smears on the stone floor. Then he again turned his attention to Masud.

"I'll tend to him," Papusza said. "You must help Norin."

"How?"

"You have to ask? Talk to her. Hold her. Show her kindness. I believe she saved all our lives, and doing so cost her much."

When Tejmur touched her, Norin leaned into him so suddenly and so heavily that he had to wrap his arms around her to keep her from falling. He picked her up, took her across the room, and sat leaning against the wall, holding her as he might hold a child. After a long moment, she began to sob quietly, her tears wetting his shirt.

"Will more of Rostam's men come?" Papusza asked.

"I think not tonight," Tejmur said. "The one who ran will fear reporting his failure. As well he should, for Rostam would kill the man.

My guess is that the assassin is somewhere tending the knife cuts Norin gave him, and that he plans to leave Baku, if he has not already done so. Rostam will know nothing until sometime tomorrow when he figures out his thieves will not return. Or until the innkeeper sends a message to him. My guess is that we're safe here for the rest of the night, but we must leave at sunup."

"Your guess? Is that the best you can do?"

"Maybe not. I have Masud's pistol, just in case."

"In case of what?"

"In case I'm wrong. How is Masud?"

"He's whispering some to me. He thinks I'm Norin, and he keeps wanting to feel my breasts—her breasts, I suppose. He's groggy and is being a pig of a man. But at least he's not dead. Though he might wish he were, if he doesn't keep his hands off me. How's Norin?"

"She weeps."

"So we are both caretakers." Papusza met his gaze in the flickering candlelight. "But I would rather it be only you and me in this room."

"You continue to surprise me," Tejmur said.

"Try to sleep. As will I."

"Sleep? While holding a woman who weeps?" Tejmur put his head back against the wall and listened to the sound of Norin breathing, feeling the pounding of his heart begin to slow.

He awakened with a start. Through the window he could see the glow from the phantom of false dawn. Norin lay draped across him as if she had been shot. Papusza slept with her head in Masud's lap. One of them snored, not loud, and Tejmur assumed it was Masud. He gave Norin a slight shake.

Norin sighed and snuggled into Tejmur, then opened her eyes. "Did you say last night you would be my slave?" she asked in a sleepy voice.

"Did I? No matter. It's time for us to find a way to leave Baku. Papusza?"

"I hear you," she said without moving or opening her eyes. "Call for me again in two hours."

"Masud. Awaken. With the coming of the sun comes much danger."

"I hate this hotel," Masud said. "Lumpy beds, terrible room service. The place stinks of blood and dung."

"You're okay, then?" Tejmur asked.

"Headache." Masud gave his head a shake and looked at Tejmur. "What are you doing holding my woman?"

"Enough clowning," Tejmur said. "Come on, Norin. Come Papusza."

They stood and dusted the straw from their clothing, then Tejmur picked up the coins from the Volta pile. Tossing aside the bits of cloth, he pocketed the money.

Masud took a few stumbling steps, then looked into the hall. "The assassins. I killed them. Both of them."

"You did not," Papusza said. "I think you struck one of them, and the other slammed your head against the wall. I think Norin picked up a dagger one of them dropped, and she stabbed two of them to death. Likely she sliced up the third man, but he ran away."

"Amazing," Masud said. "Is that what happened, Norin?"

"I think yes."

"That's wonderful." Masud said.

"No," Norin said. "It was terrible." She burst into tears. "You see? I weep at the memory of killing those men."

"I like you better now," Papusza said.

"But, Norin, you did kill the men." Masud turned to Tejmur. "Look. We killed two men, and I have not vanished. Nor you, nor Papusza."

"I don't understand." Norin sniffed and stopped crying. "Of course you didn't disappear. Why does Masud speak of disappearing?"

"I was talking about time," Masud said. "Tejmur, I was talking about time. We changed nothing. Now I know I can use my pistol to defend us." He reached behind him, felt carefully, then stared at his empty hands in what appeared to be great alarm. "My pistol. The one who ran, the third assassin you mentioned. He stole the Makarov."

"No." Tejmur handed Masud his pistol. "But the deaths of those two rogues prove nothing about how time works when we travel back. My guess is that without us, those two would have been killed by the Mongol Horde which even now rides toward Baku. If so, we merely rearranged some events here in the thirteenth century, and did so in a way that does no unraveling of the past as we know it."

"You think too much," Masud said.

"Nevertheless," Tejmur said, "don't kill anyone with that pistol."

"Not even to save our lives?"

Tejmur hesitated. "Not unless I say so."

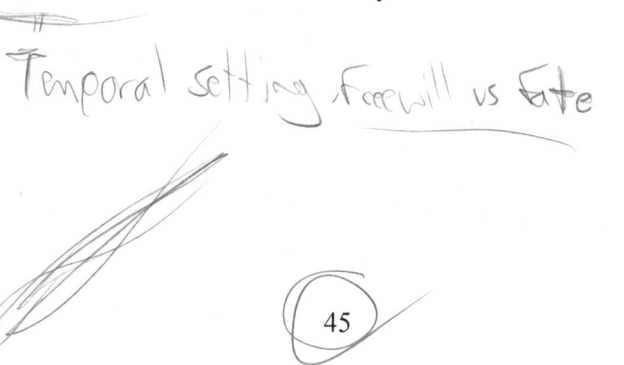

45

Chapter 9

As they left the room, Tejmur picked up the jug of water brought to them by the stable boys.

"You think we'll need water?" Papusza asked. "That means you plan on taking us beyond the walls into the desert."

"Perhaps we will go into the desert," Tejmur said. "But I need this jug for making something called a Baghdad battery. We need to find some vinegar, an iron rod, and a sheet of copper. Can we find such items in the city, Norin?"

"Yes," Norin said. "I can lead you to places where you may buy these things."

"Good. We also need food. Bread, perhaps dried fish. But we should leave soon because of the horsemen. Also before Rostam learns where we are. Papusza, bring the candle striker. It could be we will need a fire."

They found the innkeeper at the gate to the caravanserai. He turned to them, a look of amazement on his face.

"Surprised, are you?" Masud said. He pointed his pistol at the innkeeper.

"Not yet, Masud," Tejmur said. Then he scowled at the innkeeper. "You opened your door to the assassins of Rostam, and you knew they would be coming for us. Your reward for this is having to deal with the bodies of the killers. You have also earned our displeasure, and if we have more unpleasant dealings with you, they will be your last. Open the gate for us."

"But I didn't," the innkeeper sputtered. "Rostam would not do such a thing. He is an honorable man."

"You trust a man who killed his own son?" Tejmur demanded. "The gate. Open it. Now."

"You cannot take my water jug."

"We will take what we want," Masud said.

"You charged us enough to pay for the room and five jugs. Ten. Greed brings men to a bad end. Speak again to us, and your stable boys will have to haul away your dead body." Tejmur gestured toward the door. "Open the gate, or die."

As they walked into the narrow and winding streets of Baku, Masud asked, "What was that about Rostam killing his own son? Did he tell you he did that?"

"No. I was referring to a different Rostam, a character from an old story in Persian mythology. Rostam met his son on the field of battle, and they fought one-on-one. Rostam killed his son, Sohrab. But of course the warrior Rostam didn't know he was fighting his son until it

46

was too late."

"An ancient myth?" Masud waved his hand as in disgust. "No doubt it was in a literature book, and such books are filled with lies. You read too much."

"Rostam the Terrible said something similar to me only yesterday," Tejmur said.

"Rostam is a common name in Baku," Norin said. "Not all Rostams I know are terrible. But the Shah is the worst man I know. We need to leave the city. Soon."

"Is there another way out of the city other than the one we entered yesterday?" Masud asked.

"Yes," Norin said.

"Our best plan is to escape through my window," Tejmur said. "But first it must be repaired. And for that I need the vinegar, copper, and iron, as I mentioned."

"That way," Norin pointed. "I know a merchant who sells vinegar made from quince. Will that work for the magic window?"

"It will work well," Tejmur said.

Tejmur felt a bit of discomfort walking down the street where Norin led them, but he wasn't sure why. The street was narrow, lined with shops and stalls that sold everything from fresh-roasted meat to swords. Smells of food and unwashed bodies mixed together with the heavy odors of incense and perfume, and Tejmur told himself that his uneasy feeling was merely a result of unfamiliarity with the sights and smells of the thirteenth century. But as they approached the stall of a carpet vendor, Tejmur felt Papusza clutch his arm.

"That man." Papusza's voice came out in a hard whisper. "There, with the carpets. We took his silver coins." She fingered the tear on the sleeve of her blouse.

When the vendor turned toward them, Tejmur saw a heavy scar on his cheek. The man seemed to be sizing up Tejmur and his group as a merchant might in gauging the possibility of a sale. Then his face hardened.

"Thief," he said. "Thief!" And he pointed at Papusza.

"He knows," Papusza whispered.

"Deny it," Tejmur said. "We must not call attention to ourselves, not in the marketplace, not today."

Norin stepped forward. "Who am I?" she demanded of the carpet merchant.

"Ah. You're the Shah's whore. And you're keeping company with thieves. That woman stole my silver. Look, her dress, where I ripped her sleeve before the witch disappeared. Vanished right before my eyes."

"You will not call my woman a whore," Masud said in a deep and threatening voice.

"And who are you?" the merchant asked. "Her pimp?" He took a dagger from his tunic, waved it about and climbed out of his stall.

"Come closer," Masud said. "If you dare."

"Please." Papusza took Masud's arm. "Don't."

He shook her loose and turned to her with a wink. "I'll not shoot him." To the merchant, Masud said, "Put that dagger away or risk much pain."

"Strangers in Baku are all idiots," the merchant said. He stepped closer, swinging the dagger.

Masud kicked the man's knee, and he fell like a stone.

"Impressive," Tejmur said. "After what happened at the caravanserai, I was beginning to have doubts about your combat training. Now I'm convinced."

Masud seized the merchant's hand, relieved him of the dagger, and put a boot on his ribs. "Apologize for the insult to Norin," Masud said.

"The carpet merchant is named Faiq, and he is a hard man," Norin said. "He doesn't believe in apologizing."

The man grunted and uttered through clenched teeth, "Never."

"Not a good answer." Masud pulled the man's arm tight and pushed with his foot. "Speak again. But this time, speak better words."

"May sand fleas of a thousand deserts infest your crotch," the man said.

"Let him go," Norin said. "Faiq is my cousin and a bit of a fool."

"Cousin?" Masud dropped the man's hand.

The merchant sat up and clutched his knee.

"His kneecap," Masud said. Then he knelt and took the man's ankle in one hand and pushed on his knee with the other.

The man wailed, slapping the ground with one hand as Masud twisted the injured leg.

"Please," Norin said. "No more."

"But I was repairing his kneecap," Masud said. "I popped it back into place. It will hurt, of course, but there is no permanent damage." He grabbed the merchant's tunic and jerked him to his feet. "Be nicer to your cousin, Merchant Faiq."

"You took my coins." Faiq glared at Papusza.

"To the wealthy, a handful of silver coins means little." Tejmur dug in a pocket.

"To a merchant such as me," Faiq said, "a handful of coins can save my wife and children from starvation. I'm not wealthy."

"I am." Tejmur offered coins to the merchant.

48

"You have a generous soul," Papusza said.

Faiq took some limping steps toward Tejmur and accepted the coins. He examined them with elaborate care. "Some are worthless," he said.

"Not worthless. Foreign. I travel far and wide, and I pick up money from many strange people."

"Copper?" the carpet merchant held up a coin.

"There are those," Tejmur said, "who make coins of copper. Notice the cunning workmanship that went into the making of their odd money."

Faiq thrust a hand into his clothing, and the coins vanished. "But I forget myself. Thank you for your gift." He turned to Papusza. "I still want the silver you stole."

"We need bread," Norin said. "There's a bakery down this street."

"It's closed, I fear," the carpet merchant said.

"Bakeries never close," Norin said.

"The baker has taken his wife and children, and fled the city. He believes the reports that an army comes this way. An army on horseback, they say. I don't believe it. I bought much of his bread before he left, and I can give you a special deal on it."

"Are others leaving the city?" Tejmur asked.

"Some. The squeamish and the rich. The harbor is now almost empty of ships. But many think the tale of an invading army on horseback is only a rumor. Armies march on foot, and only the generals ride. I think the rumormongers lie to chase us from our homes so they can rob us."

"We must leave," Tejmur said. "Papusza, you and Norin bargain with this man for a basket and ten loaves of bread. Please."

"Maybe twenty or more loaves?" Norin said.

"I'll see that he doesn't cheat our women," Masud said.

"Our women?" Papusza sounded outraged.

"Pay him, but give no more wealth to this man," Tejmur said. "We might need all we have."

"What about finding materials you need for repairing the window?" Papusza asked.

"We'll search for what we need later," Tejmur said. "Right now we must run for our lives. The Mongol Khan and his hordes may arrive at any moment."

Chapter 10

"The man you serve," Faiq said to Papusza, "speaks with certainty. Is it true, then, that an army comes this way?"

"Yes," Papusza said. "But I serve no man."

"Hear me, Faiq. The army that comes is different from any you have ever seen. The Mongol Horde will sack Baku, and slaughter all those who are foolish enough not to flee."

Faiq bowed to Tejmur. "You shared your wealth with me, and I will share my bread with you. Take me with you when you leave, and I'll give you the loaves I bought from the baker."

"How many loaves?" Tejmur asked.

"More than twenty." Faiq shrugged. "I'm also a good fighter and can serve you with my knife."

"I don't trust him," Masud said.

Faiq eyed Masud. "You're the best fighter I've met. I would be a fool to challenge you again."

"If you come with us," Tejmur said, "you will have to leave your loved ones behind. My party needs to remain small so we can travel fast."

"My wife is dead. My children live scattered in foreign lands. My clan hates me. I'll carry the bread and follow you. The witch can keep the coins she stole from me."

Tejmur nodded, sharp and curt. "We leave now. Get the bread. Faiq, I need pots, three or four of them. Can you bring pots with us?"

"Chamber pots?" Faiq's voice carried surprise.

"Chamber pots will work. But we will use them in a different way, if I find what I hope to find on the coast."

"I sell such pots," Faiq said. "I'll get the best four I have."

"Excellent," Tejmur said. "Norin will help carry them. And Norin, which way to the nearest gate out of the city?"

When Tejmur and his group reached the gate, they found it open. Through it went small bands of people, most of them walking. Some rode in wagons drawn by horses, and a few rode camels. Rostam leaned against the gate, watching the exodus and scowling. Beside him stood three archers and the captain of his guard. When he saw Tejmur, Rostam cried out in surprise.

"Stop! I, Rostam the Great, order you and your servants to stop."

Tejmur signaled that his party should step to the side of the stream of refugees. "Masud," he said, "the pistol. Shoot the archers if I say the word. Remember, aim for their legs, and fire quickly before they can let fly their arrows."

"I'm ready," Masud said. "Why not shoot them now?"

"Wait for my word." Then, to Rostam, Tejmur said: "How might I be of service to you?"

"You steal my woman. I want her back. And I want you to tell me more about the Mongols. I have received more reports, and all speak of the coming of an army of demon soldiers on horseback."

"There's little more to tell," Tejmur said. "They'll sweep down on the city, sack it, and kill most of the citizens. The great Khan of the Mongols, the one called Genghis, will likely lead the attack. He is merciless. I advise leaving the city immediately and traveling north, as I am about to do."

"And if I order you to stay?"

"You have my respect, Rostam. But in this matter, not my obedience."

"You will obey me."

The three archers pulled arrows from the quivers strapped on their shoulders.

"I have no desire to harm your men," Tejmur said sternly. "Tell them to put away their arrows or be hurt."

Rostam raised his brows to the three archers and waved a hand toward Tejmur. The archers laughed as they nocked their arrows.

"Now, Masud," Tejmur said.

Tejmur heard three quick pistol reports, and saw the archers fall. All three men writhed in agony, clasping their legs.

"If you want," Masud said, "I'll wound this murdering king."

"Not yet," Tejmur said. "Faiq, we might need those arrows and bows. The palace guards are in no mood to object to your taking them."

Faiq grinned, the scar on his face turning white and bulging from his terrible smile. He handed his basket of bread to Papusza, and took the quivers of arrows and the bows from the fallen men.

The refugees approaching the gate fell silent and moved back. The captain of the guard pulled his sword, though he looked more terrified than fierce. He stood beside Rostam.

"My men bleed," Rostam said, "but you used no sword or spear or arrow. How is this?"

"Magic." Papusza laughed.

"Some rogue," Tejmur said, "sent three assassins to our room in the caravanserai. Two of them are now dead, and the third carries a terrible wound. Would you know of the man who sent the assassins?"

To Tejmur's surprise, Rostam remained calm. He shrugged. "Merchants with wealth often attract thieves and murderers. I'll search for them, if you want, and have the guilty punished." Rostam waved toward the refugees who were again moving toward the open gate. "It will be difficult to find anyone with all these cowards abandoning my kingdom. You will, of course, return my woman slave and give me the information you have about the Mongol army."

"I will not," Tejmur said. "But I will make a fair trade. Papusza, give Rostam the Great four silver coins, ones with the fire-worshipers stamped on one side. Then Norin will no longer be Rostam's slave."

"I'll not buy a—" Papusza began, then clamped her lips shut, produced the four coins, and held them out to Rostam.

"I'll take this as a gift," Rostam said. "But the woman isn't for sale."

"Beware," Papusza said, "Tejmur is a great magician." She gestured toward the wounded archers. "Ask them about the holes in their flesh and their pain, and be content with giving up Norin."

"Stop your yammering, woman," Rostam said. He looked at Tejmur. "What happens if I send soldiers after you? Many soldiers."

"It would grieve me to deal them or their captains more such injuries," Tejmur said. "The woman is mine now, and we're leaving to escape the horsemen. My magic can do little against tens of thousands of mounted warriors."

"Tens of thousands?" Rostam stepped back, his jaw slack.

"At least eighty thousand are coming. Perhaps as many as a hundred thousand. They have conquered peoples from China to Persia. Baku will be their northernmost move on the west side of the Caspian Sea, so I'm going north. Immediately."

"A hundred thousand." Rostam's voice carried awe. "Never have I commanded more than two thousand. My army could never repel such a force. I might do well to accompany you after all."

Tejmur nodded. "You're welcome as my guest, but not as my commander. You rule only in Baku. Tell your captain he is not to travel with us."

"I need retainers and guards and servants to set up tents and prepare meals," Rostam said. "You will wait here while I summon the proper camp followers. Never has a king slept under the stars, and prepared his own food."

"Summon them, if you like. Then try to catch up with my party, or die at the hands of the Mongols for your delay. We wait for nobody."

"You have my woman carrying chamber pots for you," Rostam said, "and you would deny me the comfort of retainers? I should have had you killed."

"I could have you killed at any moment."

"Shall I do it?" Masud pointed the pistol at Rostam.

"Not yet," Tejmur said. "First give him a chance to answer. Rostam, these are not chamber pots. They are for special use. And our survival may well depend on your guiding us to the place where we must use them. Do you know of a place nearby where black, foul water seeps thick from the ground?"

Rostam smiled in a cynical way, clearly not believing Tejmur. "Black and foul? Yes. Beyond the ridge on the edge of the sea lies a stinking pool of such stuff." He waved his hand in disgust. "I can lead you there. But I'll have at least one retainer. The captain of my guard must go with me."

"Very well. He will carry this jug of water." Tejmur thrust the jug into the captain's hands. The man struggled to hold it and his sword at the same time.

"Watch the soldier," Tejmur told Masud. "If he threatens anyone with that sword, you know what to do."

"Soldier," Masud said with a sneer, "tell me your name."

"I am Captain Amin."

"Amin," Masud said, "as soon as we walk through this gate, you are no longer a captain. You are Foot Soldier Amin. Set the jug down, sheathe your sword, unfasten your sword belt, and give your weapon to this woman." Masud turned to Norin. "She is now captain in our group, and you will take orders from Tejmur, from me, and from Captain Norin."

"Clever," Papusza said. "Though perhaps you overstep."

Norin took the scabbard belt and sword, and strapped it around her waist. "But I don't know how to use a sword," she said.

"A woman with a sword and a title?" Rostam said. "Worse, a slave woman. This is wrong."

"Less talking," Tejmur said. "More walking." As he led the group through the city gates, he pointed north. "We go that way."

"But the highway west soon turns north, and it would be easier than climbing the rocky hill with no road," Papusza said.

"Easier, perhaps, but more dangerous. Also Rostam said that the place where oil flows to the surface lies in this direction."

"Oil leaking from the ground?" Masud asked.

"Yes," Tejmur said. "In our own time, we have discovered that there is more oil under the Caspian Sea than under all of Saudi Arabia. For centuries shallow deposits of crude befouled some coastal areas of Azerbaijan before anyone understood what it was or what to do with it. Perhaps we can put it to good use when the wild horsemen find us."

Chapter 11

Climbing the hill north of Baku proved to be hot, tiring work. Rostam lagged behind, and Tejmur urged him on: "We cannot slow down for you, though you be Shah of Baku."

The hillside was steep and bare of anything but ankle-high, thorny plants and a few scattered sensitivity ferns. Tejmur wished for some trees, for cover in case the Mongols arrived before the party had cleared the ridge. The little group of refugees would be plainly visible to anyone who even glanced in their direction.

Rostam grumbled, but only in low curses aimed at no one. Masud set the pace with Norin and Papusza right behind him. Norin carried Faiq's pots. She had tied them together and slung them over her shoulders, and they clanged as she walked. Amin complained about the weight of the water jug, and the loss of his sword. Faiq grumbled about the heat and the pain in his knee.

Tejmur looked back often to observe the progress of the mass of refugees fleeing the walled city. All headed straight west, no doubt using the caravan trail carved into the desert from centuries of foot, horse, and camel traffic on the Silk Road. It struck Tejmur as most unwise for anyone to go that direction since the Mongols would no doubt travel on the same road, coming up from the south and then turning where the road split to ride east—headlong into the fleeing Azerbaijanis.

The climb grew steeper as the day advanced. Twice the group paused to drink from the jug Amin carried, and once they stopped long enough to eat some of the bread Faiq had supplied. After Norin took part of a loaf to Rostam, Papusza reminded her that she was no longer his slave.

"It's a habit," Norin said. "I suppose I'm still a bit afraid of him, even if my new master protects me."

"Tejmur is not your master," Papusza hissed.

"He bought me, so I'm his."

"You belong to no one. Ask Tejmur, and he will tell you that."

By the time Tejmur and his group reached the rocky outcrop at the top of the hill, the slant of the sun meant they had only a few hours of daylight left. They paused to rest at the summit, and Norin cried out in alarm.

"The horsemen!" She pointed.

At first all Tejmur could see was a huge cloud of dust, then mounted riders emerged from the brown cloud. The distance was so great that the Mongols looked as tiny as insects. They poured down the vast hill, breaking into small groups to chase down those who ran from the highway.

"Look, the flash of swords and lances in the sun," Rostam said. "It's true, what the messengers told me. They slaughter everyone."

"We have little time," Tejmur said. "We must hurry down the other side of the hill."

But the group didn't move. They stared in horrified fascination as horsemen reached the walled city, leaped from their horses, and pushed at the gate.

"Fools," Rostam said. "Those keeping the gate ran without securing it."

"Come," Tejmur said. "The city is lost. We have no need to see it destroyed."

The descent to the Caspian on the north side of the Asperon Peninsula was more steep than the long, slow climb to the summit from Baku. "Climbing was easier than going down," Papusza said.

"No. Going down is much easier," Masud said.

"This sharp descent is hard on my knee," Faiq grumbled.

"We need to find the tar pits where the oil leaks to the surface," Tejmur said, "and we need to find them fast. We have little time, though the coming sunset gives us a slight edge. My guess is that the Mongols saw us on the hilltop. At first light tomorrow, some of them will come after us. We must be ready for them."

"What will we do with tar pits?" Masud asked.

"We need better weapons," Tejmur said. "At the tar pits, we will make a weapon dramatic enough to frighten even the Mongol Horde."

"More dramatic than my pistol?" Masud asked.

"How many bullets do you have left?"

"The magazine holds eight, and I fired three. That leaves five plus the eight others in my pocket. I have thirteen rounds."

"Those will help, but that's hardly enough. We need the oil to make fire."

"You plan to frighten the wild horsemen? I doubt they're afraid of much," Norin said.

"Perhaps they fear nothing," Tejmur said. "But maybe we could at least startle them. Maybe we could even chance altering the future by killing the raiding party sent to murder us. That is, if the raiding party is small enough."

"Did you read in your history books about the Mongols sending horsemen to the north side of the peninsula in pursuit of people fleeing Baku?" Masud asked.

"Not exactly. While I was reading the historical account of Genghis Khan's campaign on the west side of the Caspian Sea, I thought the account of the Mongol invasion was quite detailed. But here, in the land

and time of his coming, I find the historians were too sketchy." Tejmur shrugged. "All I can do is guess on most matters and hope I have enough information to keep us alive until I get the window working again."

When they reached the edge of the sea, they found a boggy area blackened from oil seepage. The acrid scent of tar filled the air. "It smells like a road under construction," Papusza said.

"You're smelling oil thickened by the sun and sea water. It has become tar, the same stuff used on roads." Tejmur pointed toward huge rocks some thirty paces from the water. "There! The oil leaks from there."

"I cook using oil," Norin said. "But I use butterfat and the fat from cattle. That foul-smelling black stuff isn't oil."

"But it is," Tejmur said. "Oil that's a million years old. Older. It isn't something you can use for cooking."

"The world isn't a million years old," Rostam said. "Historians must have written such a lie, and I warned you not to believe historians."

"How old the oil is matters not at all," Tejmur said. "What matters is that we have it now, and can make use of it for defense."

"We should push on," Rostam said. "The edge of the sea turns north, the direction you said was safe. We could walk at least another hour before darkness. And we could walk in the dark."

"Look ahead," Tejmur said. "Can you see great distances from here?"

"Yes," Rostam admitted with reluctance.

"And from the hilltop behind us, would the horsemen not see even greater distances?"

Rostam looked glum and remained silent.

"We cannot outrun the horsemen. Even if we walked all night, they would spot us at dawn. And they would ride down upon us. We must make a stand here."

"Against an army of a hundred thousand?" Rostam asked in mock surprise.

"No," Masud said. "The army will remain in and around Baku until Genghis Khan orders them south again. No general would send a huge force after a small handful of stragglers such as ourselves."

"Masud is right," Tejmur said.

"How many, then?" Norin asked. "How many horsemen will come to slay us?"

Tejmur shrugged. "Ten, maybe. Twenty at most."

"Do you agree?" Papusza asked Masud.

"Yes. Twenty would be more than enough to subdue us. We are

only seven. Ten would be plenty to do the job. If I were a Mongol general, I would send ten or fewer."

"We're doomed," Norin said.

"No," Faiq said. "I'll fight like a demon. And this man, Masud, is even more fierce than I. Just the two of us could face ten men."

"Ten men on horseback?" Norin asked.

"Enough bickering and worry," Tejmur said. "We'll fight smart, so we'll need few fighters. If we all work together, we just might win."

"I need to eat soon," Rostam said, then corrected himself: "We should eat soon."

"A fast meal, then," Tejmur said. "Bread and water, then we get to work."

"Woman," Rostam said to Norin, "bring me food."

When Norin set down the pots and reached for the bread in Papusza's basket, Papusza caught her arm and snapped at Rostam: "She is not yours to command."

"And you, slave to Tejmur, be silent."

"Papusza is correct," Tejmur said. "Norin is no longer your slave. Get your own bread. And do it fast, for we must busy ourselves with the problem of survival."

"The Shah of Baku gets his own bread." Rostam issued a heavy and theatrical sigh. "I should have sent for retainers."

Papusza set the basket of bread on the ground, broke off a piece, and brought it to Tejmur.

"Thanks," he muttered, then picked up one of Faiq's pots and walked toward the rocks where oil seeped into the tar pit.

Chapter 12

"This," Tejmur called out from the place where oil leaked from the rocks, "is light oil, almost sweet crude. We're in luck." He scraped out a basin in the sand to catch the oil before it spilled into the marsh water, then he filled the pot.

When he rejoined the group, he set the pot on the ground and surveyed the area. The others gathered around to look at the oil.

"It looks like the foulest chamber pot in the world," Rostam said.

"It smells terrible," Papusza said, "but not so bad as a dirty chamber pot."

"That isn't oil," Norin said.

"It doesn't look like much of a weapon," Masud said. "Tejmur, how will we make this bowl of crude oil become the kind of weapon that can kill a raiding party of Mongol horsemen?"

"If the wizard Tejmur says it's such a weapon," Faiq said, "then I believe him."

"We will use the oil to make two weapons," Tejmur said, "not just one. And by using both of those weapons, we'll give ourselves a fighting chance." He swung an arm around and pointed toward the open space at the foot of the hill. "The horsemen will attack from there. With our backs to the marsh, they will have to ride toward us on that hard ground. We'll build a semicircle of fire to unnerve them and their horses."

"A wall of fire," Masud said. "Of course. But will they not cross a small wall of fire with ease?"

"We'll light it just as they approach," Tejmur said. "It will spook the horses, and make them pause or stop. Then the riders will be easy targets."

"Good, good," Masud said. "We'll use my pistol. And the arrows."

"Yes," Tejmur said.

"But who among us is skilled with shooting a bow?" Papusza asked.

"I am," Faiq said. "And Foot Soldier Amin was once captain of the palace guard. Surely he can use a bow. I have no doubt that Rostam can handle one."

"I can," Rostam said. "I'm the best archer in all of Persia."

"There it is, then," Papusza said. "We have three bows and three archers."

"For our ring of fire," Tejmur said, "we must build a canal to hold the oil, and we must carry oil to fill it. Doing so will be hard, dirty work. But we can manage it." He took a rock and scratched in the sandy loam, gouging out a channel and banking the dirt on both sides. "We do it thus," he said. "I'll mark out the place for our fire ring. Papusza and Norin, please start digging the channel as I've done here. The men will carry pots of oil to pour into it."

"Bah! This is madness," Rostam said. "The black excrement in that chamber pot will not burn."

Tejmur poured some oil on the ground. "We might as well test this now. Papusza, do you have the striker you used to light our candle in the caravanserai?"

"Of course."

"Throw some sparks on the oil I've spilled. Pretend it's a candle."

The first sparks set the oil ablaze. Rostam stepped back, eyes rounded. "You have amazed me," he said. Then he recovered his usual haughty manner. "Still, no soldiers have ever won a battle by building a small fire. I'll have nothing to do with your plan."

"You will do your part," Tejmur said, "if you want to survive."

"I am Rostam the Great, Shah of Baku, and I'll not be commanded as if I were a common servant."

"No one is commanding anyone here," Tejmur spoke with great patience, as to a child. "We're all volunteers, working for the good of the group and for our own survival. Those who do not wish to volunteer must leave the group immediately. You may return to Baku, or you may take your chances running north."

Rostam muttered and scowled, but he offered no further objections. Tejmur assigned him to stay beside the oil seepage and to fill the pots while the other men carried them to the small channel.

Amin pointed out that the oil vanished into the sandy soil when they poured it into the ditch dug by Papusza and Norin.

"It will do that at first," Tejmur said. "But the oil will seal the dirt fast enough, then it will hold."

By nightfall, they all had an abundance of sticky black oil clinging to their faces and hands. But they had a black ditch drawn around the area where Tejmur said they should make their stand when the Mongols came.

"Our final job," Tejmur said, "is to tear some of our clothing into strips and wrap the cloth around the ends of our arrows." He tore material from the bottom edge of his shirt where Masud had cut it for making the Volta battery. "Watch how it must be done." Sitting beside one of the quivers, Tejmur took an arrow and covered the area just behind its iron point with cloth, then tied the cloth in place with the twine Masud had given to Papusza for tying his hands when they first fell through the window.

"That's a stupid thing to do," Rostam said. "It will make the arrow useless. Its flight will be short and inaccurate."

"Yes, yes," Masud said. "The idea is brilliant! We soak the cloth in oil, light it, and shoot flaming arrows into the ranks of the Mongols. It will scare the hell out of them."

"Probably not," Papusza said. "My guess is that they have seen flaming arrows before, probably even used them. So they will laugh at such efforts."

"Maybe," Tejmur said. "But according to one of the histories I read, Genghis Khan learned about fire that flies during his trip to Persia. He took the weapon with him back to the East. And with it, he conquered the people who had resisted him, especially in India and China. It could be that he hasn't learned about flaming arrows yet."

"Or perhaps he learns about them from us," Papusza said. "So perhaps we are about to change history."

"Yes," Tejmur said. "It worries me. Though right now, particularly since the Mongols learned about flaming arrows on this campaign anyway, survival is a bigger concern."

"You thought about flaming arrows before we left Baku," Papusza said. "That's why you had us bring the bows and quivers."

"And it's why you asked Faiq for pots." Masud's voice carried a touch of awe. "And the flaming arrows are the second new weapon you mentioned we might use. You're good at planning ahead."

"Thanks," Tejmur said. "But if I were that good at planning, I would have in my pocket some spare batteries for the window."

"What's this window you keep talking about?" Rostam asked.

"Shall I tell him?" Masud asked.

"It won't matter," Tejmur said. "He won't believe us any more than you did when I told you that the window took us to this primitive time."

"The window," Masud told Rostam, "opens to other times. We came through it from our world, which is your world . . . but nearly a thousand years in the future."

Rostam guffawed. "The world will end before a thousand years are up."

"You are from the future?" Norin asked, her voice soft with wonder.

"Yes," Papusza said.

"Can this be?" Faiq asked.

"Faiq," Papusza said, "I'm sorry I took your silver. Tejmur thought the silver wouldn't be missed since according to our history books, the Mongol Horde would soon attack Baku and kill nearly everyone. At the time, we didn't know we would be coming into your world. I'll return your silver."

"You are an honorable woman," Faiq said. "But you and Tejmur saved my life, and for that I would gladly pay all my silver. Please keep what you still have of it."

"So I'm no longer a thief," Papusza said. "I can't tell you what a relief it is to know that."

"You're all crazy," Rostam said. "Every one of you."

"You might be right," Tejmur said. "If so, I hope we're crazy like foxes, for it will take all our cunning to survive tomorrow. Everyone should sleep now as best you can. We must greet some wild horsemen at first light."

Part Two: The Great Khan

Chapter 13

Tejmur awakened in the dark. He felt it had to be morning, or close to it; yet he saw neither stars nor any glow of predawn light. Someone snored nearby, a louder sound than he had heard the previous night in the caravanserai, so it had to be one of the men new to his group. The raw arrogance of the gurgling snore, he decided, had to come from Rostam, who no doubt found ways to be imperious and annoying even in his sleep.

It felt good to be awake before the others. Tejmur had always been an early riser; as an engineer and a scientist, he had always valued his morning solitude as the time when his mind was clearest and worked best. The idea for the time window had come to him on just such an early morning, as he sat on a park bench overlooking the Caspian Sea. It was the very bench upon which he had been sitting and drinking a bottle of vodka in celebration of the final proof of the complete functionality of his time window when the Soviet army had invaded Baku.

Now, as he struggled to survive in the past into which he had fled to escape the Soviets, he squinted against the enveloping darkness and tried to make out the lovely Caspian waters that he knew to be only meters away. The air felt thick with salt and heavy with moisture, as if the Caspian were flinging whitecaps against the shore and misting the land with such smells as could come only from a living, breathing body of salt water. But he heard no surf, and there was little wind. It would start blowing around sunrise, as it always did, sweeping across the sea from the east; though he knew waves high enough to carry the foam of whitecaps came only with storms. Most mornings the Caspian looked like a giant lake, flat and gray as a slab of stainless steel before the morning wind wrinkled it.

Fog, Tejmur thought: that had to be what made it so dark, a heavy fog sitting low on the ground, and no doubt over the water, and blocking light from the heavens. The blanket of fog must be dense indeed to so completely block out the moon and stars, and even the false dawn—that comforting harbinger of morning that in the desert of Azerbaijan often announced sunrise before winking out, leaving the world dark for long minutes as the real dawn began streaking the sky with orange and red. Despite the fog-induced darkness, Tejmur knew morning was close at hand, and he knew Genghis Khan's mop-up campaign would be underway soon. Perhaps small groups of men already moved about in the Mongol camp.

The snoring changed with a grunt to a low buzz, and Tejmur heard someone stir and cough. Moving with as little sound as possible, he stood and dusted the sand from his clothes as he looked around. To his surprise, the fog hugged the ground, the top of it just below his shoulders; and in the phantom of false dawn he could see the fogbank layered like thick putty, stretching gray-white across the marsh where taller reeds protruded moist and dark. It was beginning to dissipate already, the vapor floating across the strip of flat land between the sea and the hill. The hill stood completely above the mist, holding its rocks and dirt high into the brightening sky. The few remaining stars were winking out with the coming dawn.

"Shall I awaken the others?" Papusza spoke in a whisper. She stood and moved toward him, her head seeming to float on the fog.

His precious moment of solitude broken by Papusza's awakening, Tejmur found—again to his surprise—that he didn't mind. "Let them sleep a while more."

"What might I do to help prepare for the attack?"

"Nothing yet. When the fog lifts, you might check the arrows we laid out and make sure the basin of oil is ready for dipping their tips."

Desert air seemed to devour the fog, and the ground mist thinned into streaks and slowly vanished. Tejmur looked into the narrow ditch he had dug connecting to the wider defensive one, and nodded with satisfaction. It still held plenty of crude oil for carrying fire to the main ditch that arced around the perimeter of the spot he had chosen to make their stand. When he turned to look again at the hill, Papusza touched his shoulder.

"The weapons are in place," she said. "We're ready, I think."

"Yes," Tejmur said. "As ready as we can be to face such a danger. Barbarian horsemen seeking to murder us. It all seems so odd. Just hours ago you and I sought to escape the slaughter that was unfolding in our own time, but I managed to make things worse by taking us into the middle of an ancient war."

"You saved us from Soviet bullets. Now you're saving us again in this past world. I must admit that I liked it better before the troops came, before we opened the time window to steal from Faiq. I liked it better when I thought you courted me. Did you know that after the first few meetings, if you had tried to kiss me, I would have offered no resistance? I would have been most enthusiastic in such a kiss."

"I didn't think much about those matters." Tejmur realized as he spoke that he was not telling the whole truth.

62

"Think about them now. We should have kissed. Now our time is running out, and we might never have another chance."

"Time, in its turns and eddies, treats us in such strange and dangerous ways. Even with the window, it seems that we cannot escape them."

"I want more than mere escape," Papusza said. "Very much more."

"It seems to me that in our current situation, escape is the best outcome we can hope to achieve. What more is it that you want, Papusza?"

Papusza made an impatient gesture. "You don't know, do you? You were smart enough to build the time window, and resourceful enough to escape two massacres, and yet the nature of a woman's desires eludes you. There are only two things that I truly desire. Do you really want to know what these things are? After all, history has shown that such knowledge can be more dangerous than the Mongol Horde."

Tejmur looked into Papusza's face, her high cheekbones half-lit by the coming dawn and her eyes in shadow. It came to him that her face was only inches, now, from his own. He found himself wishing it were closer.

"I do want to know," he said. "Really. What two things do you truly desire, Papusza?"

"The first is to go to Istanbul." She looked up at him with an enigmatic half smile. "Take me there. I'll tell you the second when we arrive . . . if you haven't figured it out for yourself by then."

"Fair enough. Istanbul is as good a place as any for us to go, even when we return to our own time. Given the Russian invasion of Azerbaijan and the war they have stirred up in Karabakh, it may be the only place. But if we make our way to Istanbul now, we'll find a city named Constantinople. We would have to go there in the fifteenth century or later to be in Istanbul."

"I'll go with you to Istanbul anywhen, and it matters little to me what the city is called when we arrive. I don't like large cities, but with Istanbul I've made an exception. It's wonderful. Have you been there?"

"Yes. But if you wish to return to that great city after it has become Istanbul, we must make sure the time window survives the battle we are about to face here in the present moment." Tejmur waved toward the formation of rocks that loomed in the morning mist not far from where he and Papusza were standing. "I had thought to place the window in a protected cranny of that rock formation. When the battle is over, we can recover the window. What do you think?"

"I think that you are right."

"Then let us hide it quickly, before the others awaken."

Tejmur and Papusza worked their way carefully into a crevice between two huge rocks that still felt damp with the moisture from the fog. Near the back of the crevice, they found a small cave that continued into the heart of the formation. The cave was protected by overhanging rock, and was completely dry to the touch. They worked the case containing the time window and the peephole deep into the little cave, then piled stones in front of the opening.

"Perfect!" Papusza said, when they were finished.

"Yes, the window will be safe here from the elements, in case . . . in case we need to leave it here for some reason. And it is completely hidden from view."

"When you hesitated a moment ago, you meant to say *in case we are captured or killed.*"

"Or merely injured, and unable to travel. There could be any number of reasons we might want to leave the window here for safekeeping," Tejmur said softly. "But yes, I did mean that."

"If we do survive, and we are able to travel, you'll take me to Istanbul. Perhaps soon? I want you to promise. If we survive the battle we face, and what comes after, promise me that you'll take me to Istanbul-that-will-be."

Tejmur glanced across the narrow plain and up the hill, and he realized that the land glowed with enough light to bring the horsemen of Genghis Khan. Then he looked deep into Papusza's face, lovely in the dawn light.

"I promise," he said. "But you must also promise to reveal the second of your desires when we arrive."

"Done," Papusza said. "And now, I think, it is time to wake the others."

As Tejmur and Papusza reentered the camp, Masud sat up and yawned. "The hour is upon us."

"Not yet," Norin said. She stood and stared in the direction of the high ground. "No one is on the top of the hill."

"Shake off sleep," Tejmur said. "Eat some bread, and drink a little water. We must have steady hands and steady nerves to face the Mongols."

"And if they deem us too trivial to pursue and do not come?" Faiq asked. "How long do we wait?"

"They'll come," Norin said. "You see? They are already here." She pointed away upward, to the southeast.

The dawn grayed the land with its morning light, and horsemen stood atop the ridge above them, silhouetted against the sky. Though they were some distance away, Tejmur could see how wind from the Caspian ruffled the fur cloaks of the Mongols as they paused on the pinnacle of the hill.

Rostam laughed. "Four. They sent only four. What arrogant and stupid dogs they are."

"The horses must zigzag down the steep hill," Tejmur said. "We still have time to break our fast with a small amount of bread."

"I'm not hungry," Faiq said. "It would be best for me to string a bow and ready the arrows."

"Bring me food, slave," Rostam said to Papusza.

"If you put an arrow into one of those men," Papusza said, "I'll bring you food. Once."

"You just sealed the fate of at least one of them," Rostam said.

When the four riders reached the plain, they stilled their horses for a moment and stared. Perhaps in amazement, Tejmur thought, at the seven people standing beside the marsh, making no attempt to run. Faiq, Rostam, and Amin gripped their bows and nocked arrows, tipped with oil-soaked cloth, while Papusza knelt beside a chamber pot filled with oil.

"Now," Tejmur said, and nodded at Papusza.

Papusza flicked the candle striker to throw sparks into the pot. She then turned to the small ditch and struck sparks into it. As the three archers lighted the tips of their arrows in the pot's flames, fire ran up the small ditch to the larger one.

The Mongol warriors cried out in surprise as flames seemed to leap from the ground in front of them. "Now put arrows among them!" Tejmur shouted.

One of the arrows struck the lead Mongol, and his fur cloak burst into flame. The other arrows fell short, hitting the ground in front of the horses and becoming small puddles of fire. The horses shied and turned aside to avoid the burning ditch. The horseman who had taken the arrow threw down his lance, leaped from his horse, rolled, and stood, flailing his arms and pounding on his burning cloak.

At a command from the man on the ground, the other three controlled their horses; and with speed and agility that astonished Tejmur, they jumped to the ground and seemed to land running, all three yelling their blood-chilling war cry. One held a lance above his head. The other two held swords. They bounded over the flaming ditch and ran several more steps before two flaming arrows thudded into one of them, and a single arrow dropped another. The third, swinging his sword and yelling, kept running.

"Masud," Tejmur said, "the Makarov."

Masud was already aiming the pistol. It spat fire with a loud clap, and the man stumbled. Another shot dropped him. He made an attempt to stand, issued one more war cry, and collapsed.

The warrior standing beyond the flaming ditch had flung aside his burning cloak. He stood beside it as it smoldered. Tejmur thought the look on his face revealed no fear, but rather a savage kind of curiosity.

Chapter 14

The Mongol held out his hands as if saying he was unarmed, and he spoke in a language Tejmur did not recognize.

Rostam bent his bow. "I'll put a flaming arrow into his chest so Papusza will bring me another meal in addition to the one she promised for my killing the other warrior."

"No," Tejmur said, and "No," Masud said.

"Yes." Rostam took aim.

Faiq grabbed Rostam's arms, and forced him to unbend the bow and relinquish the weapon—along with the arrow Rostam had already nocked.

"I understood the Mongol's words," Masud said. "He spoke the language from my own tribe, but with an odd accent."

"You'll die for this," Rostam said to Faiq.

"Threaten me again," Faiq growled, "and I'll get Tejmur's permission to cut your throat."

"The horseman asked which of us is the leader of our group," Masud said.

Rostam shook free from Faiq and stepped forward. "Tell him I'm Shah of Baku."

Faiq laughed. "The king of a lost city, are you? A runaway ruler of a town now sacked and dying."

Masud spoke and pointed to Tejmur, and the Mongol warrior replied.

"He wants to bargain with you," Masud said.

"Bargain? For what?"

"For our lives, he says, in return for showing our weapons to his king."

"I say we kill him," Rostam said. "Then we go north and wait until the wild men leave Baku."

"When those men don't return to the Mongol camp," Masud said, "their commander will send a much larger group after us, one we cannot overcome even with Tejmur's tricks. Anyway, that is what I would do, if I were their commander."

Tejmur gave Masud a curt nod. "Ask what assurances we have that he can speak for the great Genghis Khan," Tejmur said. "Also ask what we must do to be allowed to live and go where we wish."

While Masud spoke and the Mongol warrior answered, Tejmur studied the man. His hair hung straight and greasy-looking, touching his shoulders, though part of the hair had been burned away by the flaming arrow. He had the bare beginnings of a beard. The arrow must have burned him at least superficially, but he seemed otherwise unharmed. He wore a leather jerkin sewn from the hide of some furred animal, leggings crisscrossed with leather strips, and a pair of soft-soled boots. His face told in numerous scars of the battles he had survived. Though he is young, this man has killed huge numbers of people, Tejmur thought, and he wouldn't hesitate a moment to kill any of us.

"He declares himself to be Iskandar, son of Jamuga," Masud said, "and his birthright gives him the ear of the Khan."

"Jamuga," Tejmur spoke in a low tone, addressing only Masud. "That name figured prominently in the history I read. I wonder—"

The Mongol warrior, Iskandar, spoke again.

Masud translated: "Iskandar claims through his army's conquest the right to the two women with us, though he promises the rest of us will be treated as guests by his great Khan, especially when we reveal to the Khan our secret of making fire fly through the air."

"Trade our lives for some information?" Rostam said. "I say we do it, and that we give the women to this man."

"We are not chattel," Papusza said. "We are not to be bartered at your whim."

"But you are," Rostam said.

"You will remain quiet," Tejmur told Rostam. Then to Masud: "Tell Iskandar that if he tries to take or even touch these two women, we will kill him immediately."

"I could shoot him right now," Masud said. "But I won't, of course, until you say." He turned to the Mongol warrior and spoke again.

The man listened, his eyes narrowing and growing smoky with anger. Then he shrugged, nodded, and replied.

Masud shook his head and turned to Tejmur. "He says that you must teach him now the art of making fire that flies."

"I'll explain it only to Genghis Khan," Tejmur said.

Masud nodded in agreement, then spoke to the Mongol warrior.

Tejmur was uncomfortable with the deal he had struck with Iskandar for many reasons—not the least of which was his fear of polluting the timeline. But he told himself, once again, the history books had said that the Mongols discovered the secret of flaming arrows on this very campaign. And Tejmur did indeed believe that, if the circumstances of their surrender to the Mongols were conveyed accurately to Genghis Khan, the leader would honor the bargain. The Khan would no doubt see the military advantage he stood to gain with the use of flying fire. The big question in Tejmur's mind was whether Iskandar would present the deal to his king.

Iskandar rounded up the horses of his dead comrades, though he made it clear that none but the men of his army were allowed to ride. As Iskandar was busy with the horses, Tejmur pulled Papusza aside. He spoke to her quietly, so that none but she and he could hear.

"Papusza, I need for you to cover the oil pot with a piece of cloth and carry it with the firestriker back to Baku in the folds of your dress. Remember to keep the oil pot swaddled in cloth. Let the Mongols think it's just water you're carrying. We will need to make fire fly again before we're through."

Tejmur and his followers found themselves retracing their steps over the hill and down into the Baku valley. The men carried the bows and quivers of arrows. Amin, upon Norin's orders, carried the jug of water. Faiq shouldered the basket of bread, and Papusza bore the cloth-covered oilpot and candle striker surreptitiously amid the folds of her skirt.

The Mongol encampment filled the flat area outside the city's walls and stretched up the surrounding hills. Never had Tejmur seen so many horses; and the black, gleaming heads of the savage horsemen seemed more numerous than the thorny plants on the hillside. In Tejmur's own time Baku had about a million people in it, but they were stacked up and hidden in high-rise apartments built by the Soviets and forbidden to assemble in crowds this large. Thus the Mongol Horde appeared vaster than the population of the huge city of his own time.

Mongol warriors shared the encampment with the dead of Baku, and the smell of death permeated the air—though not yet so bad as Tejmur knew it would be in a few days. The Mongols themselves reeked with the stink of unwashed bodies, and the camp smelled of horse dung and human excrement. Mixed into the putrid odors was the smell of roasting meat. None of the warriors appeared to notice the foul smells. Norin and Papusza pulled their sleeves across their noses, and the men in the group breathed through their mouths, sometimes holding a hand over nose and mouth. Tejmur wondered how the Mongols escaped the ravages of disease from the hostile bacteria no doubt multiplying in the filth of the camp. Perhaps they didn't escape diseases; perhaps many died, he speculated. Or perhaps their immune systems had developed resistance to many illnesses, given their lifelong immersion in such dirty conditions.

As they approached the open gate to the city, Tejmur and his party found themselves surrounded by a swarm of armed savages, all looking much like Iskandar, though most were older and had more scars on their faces and arms. At a word from Iskandar, several men seized each one of Tejmur's group.

"You promised us safe passage," Tejmur said, and Masud translated.

"He says," Masud explained, "it is the law among tribesmen of the steppes that outsiders cannot be armed. He says we will be kept free but under guard after we give up our weapons."

The warriors took the bows and quivers from Faiq, Amin, and Rostam. They also took from Faiq a long dagger and from Norin the sword that had once belonged to Amin. But Amin was left the water jug; and to Tejmur's relief, Papusza still held the cloth-swaddled oilpot and firestriker in the folds of her dress. Then the Mongol soldiers released Tejmur and his followers.

Again Iskandar spoke. Masud said, "He claims you must now tell him the secret of making flaming arrows so he will not look like a fool to Genghis Khan. He says the king will not believe him unless he has the right information."

"Tell him I'll give the information only to the Khan."

With an angry frown, Iskandar spoke again. Then he turned his horse and rode toward the center of Baku.

"He said we are to remain in this place." Masud pointed to a nearby building. "He said he will go speak to his king, though he thinks it will be pointless unless he knows your secret of flying fire. He said if we try to leave, the guards have orders to kill the men."

"The Makarov?" Tejmur asked.

"Still in my belt," Masud said. "And the second clip is still in my pocket. The monkeys looked only for knives, and they are hardly capable of the kind of frisking done by the police of our own time."

"That, at least, is a piece of good luck," Tejmur said.

Troops escorted Tejmur and his people to a small mud-brick building not far from the city gate, the same one Iskandar had indicated earlier.

"What do we do now?" Faiq asked.

"We bide our time." Tejmur entered the door of what had obviously once been a home. Inside he found four bodies and the debris of battle: blood on the floor and spattered on the walls, overturned chairs, broken pots scattered here and there. "The first thing we must do is haul these bodies out of our prison."

"I'll not do such work," Rostam said.

"Very well," Tejmur said. "But you might well come to regret not doing your part in helping us survive."

Guards, hands on the hilts of their short swords, laughed as Faiq, Amin, Masud, and Tejmur dragged the bodies into the street. Two were young men, apparently cut down trying to protect the other two, both women of considerable age. Tejmur and the others performed the grisly task with tight lips and barely controlled anger. The guards pointed to a gutter across the street. They made it clear the prisoners could go no farther with the corpses, and that they had to return to the house in short order.

As the prisoners reentered the building, Masud said, "Iskandar said one other thing. He said the women in our group are his, and he will return before long to claim them."

Chapter 15

The day stretched into evening with the sinking sun casting a long shadow from the high western hill over the ruined city and onto the sea. Tejmur saw nothing of Iskandar. Twice the prisoners ate some of Faiq's bread and drank from the water jug. Tejmur had to force himself to drink, for the water grew lumpy with backwash from others drinking, and he worried about disease from the many hands that had touched the bread.

Papusza brought Rostam bread for their first meal but refused to wait on him in the evening, and Rostam growled in discontent. And as evening turned to night, low clouds reflected thousands of flickering campfires on both sides of the city wall.

"The stench grows," Faiq said.

"It will be almost unbearable by morning," Papusza said. "When I was in the Karabakh and the Armenian shells fell on my village, nearly everyone was killed. I wandered through the rubble looking for survivors—my family, my friends, anyone. But within twenty-four hours the smell of death drove me into the desert, and I walked to Baku."

"Will Iskandar come back?" Amin asked.

"He will," Tejmur said. "But we should not trust him to deliver us to Genghis. Iskandar will be back because he wants Papusza and Norin as his personal playthings, and he will try again to pry from us the secret of our fire arrows."

Masud patted the Makarov under his shirt. "He'll find something he didn't expect. Death."

"Kill him with your magical iron finger," Rostam said, "and the others will be upon us. We'll all die. I say give him the women."

"Suggest that again," Masud said, "and I'll kill both you and Iskandar."

"When I again become Shah of Baku, I will remember your

threats, and I will take action."

"Peace," Tejmur said. "We have enough trouble without fighting among ourselves."

"What can we do tonight?" Faiq asked.

"We can sleep," Tejmur said, "or at least try. We should be rested when we deal again with Iskandar."

The night proved long and difficult. Many of the Mongol warriors amused themselves late into the night amid great laughter and shouting. Among their revelry Tejmur heard cries of anguish from women. Many women. Only in the early morning hours did the savage warriors fall into the silence of sleep. By dawn the stench of death hung over Baku like a thick fog.

Just after the sun rose, seeming to emerge from the waters of the Caspian, and the Baku winds began their steady, relentless sweep from the sea, Iskandar called from outside the building. Already awake, Tejmur and the others sat in sullen silence as Iskandar talked.

Then Masud spoke: "He says that last evening the great Genghis Khan scoffed at the idea of flying fire, that Iskandar's words carried no weight, though he is the son of Jamuga. It will be hours, he says, before the Khan will see him again."

"The name again," Tejmur muttered muttered to himself. "But I wonder if Iskandar's father is the same Jamuga that the history books speak of." Then to Masud: "Is that all?"

"He said he leaves his lieutenant here to take care of us, that the man will listen to our chatter, for he speaks our language, and that he has orders to kill anyone speaking treachery or planning to escape. He also said you must remember that escape is impossible in the midst of his vast army."

"His army," Rostam said with contempt. "He dares to call it his army."

"What else did he say?" Tejmur asked.

"He said if the great Khan again laughs at his account of the way you killed the warriors on the edge of the sea, you will have no choice but tell Iskandar the way you make the arrows. He also said he will soon claim his women."

"Did he say the name of his lieutenant who will spy on us?"

"Yes. Dajir. He leans against the building across the street and watches us even now."

When he came closer, Tejmur thought, there would be much to say to this Dajir, if he would listen—particularly if the father of Iskandar was the same Jamuga of whom Tejmur had read.

Steady winds blew the stench of Baku's dead and the Mongol army west; and a rolling cloud cover, low and heavy, kept the city cool.

Tejmur spent some time examining the house that was their prison, though he returned repeatedly to the doorway hoping that Dajir would approach. Perhaps, Tejmur told himself, he might get lucky and find in one of the rooms something made of copper that he could hammer into a sheet. Then for the Baghdad battery he would need a pot, some acid, and an iron rod. Obtaining those things would be easy, under normal circumstances: for the iron he could use a dagger, and uric acid would work for the electrolyte. But these are not normal circumstances, he reminded himself.

The house contained nothing made from copper. Tejmur wandered from window to window where he found Iskandar's guards grinning, hands on their swords as if they wished he would try to climb out a window so they could cut him down. Nothing in the streets and nothing in the crude dress of the Mongol guards suggested that finding copper would be easy.

When Tejmur returned to the main room, he found Dajir lounging in the doorway, looking bored.

"We have bread," Tejmur told him. "Enough to share with you, if you want."

"Bread?" Dajir looked in astonishment at Tejmur. "You are about to die, and you offer to share your bread?"

"Iskandar promised to deliver a message to your great king that he should spare our lives."

"You lie. Iskandar would never say such a thing, nor approach Genghis Khan with any message of that sort. Still, you are a generous man to offer bread. If only you had wine or even some of the terrible beer brewed in loaves of old bread. I have had nothing but water since we left the desert cities in the south."

"I have something better than foul beer, better even than good wine." Tejmur took the flask that he had been carrying since the Soviet invasion of Baku from his pocket. "In my country, we call this vodka."

"What?" Dajir stared. "You would poison me."

Tejmur took a drink and offered the flask. "You see? I have no fear of vodka, and I will gladly share with you."

Dajir took the flask, sniffed it, then took a tentative taste. "Strong," he said. "Good." He tilted the flask for a long drink.

"Careful," Tejmur said. "Vodka will spin your head much faster than wine or beer. It's a drink to sip a little at a time."

"Sip?" The notion seemed to amaze Dajir. "Sip?" He took another gurgling drink.

"Good, yes?" Tejmur asked. He waited while Dajir took another drink. "Enough," Tejmur cautioned. "You have downed what amounts to many tankards of stout wine."

"Yes," Dajir agreed, and he laughed. "Yes." He handed the flask to Tejmur.

"I know of the traitorous acts of Jamuga," Tejmur said.

"Jamuga?" Dajir shook his head as though trying to fling the word away. "Jamuga is not a name we speak."

"Iskandar spoke of him and called him father."

"And a fool he is to do so." Dajir seemed to make an effort at looking serious, then threw his head back and laughed. "Many tankards of wine. I feel them. Many."

"Iskandar is also a traitor," Tejmur said. "He betrays the great Khan's trust, for he seeks to learn from me the secret of sending fire into the sky on the backs of arrows. And he plans to keep the knowledge to himself."

"Fire? Flying like arrows? You jest."

"Did you not see the burnt hair on the side of Iskandar's head? My men scorched him with one of our flaming arrows."

"I thank you for the drink, but it puts me under no obligation to you. Speak no more lies about Iskandar lest I draw out your blood upon my blade. He is my captain, and I'll hear no more." Dajir stomped across the street.

"What did you accomplish there?" Rostam asked. "Now Iskandar will kill us as soon as he can, and he will take joy in the killing. If I had my retainers about me right now, I would have you gibbeted for being such a fool."

"Watch your tongue," Masud growled.

"Maybe Rostam is right," Tejmur said. "But then again, maybe I planted enough doubt in Dajir's mind to make him useful when we must deal with Iskandar."

"That time is upon us," Papusza said. "Look. He comes, and he does not look happy."

Chapter 16

As he approached, Iskandar called out to Dajir.

"He told Dajir to have his sword ready." Masud took the Makarov from his belt.

"Stand over there," Tejmur said, "in the shadows. When I point at Iskandar, shoot him, then put the pistol out of sight, fast. The rest of you move back out of reach of a sword."

"Tejmur!" Papusza nodded at the oil pot, picked up the candle striker, and raised her eyebrows in an unspoken question.

"Not yet," Tejmur leaned toward her and whispered. "But if Masud and I go down, light the oil and use the fire as a weapon of last resort."

On the far side of the threshold, Dajir drew his sword and followed his captain into the prison house.

"It's time," Iskandar said and Masud translated, "for you to tell me the way of fire that flies. If you do not, Dajir and I will cut pieces from your body and the bodies of your followers until you speak."

Iskandar drew his sword.

"Tell him," Tejmur said to Masud, "that he must confess he that he lied to me when he promised to talk with Genghis Khan about us and our use of flying fire."

Masud spoke and Iskandar laughed, then answered. Masud translated: "I did not bother the great Khan with petty matters."

As Iskandar moved closer, holding out his blade and seeming to enjoy his threat, Tejmur said to Dajir, "You heard his confession. Your captain has betrayed me, and he has betrayed your king. I will now kill him. Afterward, you can take us to the Khan and win his gratitude. For I know that Genghis Khan values loyalty above all else."

Iskandar stepped toward Tejmur, who pointed his finger in a dramatic gesture, and Masud fired the Makarov. The report of the pistol, and the hole that appeared in Iskandar's forehead before he crumpled to the floor, startled Dajir. He drew back, sword ready, but with his body half turned toward the doorway. Masud tucked the Makarov under his shirt and put his hands in plain view—as if he had done nothing. The guards, responding to the sound of the pistol, crowded around the entrance, trying to see past Dajir.

Tejmur pointed his finger at Dajir. "Tell them," Tejmur said, "to go back to their duties. Tell them the noise was nothing. And tell them now, or you will join Iskandar there on the floor with a magic hole in your head."

A few rasping words from Dajir sent the men back into the street. He stood by the door, looking confused and dizzy.

It took little prodding for Tejmur to get Dajir to lead the group through the narrow streets to meet Genghis Khan. Papusza carried the oilpot and candle striker, and Masud had his pistol; but the rest of them were unarmed and empty-handed. Wind from the Caspian had pushed away much of the odor of decaying corpses, though the smell still caused Tejmur and his followers to cover their noses. Mongol soldiers pointed at them and laughed as they passed, for the horsemen were immune to the stench. Bodies of slain Baku citizens seemed to have been tossed about in the street. There were very few dead Mongols. Doors and windows to houses stood open, and the smell of death came from them. Smoke drifted from some houses, and everywhere was evidence that the city had been looted.

"The citizens fought us," Dajir said. "That was their mistake. We had orders to spare them unless they took up arms."

"They fought?" Rostam asked, surprised. "I tried to get them to leave the city because I thought them all cowards."

"Not cowards," Faiq said. "Brave defenders. And now they are brave and dead. But my memory says you made no effort to warn your people to leave."

"One day," Rostam muttered to Faiq, "I will find a way to make you suffer before I have you killed."

"Enough of such talk," Tejmur said, as they stepped into a large courtyard that he remembered.

"My tent!" Rostam howled. "That scoundrel has taken over my tent."

"Silence," Tejmur said. "Talking like that will get us all killed."

Guards stopped them at the entrance of what had once been Rostam's tent, but was now occupied by Mongols. Dajir spoke to the guards with a great waving of his arms. Then he pointed his finger, touched his forehead, and mimed being wounded.

Masud started to translate, but Tejmur stopped him. "I could see what he said."

Six Mongols crowded around Tejmur and his group, and escorted them into the tent. They came to a halt on the carpet in front of the chair on which Rostam had once sat in state. Sitting on the chair now, much to Tejmur's astonishment, was one of the most beautiful Persian women he had ever seen. She had long hair with a clean raven-like sheen, black eyes that blazed with intelligence and passion, high cheekbones, and a tiny body covered in elegant red silk. Her demeanor said she was accustomed to being obeyed.

This is not, Tejmur thought, a person to trifle with. She signaled them to kneel on the small carpet spread before her chair, and she examined them with a look of imperious disdain.

All knelt except for Rostam. A guard pushed him to his knees.

"What a strange-looking group you are," the woman said in Azeri. "Which is your leader?"

"I am." Rostam stood up. "We have come to bargain with Genghis Khan."

"You're no leader," the woman said. "You're little more than a fool. On your knees."

Rostam bared his teeth. "A Persian dancing girl commands me to kneel on my own carpet? Look, woman, at the cunning workmanship of this small rug. Those are golden threads woven into it. I paid more for this carpet than you are worth in any slave market."

"Careful," Tejmur warned.

"You own nothing here," the woman snapped. She gestured, and a guard forced Rostam to kneel. Then she looked directly at Tejmur. "Call me Dinarzad when you find your tongue."

"Dinarzad," Tejmur said. "I know that name."

"You do not," Dinarzad snapped. "You are a stranger to me, and be advised not to pretend otherwise."

"I meant no insult and no wheedling," Tejmur said. "I know the name only from an ancient story of two sisters, Dinarzad and Shahrazad, who were daughters of a vizier."

"I know that story." Dinarzad's tone softened. "It's a favorite of mine, for it tells of a woman who is far more clever than her father the vizier."

"And far more clever than the Shah whom her father served," Tejmur said.

"Speak with care." Dinarzad glanced about as if checking for someone who might be listening.

Tejmur looked at a group of men standing in a loose circle deeper within the vast tent. They spoke in loud voices and did much laughing. One of them, a man stocky with muscles and wearing bracelets of brass, appeared to be dividing his attention between the men and Dinarzad.

"That was a kind warning," Tejmur said, "and I thank you."

"I heard this man," Dinarzad gestured toward Dajir, "claim that you are a great sorcerer who can kill by pointing your finger, that fire erupts from your hand with a clap of thunder, and that men fall dead."

"I'm not a magician," Tejmur said. "But I do have some information that will be of great use to a certain Mongol leader, a man who was once called Temujin, and is now honored with the title Genghis Khan."

"I've never heard that name, Temujin," Dinarzad said. "Perhaps it would be best for you not to speak thus." Dinarzad looked at Norin. "Stand, girl. Approach me."

Clearly startled, Norin stood with great hesitancy. Then she bowed and approached Dinarzad.

"You're Persian, like me," Dinarzad said. "Have these men treated you well?"

"Tejmur and his friends give me great respect."

"And that fool who thinks himself a leader?" Dinarzad pointed at Rostam.

"Rostam?" Norin hesitated. "He is . . . I mean, he—"

"You fear him."

Norin bowed her head. "Tejmur the magician protects me."

"So the foreigner does have magic," Dinarzad said. "What sort of magic does he wield?"

"He knows the art of sending fire through the air. I've seen him and his lieutenant kill using some kind of magical thunder. But they are good men and kill only to protect those they care about."

"So they care about you?"

"Yes. And the pretty woman called Papusza. And Faiq. Perhaps Amin, once captain to Rostam. Sometimes they seem to care about Rostam, though I see no sense in that."

The man wearing bracelets of brass broke away from the circle of Mongols deeper in the tent and put a hand on Dinarzad's shoulder.

"You have done well," he said.

"This man," Dinarzad nodded toward Tejmur, "and his followers are good people. You must spare their lives, except perhaps for that fool Rostam."

"Must I, then? I've warned you not to count too much on your beauty to spare you from my wrath. You have been useful to me. But you are a slave, and I am the great Khan. Remember your place." The man turned to Tejmur. "You spoke the name given to me at birth. How did you come to know it?"

"Genghis Khan," Masud said, his voice laced with awe. "The greatest of the Mongols, and you speak Azeri."

A smile seemed to flicker across Genghis's face and vanish so fast that Tejmur wasn't sure the man had smiled at all.

"In my travels," Genghis said, "I've come across many strange tongues. Some of them I learn, for such words usually come easily to me, though not the odd speech of the Chinese. They sing when they speak, and I make little sense of them. You—Tejmur, is it?—you knew my birth name. How?"

"I have read many books," Tejmur said.

"There are already books about me?"

"He knows much about the future as well as the past," Papusza said.

"Speak little," Dinarzad warned.

"Speak not at all," Genghis growled to Dinarzad.

"He knows magic of great use to you," Papusza said.

"Is he a shaman?" Genghis asked Papusza. "Does he divine the future by tossing sticks and pebbles, or reading the entrails of slain animals?"

"Yes," Papusza said, and "No," Tejmur said.

Genghis scowled his displeasure. Dinarzad's hand flew to her mouth, and her eyes went round in alarm.

Chapter 17

The great Khan laughed, and the sound sent a chill up Tejmur's spine.

"My guests disagree," Genghis said. "I see that I must put you to a test, Tejmur who knows so much but is no shaman. My weak fondness for wizards and shamans, for mages of all sorts, is matched only by my displeasure with those who tell lies to curry favor." The Khan's eyes glinted with a cold fire. "Perhaps I should have you meet my Chinese wizard. You might be amused by his riddles. But first, you who seem to have the knowledge of a shaman but proclaim that you are not, tell me something no others in this tent know about me."

"Your father's name is Yesugei."

"Good, but hardly something to brag about knowing. Tell me something else."

"The mother of your sons is Bortei. Her father gave you the gift of a rare black sable fur. Your good friend Bogurchi helped you retrieve some stolen horses."

"Enough. You have strange powers, for who among you could know such things?"

"But he reads books of historians and other fools," Rostam said, "so what he seems to know is mostly falsehoods leavened with some truth. I say beware of such knowledge."

"Ah?" Genghis turned a hard face to Rostam. "Who are you to make such pronouncements?"

"Rostam the Great, Shah of Baku."

"Could this be true?" Genghis demanded of Tejmur.

"It was once. Rostam was Shah of Baku before your armies came."

"And this was your tent, and these your royal carpets?" Genghis turned to Dajir. "Your name?"

"Dajir, Lieutenant to Iskandar."

"My lieutenant, then. You and these guards, take this fool shah outside. Take that carpet," Genghis pointed at the small carpet in front of the chair where Dinarzad sat, "and roll his highness into it. Leave him to warm in the sun. Perhaps those golden threads sewn into his beloved carpet will give him comfort."

The men in the back of the tent chuckled—a low, sinister sound—and Tejmur felt the chill in his spine deepen into a prickle of real fear. He watched Dajir and another Mongol warrior drag Rostam outside, while a couple of the others rolled up the carpet Genghis had pointed to.

"May I make a plea for Rostam's life, and for the lives of my friends?" Tejmur asked.

"Were you among the foolish people of this city who resisted my army?"

"No. We knew you were coming, and we tried to flee. But Iskandar, son of Jamuga, captured us beyond the hill to the north. I asked him to tell you of our use of fire that flies as a weapon."

"Fire that flies?" Genghis's eyes hardened. "Iskandar said nothing of such a weapon."

"He gave me his word that he would talk to you of our weapon, but he lied." Tejmur decided it was time to take a chance, one that could win safe passage out of Baku. But he also knew that if he chose his words poorly, his talking would earn only death for himself and his party. Speak now, he told himself, then blurted out, "Iskandar is dead."

Genghis nodded, his face showing no emotion. "You killed him with your magic weapon, then, you who are no shaman."

"The weapon I spoke of is a sending of fire through the air on the tips of arrows. It is a device you will use to subdue the Chinese."

"*Will* use, not *can* use." Genghis rubbed his chin. "You know something of the future, then. Or perhaps you seek to flatter me. Be warned that I have sent many flatterers to their deaths."

Tejmur swallowed hard. "I do know a great deal about your future."

"Will it serve me well to hear what you know?" Genghis sounded genuine in his question. "Do you see the time and way of my death?"

Dinarzad gasped, and spoke in a trembling voice. "But you will not die. You must not die."

"All men die. So Shaman Tejmur, do you foresee the way and time of it?"

"Yes," Tejmur said. "I know the time, the place, and the circumstances."

"Then, on pain of death, you will not tell me."

"What I have to offer you now is not predictions. Perhaps, after you have seen the weapon, you will be more interested in what I have to say about the shape of things to come. But for the present, I offer the secret of the fire that flies . . . in exchange for the lives of myself and my companions, and for safe passage away from Baku."

"You will demonstrate the weapon, of course."

"Of course."

"Now."

"I'll need a bow, some arrows, and some rags. But I ask again for our lives, and safe passage, in exchange for showing you the secret of the weapon."

"We will speak later of favors, if your weapon pleases me." Genghis barked an order in a language Tejmur did not understand, and several men jumped to obey.

The Mongol warriors returned carrying a bow, arrows, and some strips of cloth crusted with dark stains that Tejmur realized with a shudder had been made by the blood of dead citizens of Baku.

"You have what you asked for," Genghis said. "Proceed."

Tejmur stole a furtive glance toward the oil pot and candle striker that Papusza still hid in the folds of the dress that bunched around her crossed legs. She sat on the carpet nearby, and he made eye contact with her before he turned back to the man on whom all their fates rested.

"I'll need a moment to prepare."

"Alone?"

"No. With my apprentice Masud, and this woman here." Tejmur nodded at Papusza.

"Not alone," the Khan said thoughtfully. "And not with your apprentice. I won't leave you to your own devices with another who knows so much of your magic." Genghis stretched his lips into an ironical smile and studied Masud for a long moment. "I don't want to wind up like Iskandar."

"Just the woman, then."

"Very well. But be warned, shaman, all who have sought to cheat Genghis Khan have paid the price of their dishonor with agony and humiliation that made death welcome when it finally came."

"I have heard that Genghis Khan is a man of honor, a man who rewards the loyalty of those who serve him well. I am also a man of honor, and I have much to offer that the great Khan will find useful."

"Remember that your life, and the lives of those who follow you, depend upon that." With that, Genghis barked a series of commands and all the occupants of the tent scurried for the front entrance—all except for Dinarzad, who remained standing a few feet from where Tejmur stood and Papusza sat.

Dinarzad met Tejmur's questioning glance with a steady stare, her black eyes wide with a mix of awe and suspicion. "The Great Khan has tasked me with making sure you do not vanish into thin air, or fly away over the battlements of Baku."

"Surely," Tejmur said, "he does not believe such things are possible. And I know that you do not."

"I do not presume to speak of what the Great Khan believes or disbelieves. Nor should you, if you mean to leave this place alive."

Papusza stood and took a slow step toward the Persian courtesan. "Will he keep his word? Let us speak plainly, woman to woman. If we give him what he asks, will the Khan allow us to go on our way?"

"Woman to woman, then. I have never seen the Khan deal unjustly with those who have dealt justly with him. Anyway, not with men. He regards women in a different way." Dinarzad shuddered as she shifted her glance to Tejmur. "Now you must hurry. You have little time left before I must take you outside to meet your fate."

Tejmur and Papusza wasted no time wrapping the tips of the arrows with the blood-stained cloth and tying the wrappings firmly to the arrow shafts. Dinarzad watched them carefully, stepping closer as Papusza uncovered the oilpot and candle striker. Papusza held the oil pot while Tejmur dipped each arrow in the sticky black crude. When the last of the arrows had been dipped in oil, Papusza swaddled the oil pot and firestriker again and returned them to the folds of her dress.

"We are ready," Tejmur said.

"Good. It is time."

Dinarzad escorted them out the front entrance of the tent, into the blinding afternoon sun and the smell of death that wafted on the cool sea breeze. The Mongol warriors who had been evicted from the tent had been formed into a wide circle to create a kind of arena. Masud, Faiq, Norin, and Amin sat in a tight group at the far edge of the open space, watched by a pair of Mongols whose swords were bared. A short distance from them, a pair of corpses, naked and bloating in the afternoon sun, showed Tejmur where the strips of blood-crusted cloth had come from—and reminded him of the price they would all pay if he failed to make the fire fly as he had promised.

"Are you ready then, shaman?" Genghis's brass bracelets clanked as he strode across the open ground toward Tejmur and Papusza. He stopped about a meter away, and made eye contact with Dinarzad, who nodded.

"I will need a target," Tejmur said. "Something that will burn without setting the city ablaze. And it would be better if you allowed one of my men to do the shooting. I'm not much of an archer."

"All the better. I have in mind a challenge, one that will make your demonstration more entertaining. If you can set that carpet ablaze from the far side of the circle, in addition to your freedom, I will reward you with any gift you desire from within the walls of Baku."

"Carpet?"

Genghis barked a command and flung an arm at the far side of the circle. The warriors who had been standing there leaped back, revealing the carpet in which Rostam had been rolled up earlier and left to bake in the sun.

"How does that sound, Rostam?" Genghis roared. "I'll reward the shaman here for roasting you alive by giving him the treasure he most desires from among all the things that once were yours and now are mine."

A series of muffled screams emerged from the carpet, which commenced to flop about like a wounded caterpillar. The ring of Mongol warriors roared with laughter, either at Genghis's challenge or Rostam's response—or both.

Tejmur was not amused; nor, he noticed, was Papusza. Tejmur glanced from Papusza to the little group of captives, studying faces. Only Faiq seemed to share the amusement of the Mongol warriors, his wolfish grin mirroring the expressions of the sword-wielding barbarians who guarded him.

"I have a counteroffer," Tejmur said. "I will trade my knowledge of the future for Rostam's life."

"That would be a fool's bargain," Genghis said, the undertone of his voice as cruel and ironical as his smile. "We live among death and pain. The future promises even more suffering. You have heard my offer. Now burn Rostam and his carpet."

Tejmur looked at the carpet where Rostam still jerked and bucked, his desperate remonstrations muffled by the cloth. Then Tejmur shifted his glance to where Masud, Norin, Amin, and Faiq sat huddled under the eager swords of two Mongol warriors. He looked at Papusza, remembering his desire to kiss her in the mist that rose off the Caspian Sea and his promise to take her to Constantinople. In his mind's eye, he saw the sheet of copper he needed to make the battery that would revive his time window and saw the window open onto his own time. He nocked an arrow on the bowstring, letting the shaft rest on the bow.

"Papusza," he said, "light the arrow."

"Surely you are not going to burn Rostam alive?" Papusza's voice quavered with emotion. "The man who brought me bread and tea, and who talked with me like an equal on that bench by the Caspian Sea, would never do such a thing."

"Light the arrow, Papusza."

"I will not."

"Silence, woman!" Genghis shouted. "You will do as he commands, or all of you die."

Papusza lifted the candle striker, and the arrow flamed to life. Tejmur drew the bowstring back, sighting down the arrow shaft at the carpet that held the man whose death would give all of his companions their lives and freedom—the same man who had tried to have them all killed in their sleep. Then he took the deepest breath of his life, raised the bow high, and fired the flaming arrow above the ring of Mongol warriors where its fiery path would end in the Caspian just beyond the city's wall. The warriors yelped in surprise to watch fire fly over their heads.

"Thank you," Papusza whispered.

"You're a dead man," Dinarzad said.

"I wish you had not done that," Masud said, pulling the Makarov from beneath his shirt and checking its safety.

Chapter 18

"I doubt," Genghis said, "the ocean will burn." He strode to the rolled-up carpet, picked up the edge, and gave it a shake. Rostam went spinning into the dust, an event that brought waves of laughter from the Mongol warriors. Rostam, caked with sweat and dust, crawled toward the city wall.

Then Genghis laughed as well, a barking sound devoid of humor.

Tejmur's relief at their momentary reprieve spurred him into quick action. "The Makarov," he gestured to Masud, who looked at the pistol as if he were surprised to see it in his hand. He tucked it again into his shirt.

Genghis spat rapid orders to the men near him, and a great wave of activity swept across the open area in front of the tent that had once been Rostam's. Tejmur stepped back among his friends, surprised to see Dinarzad among them.

"The Khan," Masud said, "has ordered a hay rick brought to us."

"So he still wants to see the fire that flies," Tejmur said.

"Yes." Dinarzad nodded. "Somehow your act of defiance has pleased Genghis. I do not understand men."

"Nor I," Norin said.

"I understand this man." Papusza took Tejmur's hand and brought it to her lips, then she dropped his hand and gave her attention to tying strips of cloth onto an arrow. She turned her back, produced the oil pot, and poured some onto the wrapped arrow.

Two Mongols pushed a cart heaped with straw into the courtyard near the discarded carpet. Rostam, to the amusement and jeers of the warriors, continued to crawl.

"Stop that!" Faiq said. "You dishonor yourself. You dishonor your city."

"Shaman Tejmur," Genghis called out. "Tell your woman to strike fire onto another arrow. Burn this straw."

Papusza brought the arrow dripping with oil.

"I'll miss," Tejmur said.

"Miss, and this time you will be a dead man for sure," Dinarzad said.

Masud took the bow and nocked the blackened arrow. "I will not miss. Papusza, light the fire."

Tejmur had expected someone to rake the straw onto the ground. He was a bit surprised to realize that Masud's instinct as a soldier was superior in this instance to his own trained mind. Masud had understood at once that straw and cart alike were the target, and that both should burn.

Masud drew the bow and released the arrow that Papusza had lit.

An awed silence fell over the Mongol warriors as they watched the flaming arrow thud into the bed of the cart, the fire spreading fast and sending dark smoke into the air.

"So you see," Tejmur called to Genghis, "it takes no shaman to send fire flying toward your enemy. Any man can do it."

"Any man?" Dinarzad said. "It seems to me that the woman played a larger part."

Looking fierce and not at all amused, Genghis strode to Tejmur and clapped a heavy hand on his shoulder. "You are truly a man of honor, and a wizard armed with fire."

"You never expected me to kill Rostam," Tejmur said.

"I never expect anything." Genghis glanced at Dinarzad. "Those who do are too often disappointed."

"It was all a test, then."

"All of life is a test. The fools who fail when I test them die." Genghis shrugged. "Most of them. I admire loyalty of the type you showed to that pitiful man." He gestured toward Rostam, who had reached a thin strip of shade at the base of the city wall and sat panting and glaring at the Mongol warriors.

"Woman," Genghis turned to Papusza. "Show me the bottle of magic water you poured on the arrow."

Papusza drew her dress about her and shook her head.

"Do it," Dinarzad hissed through her teeth.

"Papusza," Tejmur said gently, "give him the bottle."

When Papusza handed him the oil pot, Genghis sniffed it, and poured some in a hand. "The smell." He shook his head.

"Not pleasant," Tejmur agreed.

"And yet that black water understands fire and likes the heat of it."

"Yes," Tejmur said. "In large amounts, and spread properly, it can set rock walls afire and bring flame to anything made from wood."

"Flesh?"

"Yes. It can burn flesh. Your hand would burn even now, if someone dropped sparks into the black stuff that sticks to your skin."

"Good," Genghis said. "You, Papusza, wrap another arrow with strips of cloth from the dead of Baku."

"Why?" Dinarzad demanded.

Genghis gave Dinarzad a hard look, and she stepped back. Tejmur noticed a quick flash of terror on her face, though she found composure immediately.

"You wish to send fire into the sky yourself, of course," Dinarzad said.

Papusza quickly wrapped another arrow.

Genghis wiped his hand on a piece of cloth and turned to Tejmur. "You will show me the secret of making the black water that loves fire."

"We did not make the black water. We found it."

"Far from here?"

"Over the high bluff to the north." Tejmur pointed.

"Is there enough for my men to use in laying siege to a stubborn city?"

"Enough for a hundred such cities."

"You will show me where."

"Of course."

Papusza handed him the arrow. Genghis poured oil onto it, and set the oilpot on the ground. Then he took the bow from Masud, nocked the arrow, and turned in silence to Papusza.

She struck the candle lighter, and the arrow blazed.

With a swiftness of motion that startled Tejmur, Genghis swung around, jerked the bowstring back, and fired the flaming arrow into Dinarzad.

She crumpled to her knees, a look of shock on her face, then pitched forward into the dirt.

"Her flesh does not burn," Genghis said. He sounded surprised and disappointed.

The Mongol warriors cheered.

"Lickspittals," Tejmur murmured and turned to Papusza, who had fallen to her knees. They both looked at Dinarzad, the shock on her face fading to resignation as the light faded from her eyes.

"Right now more than ever," Masud said softly, "I would like to use the Makarov."

"As would I. But do not." Tejmur gestured toward the Mongol warriors in the courtyard.

"You speak of my men," Genghis said.

"They cheered the killing of your woman." Tejmur tried to keep the disgust from his voice—disgust for both Genghis Khan and the warriors.

"They cheer whatever I do, of course. Unless I were to show weakness, such as enduring for long the sharp and commanding tongue of a woman slave." Genghis chuckled. "And yet her flesh did not burn. It did not burn, as you said it would."

"The blood in her body quenched the fire," Tejmur said. "And there was too little of the black water to burn her body."

"The bottle, woman," Genghis said. "Pour the rest of the black water that loves fire on her."

Papusza, still kneeling, seemed not to hear.

Beside her, Norin sat with her head in her hands as her shoulders heaved with great sobs. Amin stared dully at the body of Dinarzad. Only Faiq seemed unmoved.

"Woman of Tejmur!" Genghis barked in a commanding tone.

Suddenly, Faiq snatched the bottle from Papusza and poured its contents on the back of the dead courtesan.

"Good man. Now drop the sparks on her."

Faiq took the candle striker from Papusza and set the corpse to burning.

"No," Papusza moaned, and she struggled to her feet.

Tejmur took her arm, drew her to him. "Do nothing," he warned. "Don't watch. Turn your back. Think of Constantinople. You must stay still for now, and stay silent."

"You have wisdom," Genghis said to Tejmur, "about women, and about the black water that loves fire." He pointed to the body of Dinarzad, which was now covered in flame. "As you said, even flesh burns when there is enough of the black water. This weapon of yours pleases me mightily. You will show me where to find the magic water."

Tejmur stared at what had once been the lovely Dinarzad but was now a mass of charred flesh. The stench of burned meat rose from the body in a cloud of dirty smoke that made his gorge rise, choking off his first attempt at speech. At last, Tejmur swallowed hard, then managed a shrug.

"I will show you . . . if I must."

"Of course you must. Tomorrow. Tonight I dine. And you, Shaman Tejmur, will be my honored guest. Until then, I offer you the shade of a clean tent and the comfort of the city's best carpets covering the sand. And you will have water, as much as you desire." He gestured toward a smaller tent across the courtyard from the one formerly belonging to Rostam.

"And my people?"

"Ah. Of course. The shaman is loyal to those who serve him. They will share in his good fortune. I suppose you would invite that dog, Rostam, he of the carpet with golden threads?"

"No," Norin muttered, raising her tear-streaked face and staring at Rostam, and "No," Masud whispered.

"Him too, yes," Tejmur said. "Although he is indeed a dog."

"Wisely put." Genghis gestured and two Mongol warriors dragged

Rostam to his feet, pulling him toward the smaller tent. "But for dinner with me tonight, only you." Genghis laughed again, and again Tejmur heard no humor in the laughter.

Chapter 19

The two Mongol warriors who had stood watch over the company while Tejmur showed Genghis Khan the secret of flying fire herded them all into the small tent where the guards had already dragged Rostam. Then both guards sheathed their swords and withdrew. As the Khan had promised, the floor was covered in beautiful carpets, and there were great earthenware jugs of water in a corner. They found Rostam sprawled next to the water jugs, draining cup after cup—between bouts of dousing his head and body with the life-restoring liquid.

"Make way, dog!" Faiq dragged Rostam away from the water, stopping at intervals to kick the struggling former Shah of Baku, finally depositing him in a heap near the entrance to the tent. "You have dishonored us all with your cowardice. I would gut you like the cur you are, if only I had my knife." With that, Faiq began kicking Rostam again.

"Faiq!" Tejmur said, his voice calm but firm. "Leave him—"

But Tejmur's remonstrance was interrupted by Amin, who leaped across the tent and drove a shoulder into Faiq's back, carrying him to the ground. The two men rolled over and over, their hands finding each other's throats—first Faiq on top, then Amin—until they threatened to overturn the water jugs.

"Stop this!" Tejmur shouted.

But both Faiq and Amin, who was now astride him, continued to do their best to choke the life out of each other.

"Stop now, or die." Masud said in a voice as cold and hard as the Makarov clenched in his fist.

It came to Tejmur that Masud's voice sounded just like Genghis Khan's as he spoke of killing Dinarzad. That thought chilled Tejmur almost as much as the sight of the company literally at each other's throats. Despite the pall of heat that hung in the tent, he found himself frozen.

Everyone in the tent fell silent, as completely still as Tejmur himself. Papusza and Norin stood against the wall of the tent, as far from the melee as they could get. Rostam lay on his belly next to the water jugs. Masud leveled his Makarov at Amin and Faiq.

"Decide," Masud said in that same cold voice.

"He will not lay hands on Rostam," Amin managed to choke out, through the grip that Faiq still had on his throat. "He may not be a . . . man of honor, but he is my former commander."

"I will bury my knife in his guts," Faiq grunted in reply.

"Then you die," Masud said.

"Animals," Papusza hissed, advancing to stand between Masud's Makarov and the men on the floor of the tent. "You are all acting like animals. As bad as the Mongols. If we turn on each other, we will all die like Dinarzad, at the hands of that monster out there."

To Tejmur's horror, Papusza was standing directly in front of the Makarov's muzzle. "Papusza is right," he found himself saying. The sight of Papusza standing in front of Masud's still-leveled pistol, he guessed, had melted the ice that had frozen his brain. "We have every chance of escaping Baku with our lives and the means to go where we will. But to make that happen, we must all work together."

"You I trust," Masud said, shifting his glance to take in Tejmur. "And you." Masud nodded at Papusza, who still stood in front of the gun. "But the rest of you, I know nothing of. And although I take no pleasure in killing, I will not place my life in your hands."

Norin moved toward Masud, both hands held palm up in front of her. "What about me?" she whispered. "If not with your life, will you trust me with the awful power of the weapon in your hand?"

"You don't even know how to use it."

"Then teach me." Norin knelt next to Masud, stretching both hands up as if in prayer. "Teach me to fight, as you were taught in that world of wonders you came from. In return, I will teach you the ways of my world. Perhaps in this way, we can come to know one another in a fashion that will benefit us both."

Masud lowered the barrel of the Makarov, then placed the butt into Norin's outstretched hands. "Let it be so," he said.

"Amin! Faiq!" Papusza said firmly, as soon as the pistol was safely in Norin's possession. "Release each other, and get up. This idiocy ends now."

To Tejmur's surprise, both men complied. They released each other and stood slowly, shaking their heads and blinking their eyes as if waking up from a long sleep. Then each man walked to opposite sides of the tent.

As if Amin and Faiq's fight had been a signal, the entire company divided upon itself. Papusza, Masud, Norin, and Tejmur seated themselves in a loose circle near the opening of the tent. Amin joined Rostam over by the water jugs. Faiq sat alone on the far side of the tent, sipping water and keeping to himself. And although Tejmur was uncomfortable with the divisions that had suddenly threatened to split their company beyond repair, he had no idea how to go about bridging those gaps and bringing everyone together. Perhaps, he thought, it might be best just to let fatigue and hunger work awhile to lower the energy levels of his companions. At least that might keep them from trying to kill each other until an opportunity presented itself to bring them back together again.

To Tejmur's relief, such an opportunity was not long in coming. The two Mongol warriors who had escorted the group into the tent reappeared in the opening, which the guards spread wide to allow the entry of a half-dozen women. All of the women carried large bowls of what looked to be beaten silver, and that each deposited in turn at the center of the tent in a circle on the carpeted floor. The women, who looked to Tejmur like locals who had survived the slaughter, said nothing. Nor did the guards. When the last of the bowls had been placed on the floor, both the women and the Mongol guards withdrew.

As the last of the slave women exited, Tejmur stood. The delicate odor of food, overpowering even the stench of death and destruction that still hung like a pall over the city of Baku, wafted through the tent. In the bowls Tejmur made out cheese, strips of dried meat, and what looked like yogurt. The sight and scent of the food unleashed a wave of hunger that centered on his grumbling belly and seemed to stretch through his entire being. He couldn't remember the last time he'd tasted food—real food, and not just the crusty bread Faiq had supplied. But in spite of his eagerness to eat, Tejmur knew that he had to seize the moment.

"We've been at each other's throats," Tejmur said, "literally. Now let's gather together in fellowship and share this gift of food equally." He looked from face to face, seeing the odor of the food at his feet begin to work its magic on the senses of each member of the company. "As equals. Once we've all filled our bellies, we need to use our minds. We've got to decide what to do once I've won our freedom. In this discussion, as with the meal, everyone will share equally. All will be heard. Agreed?"

Sounds of assent from each member of the company were followed by a general movement toward the circle of bowls at Tejmur's feet. For a long time, the only sounds were of chewing and swallowing. The meal was surprisingly good. There were two types of cheese with which Tejmur was unfamiliar—one with a sharp taste, and a hard, crumbly texture; the other softer and mellower—but both of which he found delicious. The dried meat was chewy and incredibly salty, but savory. Tejmur didn't want to think about what kind of animal the meat had come from. The yogurt was slightly sweet, and made an excellent contrast to the cheese and meat; but the lack of eating utensils made him stick with a single fingerdip from the yogurt bowl. His fear of disease outweighed his desire to cleanse his palate.

Like Tejmur, Papusza and Masud and Norin settled for a single taste of the yogurt. But the rest of the company dipped their fingers into the bowl until it was literally wiped clean. Tejmur found himself watching with distaste as Rostam, Amin, and Faiq ate like the animals Papusza had called them earlier, wiping their dirty hands upon their filthy clothes between bites of cheese, meat, and yogurt.

"We have eaten," Tejmur said, rising as the last bit of the food in the bowls had been consumed. "Now let us weigh our options." Tejmur took one of the earthen waterbowls, carried it back to his place next to Papusza in the center of the tent, and proceeded to clean his hands. Papusza, Masud, and Norin followed suit. "Who wishes to speak first about our plans for the future?"

"What makes you so sure we will have a future, shaman?" Rostam sneered from his place beside the water jugs. "Now that Genghis Khan has the secret of the fire that flies, what will keep him from using it on us in the same way he used it on his own concubine?"

All eyes turned to Tejmur.

"A fair question." Tejmur spoke evenly, careful not to allow the lack of confidence he saw in many of the faces around him to creep into his own voice. "But one for which I have two very good answers."

"Then let us hear them," Rostam said.

"First, Genghis Khan does not yet have the full secret of the fire that flies. There is yet much that he does not know, and this gives me power with which to strike a bargain. I believe that I can win much more than mere freedom for the knowledge I carry. We will need money for the road ahead, and an escort to carry us safely through Mongol-held territory."

"Mere words," Rostam sneered. "The moment you are done talking, the Khan will slit all our throats."

"Words indeed. But words have great power when spoken by those with deep knowledge—and when heard by those with the honor to keep a bargain. In all that I have read of Genghis Khan, I have learned of a man who keeps the bargains he makes, and who values honesty and honor above all. And the Khan also reveres those who have knowledge. The histories say that he was very tolerant religiously, and interested to learn philosophical and moral lessons. He consulted Christian missionaries, Muslim merchants, and even the Taoist monk Qiu Chuji."

"We hear you," Faiq said, from his solitary place across the tent. "I for one believe that the shaman is our only hope for leaving this place alive. I say that we all speak now, for or against placing our lives in the hands of Tejmur."

"Agreed," Masud said, and "Agreed," Papusza and Norin echoed.

"I also agree to place my trust in Tejmur," Amin said.

Rostam smirked and nodded with what seemed great reluctance. "Very well. For now. But when we are in lands outside Mongol control, we will have another such counsel."

"Agreed," Tejmur said. "But in anticipation of that moment, it would be wise to get a rough idea of each person's goals for what lies ahead . . . as Rostam says, outside of Mongol lands. As for myself, I have promised Papusza that I will take her to Constantinople. This is a promise that I intend to keep, if she is still interested in going with me."

"Your promise," Papusza said, "is the only thing that has kept me alive through all of this horror."

"I also go with Tejmur," Masud said.

"And I," Norin said.

"Tejmur has hopes of winning money from the Khan, as well as safe passage," Faiq said. "I go where the money goes."

"As for the money," Rostam said, "any booty that Genghis Khan bestows upon Tejmur will almost certainly once have belonged to me. And I will demand my fair share. And as for my plans, I plan to go to Ardebil and raise an army. Then I shall return to Baku to take my revenge on these barbarians and reclaim my place as Shah."

"I also crave revenge on these barbarians," Amin said. "But until we are free of their influence, Tejmur, I am yours to command."

"Then we are agreed," Tejmur said, surprised and relieved at the ease with which unanimity had been restored, at least for the moment. "I will make the best bargain I can for all of us, and we will speak again when all of us are free."

Chapter 20

When the two Mongol warriors came to escort Tejmur to the tent of Genghis Khan, Masud spoke to them in their own language. Clearly startled, the warriors responded with angry gestures that made Tejmur fear for Masud's life.

"What's going on?" Tejmur demanded.

"I told them that I'm going with you, and they say no," Masud said.

"Then you cannot go."

Masud shook his head. "That barbarian Genghis may well murder you, despite his words about rewarding loyalty. You need me along to protect you."

"There seems to be no choice. I go alone."

"Then you take the Makarov."

"A few bullets against a hundred thousand Mongols? All I could do with that pistol is get us all killed."

"I say again, that barbarian will kill you as readily as he murdered Dinarzad."

"Not likely. Remember that I have something he wants. And there is more—"

"I agree with Masud," Papusza interrupted. "He should go with you."

"We should all stay together in this wild land, when we can. But I will be safe enough, for Genghis Khan needs to learn much additional information about the fire that flies. And as I said, there is something more that he wants from me—a piece of information that he will pay richly for, over and above the price of our lives."

One of the warriors spoke in an impatient tone, and Masud said, "These men are on the verge of violence." He took the Makarov from his belt.

"Put that away," Tejmur said.

"Take it with you," Masud said. "For my peace of mind."

"And mine," Papusza said.

Astonished, Tejmur turned to her. "Are you urging me to carry the implement of violence and death?"

"Only because I fear for you. Only that."

"Then, Masud, give me the pistol. Though of course I cannot use it. I will be back, I assure you."

Masud handed Tejmur the Makarov, and he put it under his belt, beneath his shirt.

"And if you do not return?" Norin asked.

"Then may the spirits of the desert have mercy on our souls," Faiq said.

As the warriors escorted Tejmur from the tent, Papusza said, "You claimed there is more. What did you mean?"

"I know his future." Tejmur spoke over his shoulder. "And besides, the great leader has a keen sense of honor, one I think I understand better than he knows."

"That man is without honor," Rostam said.

"We must trust Tejmur's judgment," Papusza said.

Tejmur could hear the resignation in her voice, and her fear for his safety. And as he moved toward the entrance to the tent, the thought of Papusza's concern for his well being brought a smile to Tejmur's face.

The two guards took Tejmur's arms and pulled him across the

courtyard, past a fire where two women tended skewers of meat. The skewers crackled and hissed, and the meat smelled good. Tejmur looked around, wondering what kind of animal had supplied the flesh on the skewers. Camel, maybe, he thought. Or perhaps the soldiers had slaughtered one of the goats he had seen when he first entered the city. The women looked bruised and dirty. One looked directly at Tejmur, and he was startled to see she had blue-gray eyes instead of the black and dark brown eyes he had seen in all the other citizens of that ancient city. The women continued to cast furtive glances at Tejmur and the guards, who shoved Tejmur into the tent of Genghis Khan.

Genghis, sitting cross-legged on one of Rostam's elegant Persian carpets, snapped a command. Tejmur's escorts backed out of the tent, bowing and touching their right hands to their hearts.

Beside the Mongol leader sat a man with a heavy, down-turned moustache and a handsome oriental face. His eyes seemed to take in every detail about Tejmur, and to weigh what they saw with a vast intelligence.

Genghis Khan gestured, and Tejmur took a seat on the carpet. "This," Genghis said, "is Qui Chuji, the wizard I mentioned. Though he deals in ideas and riddles and not magic or weaponry. Qui said he would like to hear what you know about the tower, the one you called the Maiden's Tower."

"I know your name," Tejmur said. "There are many who call you a Taoist wizard. I have heard that you are a great and wise teacher. But of course you speak Chinese and not Azeri, so I waste my breath in addressing you. Despite your great wisdom, simple geography makes it impossible for you to be other than ignorant of the Azeri language."

"You have heard incorrectly about my great wisdom," Qui Chuji said. "And your assumption about my ignorance is also misguided."

"Persian," Tejmur said in astonishment. "You speak one of the languages of Persia."

"Like me," Genghis said, "Qui has the gift for learning tongues. What else have you heard about him?"

"Not much. That he sometimes travels with you, for he loves to learn about other peoples beyond China. That he can recite Lao Tzu. That he understands the mysteries of the Tao. Other than that, my ignorance is complete."

Qui Chuji looked amused. "Complete, is it? I have struggled for years to gain ignorance, and I hardly have enough to mention, much less brag about."

"You see?" Genghis looked pleased. "He speaks in riddles, ones I find amusing to ponder."

"You would learn the truth about the Maiden's Tower?" Tejmur asked.

"Truth and falsehood slip past one another like eels in a lake. I would learn of that tower, yes, be it truth or lies."

"It is today about a hundred years old. That I believe to be a truth. The story in my country is that it was built by a king who wanted to marry his daughter."

"Many kings want to marry their daughters to the wealthy," Genghis said.

"This king wanted the girl for himself, to mate with her, to make her bear his children."

"Disgusting," Genghis said.

"The maiden thought so, too. She told her father she would not consider marriage until she had a proper tower built on the edge of the sea. So the king ordered his architects, his stone masons, his artisans, and his slaves to build such a tower. It took many years to complete. The first part built by the stone masons was the round tower, so like the corner of many castles in Europe. The second part is the odd protrusion from the round tower, stuck to the side like an afterthought."

"This is a good story and true," Qui said.

"It is not true at all," Tejmur said. "It is a myth. But the story goes that the maiden put off her father's advances until the tower was complete, then he came for her. She fled to the top of the tower and flung herself into the sea, for she preferred death to the dishonor of mating with her father."

"That part of the myth is foolish," Qui said. "But the rest is true, for it speaks wisdom that is worthy of the Tao."

"I like best the foolish part of the story," Genghis said. "A woman who chooses death over dishonor is a good woman. If I had been there, I would have saved her the terror of leaping into the sea. I'd have taken her life with my sword. Then I would have found the father and made him suffer much before granting him death."

"How is the first part of the story true?" Tejmur asked.

"The maid's father approached her with a disgusting offer of marriage, and she did not say no. She also did not say yes. She did nothing. It is the way of the Tao. By doing nothing, everything gets accomplished."

"That's a riddle I don't understand," Genghis said.

"But she did something," Tejmur said. "She had the tower built."

"She herself did nothing. And that is good, for nothing and something create each other."

"Yet another strange riddle," Genghis said.

"You bring flying fire to this leader," Qui said. "It is a great war weapon. But wise leaders do not use weapons of war."

"And if my enemies attacked me with flying fire?" Genghis asked. "Would I be unwise to answer them with such fire?"

"When such weapons are necessary," Qui said, "the wisest leaders use them with calm restraint."

"Good, good." Genghis clapped his hands. "Finally a riddle I can understand. I, of course, always use calm restraint in all wars."

Tejmur looked hard at Genghis. Was the man serious? And did Tejmur dare challenge him about the matter—or any matter, given his murderous nature?

"You put nine out of every ten people to death in the lands you conquer," Tejmur said at last. "How is that calm restraint?

"I always spare the cities where the people do not oppose me."

"But most do oppose you."

"Yes. The fools. The cities I conquer are full of people who hoard and sleep and feed and know not me—and when I appear before their gates with my golden horde of horsemen, they resist me. And yet I do not kill them all. This, I say, is calm restraint. With your gift of fire that flies, I can observe even more calm restraint. Great fires strike fear into the hearts of even the most hardened fools, and people will learn not to resist me, so I will kill fewer of them."

Tejmur looked at Qui Chuji to see if he agreed, but the Taoist master's face showed nothing.

"You look to him," Genghis said, "to see if he fears me. He does not. Nor do you. And I respect you both for the way you look me in the eye without fear. Even my bravest soldiers cannot do that."

"Perhaps our fear hides itself in our bravery," Qui said.

"Another riddle? Ah, but no man or wizard or shaman can hide fear. No woman can hide her fear either, not for long. Your women fear me, Tejmur, and that is good. They should fear me, for I will kill them as readily as I kill flies or moths should they displease me. I might kill them if you displease me—but you know that. It is my way of ensuring your obedience, though you do not fear me for yourself."

"All men have fears," Tejmur said. "Fear of the unknown. Fear of death. The way in which we choose to deal with these fears is a great part of what defines us as men."

"As you have seen, I am not as other men," Genghis said. "And the greatest reason for this is that I choose to be careful instead of fearful."

"Now it is the Khan who speaks in riddles," Qui said.

"Bah! But if you choose to indulge me, I will tell you a tale."

"Please," Tejmur said, and "Please," Qui echoed.

"Very well. I will share the tale of the Khan and the badarcin," Genghis said, and turned a sly smile on Tejmur. "A badarcin is a wandering monk, who is clever in ways that teach lessons to those with ears to hear and the wisdom to listen. But he always exacts a reward. In this, he reminds me much of you, Tejmur. But on with the tale.

"There once lived a khan whose domain stretched across the Steppe from the sunrise to the sunset. But he had no son to pass his kingdom to, and he was beginning to feel the cold fist of age close upon him. One day he announced: 'I will leave my throne to the man telling a lie which makes a sitting man stand up and wakes up a sleeping man.'

"A tailor heard this and came before the khan. 'Great khan! In the heavy rain of yesterday the last of the edges of the heaven got torn and I went and sewed them up again using the tendons of a louse,' he lied and thought: now I have surely told a lie which will make a sitting man stand up and wake up a sleeping one.

"But the khan said: 'Bah, you sewed it up badly. After all, it rained again this morning.' The tailor left the room in silence.

"Then a herdsman stepped in front of the khan and told him: 'Great khan! My deceased father owned a whip with which he struck the stars from the sky.'

"The khan answered: 'That's nothing. My own deceased father, the former khan, owned a pipe. When he lit it up, the smoke curled around the stars in the sky and tied them all together.' The herdsman didn't know what to say to that and went away in silence.

"Just then a badarcin came into the room carrying a bucket. The khan asked him: 'Badarcin, what do you want?'

"'What, don't you recognize me?' asked the badarcin. 'After all, you borrowed a bucket full of gold from me. I have come to get my gold back.'

"The khan jumped out of his seat and said: 'When did I borrow that gold from you? You are lying!' The noise woke up the guard, who had been sleeping nearby. 'You are lying when you claim to have loaned me gold. Beat him!' the khan yelled to the guard.

"The badarcin said: 'If I am lying, then leave me your throne, great khan.'

"The khan thought about that for a moment and then he replied: 'Wait a moment! You are telling the truth. I did borrow the gold from you. I just remembered.'

"'Then give me my gold!' the badarcin demanded.

"Thus the badarcin told a lie which made a sitting man stand up and woke up a sleeping man. He gained a bucket of gold and taught the careless khan a lesson."

"A wonderful tale," Tejmur said. "Thank you for sharing it. But I do not agree with you that I am like the badarcin. It is not gold I seek, or a throne. It is my freedom, and the safety of those who travel with me."

"Is not a reward a reward?" Qui asked. "Which is the more valuable: gold or freedom, a throne or the safety of those you love?"

"Or ignorance or wisdom?" Tejmur replied, meeting Qui eye to eye. "You see, I could ask you the same question, badarcin."

"But I have an answer," Qui said, and his eyes were as deep and dark as the night sky. "If one would take, one must first give. This is the beginning of true intelligence."

Tejmur sat silent, feeling as though he had seen a great light and been momentarily blinded. "I have heard you," he said at last.

"And I have heard enough of tales and riddles," Genghis barked. "Now we dine!"

Genghis clapped his hands and the two women Tejmur had seen tending a fire outside the tent came in, one carrying skewers of roasted meat, the other a silver bowl of what smelled to Tejmur like soured milk. The women looked down, seemingly terrified and not daring to make eye contact with the three men they served.

One of the women—who was not more than a child, Tejmur observed, as she leaned toward him—whispered, "Save me and my sister." The girl's whisper seemed filled with both fear and determination. Her eyes flashed smoky and blue gray when she looked at him.

"Do you like the women?" Genghis asked.

It took a moment for Tejmur to realize that the Khan had spoken to him. He tried for a shrug.

"They are pretty enough."

"Then you must mate with them." Genghis laughed, an unpleasant sound that quieted the tent and stilled all motion.

Then the woman who had spoken stepped back, her blue-gray eyes showing only fear.

"Mate? With them? I don't find them attractive in that way."

"They are not your daughters. But I understand. Different men find different women attractive, especially when it comes to mating. They are not my daughters either, and I do find them pretty enough for my needs. Woman!" Genghis snapped at the one who had whispered. "On your life, say not another word. Serve our food. Now."

The woman handed Tejmur a skewer of something roasted.

"Fresh meat," Tejmur said. He wanted to shift the conversation away from the suffering servant lest he be the cause of her suffering even more.

"Horse," Genghis said. "The horses we ride into battle sometimes supply us with brown food such as this, and of course sausage, though goats and oxen are better for making sausage than horses. We call the sausage *blood pudding*, for it is mostly blood. Usually I eat white food—milk from mares that has been cured into cheese or yogurt. I ordered the brown food as a special treat for me and my two wizards." Genghis laughed loud and without humor. "After we eat, Wizard Tejmur, you will show me the black water that makes fire fly and burns flesh. We will ride together, you and I, to the place where Iskandar found you beyond the hill."

Chapter 21

Tejmur had never tasted horsemeat, but he found it tender and flavorful—a mix of salt and smoke and savory spices, cooked with garlic and onions—and he ate until his belly was full in a way it had not been full since he had fallen into the past. Afterward, as he sat on the soft carpet in the dimness of the firelight, he found himself fighting sleep. How long, he wondered, had it been since he had slept deep and dreamlessly, and awoken with his mind clear and at peace?

But just as Tejmur felt his eyelids growing too heavy to raise, he was startled into wakefulness by a sudden motion.

"Up, Shaman Tejmur," the voice of Genghis Khan rang out, above him. "It is time to ride."

Tejmur dragged himself to his feet, aware of the Makarov, cold and metallic, riding under his belt like a tumor. It was foolish to have brought the weapon, he told himself. Leaving Qui Chuji sitting beside the fire, Tejmur followed Genghis out through the tentflap and into the late afternoon light.

Outside the tent stood two horses without riders in a loose semi-circle of about two dozen Mongol warriors on horseback. Both riderless horses were tall compared to the other Mongol mounts; about fifteen hands high, Tejmur guessed. One magnificent black horse bore a saddle made of gold and silver and polished dark wood that glittered in the late afternoon sun. The other horse was a dun. It had a leather saddle with a plain wooden seat shaped like a crescent moon and covered with a thick felt pad. Metal stirrups hung from the saddle on leather straps. The reins were made of braided horsehair.

"Mount!" Genghis moved like quicksilver, seeming almost to flow into his saddle against the force of gravity. Then a warrior handed the Khan two curved bows, one of which he strapped unstrung onto the back of his saddle and the other he strung effortlessly and slid across his shoulder so that the arms of the bow, made of gold-and-silver-embossed horn, stretched across his back.

Despite the Khan's order, Tejmur felt himself hesitate. It had been many years since he'd been on a horse, and he had never sat on a saddle like this one. He sensed Genghis watching him, and felt the measuring eyes of the Mongol warriors. A strange feeling came over Tejmur that something was afoot. So instead of stepping into the stirrup, he raised it—and checked the cinch before attempting to climb aboard. Sure enough, the cinch was loose. Tejmur smiled to himself as he tightened the leather strap, then stepped into the stirrup and hauled himself up into the crescent moon of a saddle.

Genghis belly-laughed, spoke to the surrounding warriors, then nodded approval at Tejmur. "It's an old Mongol trick often played on young warriors when they first ride with the horde," Genghis said. "You have passed the test. Now let us ride like the north wind."

With that, Tejmur suddenly found himself alone in a cloud of dust beside the tent. Then he felt a surge that almost tumbled him out of the saddle as his dun mount leaped after the party of Mongols who were already approaching the city gate. Floundering in the unfamiliar saddle, Tejmur gripped his legs against the ribs of the dun. He realized, as he felt the horse leap forward again with a burst of speed that nearly unseated him, that this must have been a signal to accelerate into a dead run. He had much to learn and not much time in which to educate himself. And for a long moment, his attention was fixed on gripping the awkward front tip of the crescent saddle and trying not to look at the ground that whizzed with a sickening rapidity beneath his feet.

By the time he recovered himself enough to look up, Tejmur could see the Mongols far in the distance. They were already cresting the ridge that lay between Baku and the oil seep. The group of horsemen paused at the ridgeline and waited for Tejmur, whose horse had only just begun to ascend the steep upslope. Despite the mix of rock and sand and dried grasses at its feet, the Mongol horse seemed to pick up speed as it gained altitude. Like riding a mountain goat, Tejmur thought.

Knowing enough about horsemanship to trust his mount to negotiate the tricky upgrade, Tejmur studied the Mongols atop the ridge. Genghis gleamed gold and silver in the late afternoon light like a demigod, surrounded by the rest of the warriors in their leather armor and with their steel helmets glittering in the sun. The men were one with their horses, in absolute command of all they surveyed. Tejmur saw the Mongols for the first time not as murderers or thieves, but as conquerors. He understood completely, at that moment, why these people would come to rule virtually all of their world. How could anyone stand against them?

The Mongol warriors were talking and laughing among themselves as Tejmur finally crested the ridge. Although he couldn't understand the words, Tejmur made out the mocking tone of their voices—

and he felt himself bristle.

"They say you ride like a woman," Genghis said.

"What do you say?"

"You passed the test outside the tent," Genghis replied, "which tells me that you have the wisdom of a man who has lived much life." Then the Khan smiled a sly smile. "But I must agree with my warriors' estimation of your horsemanship."

To Tejmur's surprise, he found himself smiling with the Khan. "I fear I must agree with them as well," Tejmur said.

Genghis smiled broadly and nodded at Tejmur. "Good. As Qui Chuji would say, admitting ignorance is the first step in attaining knowledge. Let us begin your education!" the Khan shouted. And just as quickly, he vanished over the crest of the ridge.

Again trusting his dun mountain goat of a horse to negotiate the tricky slope, Tejmur watched the Mongols as they descended the downgrade and approached the tar pit that marked the oil seep. Seeing the golden Khan surrounded by his invincible warriors, Tejmur found himself thinking again of all those who would face the Mongol Horde in battle—and be slaughtered. How many, he wondered, would face brutal murder or a lifetime of servitude? Hundreds of thousands? Millions?

Despite the repugnance he felt for violence—or perhaps, because of it—Tejmur's thoughts shifted to the Makarov so easliy accessable beneath his shirt. He could draw it with ease, and point it at Genghis with no one becoming alarmed because of their ignorance of the pistol's power. He put his hand on the pistol, and drew it partway from his belt. With a single bullet, he could kill Genghis Khan and save all those lives. And not just the lives of the victims that the Khan would kill directly, but the entire lineage of those people's descendants as well. How many millions would he save by pulling the trigger?

Tejmur felt staggered at the possibility. He would change history. All that he knew would be swept away. Was even saving millions of lives worth that? Maybe, he told himself. But what of his promise to Genghis Khan? Was there honor in honoring his word to a mass murderer?

No, he concluded, and pulled the pistol from his belt.

But what of the lives of those in his party, lives he was now trying to save? He had promised all of them to make the best deal he could to ensure their freedom and their safe passage—and where was the honor in betraying them?

"And perhaps above all, what of Papusza?" Tejmur asked himself.

Papusza's fate would be sealed if he used the pistol, Tejmur knew; and a painful, unpleasant fate it would be. In his mind's eye, he pictured what the horde would do to her if Tejmur slew the Khan. He felt himself shudder to the core of his being. No, he thought. That was a thing not to be borne.

He shoved the Makarov back under his belt and guided his mount clear of the downslope, running breakneck toward the band of warriors waiting at the base of the rock formation on the shores of the Caspian Sea.

"So, Shaman Tejmur," Genghis called, as Tejmur rode in among the Mongol warriors. "The time has come to keep your promise."

"So it has," Tejmur said, thinking not of oil or flaming arrows, but of Papusza. "Come. I will show you where to find the oil, and how to harvest it."

Tejmur dismounted and threaded his way through the mounts of the Mongol warriors to the boggy area between the rocks and the sea, blackened from oil seepage. The acrid scent of tar filled the air, and Tejmur saw the Khan's nose wrinkle at the petroleum smell.

"Disgusting!" the Khan spat.

"Yes. But this is the scent of the power you seek. Anywhere you find a tar pit such as this, with seepage like that," Tejmur pointed to the spot where the oil leaked from the beneath the rocks into the tar pit, "you will find crude oil. This is the secret of the fire that flies."

Genghis breathed deep, staring at the light sweet crude. "Sorcery."

"No, science," Tejmur said. "The oil is merely a tool. I will teach you the working of it. But I will need one of your men's helmets."

The Khan barked an order, and one of the leather-armored warriors rushed to his side bareheaded, helmet in hand. "Then teach me," Genghis said.

"Watch and learn." Tejmur again scraped out the basin in the sand they had made before the battle with Iskandar, and showed the Khan how to catch the oil before it spilled into the marsh water. Then Tejmur filled the helmet with oil from the basin. Finally, he handed the oil-filled helmet to Genghis Khan. "I give you the world," Tejmur said with a sinking feeling. "Armed with this, no one will be able to stand against you."

Genghis held the oil-filled helmet up to the sky, muttering words that Tejmur could not understand. Then the Khan lowered the helmet and led the way back to the group of warriors, set the helmet on the ground, and stepped back. The mounted warriors edged their horses closer to look at the oil, as Genghis led Tejmur away upwind of the tar pit.

"I cannot carry enough of this oil for all of my troops," the Khan said.

"That is not a problem," Tejmur replied. "There are many such seeps, spread throughout the world that you have set out to conquer.

And I have showed you how to find them."

"Nevertheless, to lay siege to a great city, I will need cauldrons of such oil."

"Indeed. You can carry it in pots on wagons, for dipping onto arrows and for use with siege engines as well. For the siege engines, you should always use crude oil such as this. But for fire arrows, other types of oil will work in a pinch. Butter fat, whale oil, anything that will burn in a lantern or on a torch will work for a fire arrow. However, the crude oil will always burn hotter and last longer."

"Good enough," Genghis nodded, resting his hand for a moment on Tejmur's shoulder. "You have won your freedom, Shaman Tejmur, and the freedom of those in your party. I will give you horses, and my warriors will escort you to the border of my new kingdom."

"For all of this, I thank you," Tejmur said. His freedom won, and the freedom and safe passage of the party assured, his thoughts turned now to the time window that lay hidden in the rock cave only a few meters from where he and Genghis stood. "But as I told you when we first met, I have more to offer."

"Ah, yes." Genghis said thoughtfully. "You spoke of my future, and said you had information about the things that are to come."

"I do."

"And for this information, I suppose that you will require an additional reward."

Tejmur thought back to the story of the badarcin, and what Qui had said about giving before taking. "No," he said. "I offer this information without the promise of a reward. Free of charge."

"What kind of information?"

"News of future conquests, and of the people in your life."

"Sorcery," Genghis said. "I have already told you that I do not wish to know the circumstances of my death."

"Sorcery of a sort, I suppose," Tejmur acknowledged. "And I understand that you do not wish to hear news of your death. But there is much to learn of life between the present moment and the day you leave this world for the next."

"Very well, wizard. Tell me what you see."

Tejmur took a deep breath, and surveyed his surroundings. Next to him, the rock formation that hid the time window was now mostly in shadow. The sun was behind the ridge they had ridden over, and darkness would soon descend.

"Would it not be better to wait until the morning?" Tejmur asked.

"In the morning, I will be gone. I leave this place before dawn."

"Very well. What is it that you wish to know?"

"Will I conquer China?"

"Much of it," Tejmur answered, "and you will accomplish that conquest with the aid of the fire that flies."
"Much of China, you say. But not all?"
"No. Not all."
"And my sons after me?"
"Not they," Tejmur said. "But your grandson, who will be called Kublai Khan, will complete the conquest of China that you now ride east to begin."
The Khan's face spread into a fierce grin. "That is acceptable. Reveal no more of this to me, except the answer to my next question."
"Yes?"
"Will my grandson be as great a conqueror as me?"
Tejmur hesitated. "Your grandson will rule over the greatest land empire that the world will ever see. But he will be known more as the one who consolidated and extended the empire that you established. You will be known to history as the greatest conqueror who ever lived."
The grin on Genghis's face spread even wider, and his eyes seemed to burn in the gathering darkness. "Then my life's work will be accomplished," he whispered fiercely. "It is well."
"But I must warn you, great Khan, that not all will go smoothly with your family."
"What do you mean?"
"Your eldest son, Jochi, is not your own by blood. If power passes to Jochi, the empire will splinter. The conquest of China will never be achieved."
"Of Jochi's true lineage I knew already," Genghis said. "But you have risked a great deal by being honest with me. Very few men would take such a risk, for the sake of honesty. Or honor."
"I have given you my word," Tejmur said simply.
"I have an offer to make," the Khan said. "I will make such an offer only once, so think carefully before you reply. I would like you to ride east with me, and to become my chief advisor. With such a position would come immense power, and the wealth that goes with it. Power and wealth, perhaps, beyond your imagination."
Tejmur stood silent for a long time, overwhelmed with the possibilities that the Khan's offer entailed. With his help, Tejmur knew, Genghis Khan could complete the conquest of China in a single lifetime. And perhaps Tejmur could help to lessen the toll such a conquest would take upon the conquered. But drowning out the visions of the East at his feet and the dizzying temptation to change the course of history, the face of Papusza suddenly filled Tejmur's mind—and he knew what his answer must be.
"Great Khan," Tejmur chose his words with care, "I am honored

beyond imagination at the offer you have made me. But I have made a promise that I must keep. And to keep that promise, I must ride now to Constantinople."

"A man of honor in truth." Genghis nodded in approval. "Shaman Tejmur, this is a thing I understand. But in return for the information you have given me, I will make you a gift that should guarantee an honorable and a wise man such as yourself a long and a prosperous life. That is, if you will answer one more question."

"Of course."

"It is about my death. I do not wish to know the hour or the means, but I want to know this: Will I die in battle?"

"No."

"Fair enough. You have done all that I asked, and more. It is time to return to the city."

"Before we leave, great Khan, there is something of mine hidden among these rocks that I will need when I reach Constantinople. With your permission, I will recover my property before we depart."

"Very well, but do it quickly. It will be dark before we are again inside the walls of Baku."

Chapter 22

Long after darkness had fallen over Baku, Tejmur lay awake in the small tent with his party around him sleeping with the kind of peace that only those who have been given a reprieve from certain death can know. But Tejmur could not get to sleep himself. Mostly, he decided, it was the smell that disturbed him and not the sense of foreboding which had wracked him since first seeing the Mongol Horde ride into the Baku valley. The usual stiff winds from the Caspian had up to now masked the stench of death almost completely—at least, here on the city's edge that was closest to the shore; but with each passing hour, the smell became more intense. He kept close to him the small case that contained the time window and the peephole.

In the predawn light, a small band of Mongols pulled Tejmur and his followers from their tent and pushed them toward Genghis Khan. The Khan stood beside his huge horse in front of what was once Rostam's tent. Even in the dim light, Tejmur could read both determination and amusement on the man's face.

"Horses," Genghis waved his hand, and Tejmur saw them in the courtyard. There was a mount for each member of his party, even the women. Among them was the big dun Tejmur had ridden the day before.

"I am grateful," Tejmur said.

"You give me most of China with the gift of fire that flies, and I give you a few horses. I call that a good trade. For your honesty and honorable ways I also give you a mule, there among your horses, a beast that carries a burden of supplies. The mule, and all she carries, belongs to you and you alone. Do with it as you please."

With that, Genghis Khan mounted his horse with the same quicksilver motion Tejmur had seen yesterday, and rode from the courtyard toward the city gate surrounded by a band of mounted horsemen. Only four Mongols remained. They stood among the horses, and Tejmur understood them to be the escort to the border promised to him last evening when he and Genghis had stood beside the seeping oil.

Had he truly given Genghis Khan most of China? Tejmur wondered. And was his presence in the past what had caused the conqueror to learn of the fire that flies so he could ride east again to extend his conquests? Tejmur knew that time did not flow in a straight line. This was the key to the operation of his time window; it was the bends and curves in the flow of time that allowed him to find parallel hours, those narrow gaps between present and past that the window could tunnel through. And he knew that things like mass, velocity, and gravity affected the flow of time. But now Tejmur found himself wondering about the relationship between time itself and the events that occurred within its current—and how his own movements back and forth might affect that relationship. The history books reported that Genghis Khan had learned the secret of flying fire on his campaign in Persia. Were those reports based on Tejmur's own gift? If so, did that mean there was some sort of force—a power some would call Fate, but that Tejmur preferred to think of in more scientific terms—driving history? And more importantly, would the existence of such a force mean that he had no choice in what he did?

But this was a possibility Tejmur quickly rejected. He could not bring himself to believe that every action of every person who had ever lived, and who ever would live, was predetermined by some outside force—no matter what name such a force might be known by. Tejmur firmly believed in free will.

An alarmed shout from Rostam inside the tent in which Tejmur and Qui Chuji had feasted with the Khan the day before aroused Tejmur from his reverie. He hurried inside, Papusza and Masud beside him and the rest of their party right behind. The Mongols had left torches burning within the tent, and bodies lay on the very carpet where Tejmur had shared the meal with Genghis Khan and Qui Chuji.

"The pigs!" Rostam shouted again and again. "The pigs!"

"Why the shouting?" Tejmur asked. "At least you live, I've seen to that."

"You call this living?" Rostam waved his arms. "The pigs have destroyed my carpets, and desecrated my tent with blood and an abundance of corpses."

"There are only two," Faiq said. "But they are grisly corpses."

"And both are women." Papusza spoke with an intake of breath.

In the flicker of the torchlight Tejmur could see one of the women, lying on her back with her head at an impossible angle to her body and seeming to fix him with smoky, gray-blue eyes. She and her companion in violent death lay nude, wounded in unspeakable ways, and flung to the floor like so much garbage.

Tejmur felt himself stagger at the sight, overcome by a wave of despair and guilt. "I might have saved her," he muttered.

"No." Papusza gripped his arm. "No one could save her from that terrible man."

"We must leave," Tejmur said. "Now."

"Yes," Papusza said. "Leave this tent, this awful city, this terrible past."

Outside Tejmur found the four warriors laughing among themselves, clearly amused by his group's responses to the corpses.

As he emerged from the tent, Rostam said, "I'll take my horses now. Captain Amin and I have work to do. We will seek vengeance against the barbarian invaders." He strode toward the horses, and the four warriors blocked his way with drawn knives.

"These are not your horses," Masud said.

"Tell these barbarians to stand down," Rostam said.

"A word from Tejmur," Masud said, "and they will kill you. Or I will."

"Go among the horses," Tejmur said, addressing his small group. "The dun is mine. Choose from among the others the one that you wish to ride. Faiq, see to it that the mule stays beside you and the horse you choose. Rostam, cease talking. Papusza, can you ride a horse?"

"I'm a Gypsy, remember? Or course I can ride a horse."

"Masud? Do you ride?"

"You ask that of a Cossack?"

"Norin?"

"You ask because I was a courtesan, and such women know nothing of horses? But I know. Yes. I have ridden horses."

"Masud, check the saddles. Make sure all are cinched properly."

The four Mongol warriors made it clear that the group had to stay in the courtyard while Genghis and his army moved toward the crest of the hill. The dust of their passing was like a funeral pall that settled slowly upon the slaughterhouse they had made of Baku.

At last, the little group began to move in silence with two Mongol warriors riding before them and two behind. Tejmur breathed through his mouth and made a futile effort not to see the bloated corpses scattered in what Genghis Khan had left of the once-proud city of Baku. Outside the city gates he could see the vast Mongol army high above the Caspian, and he could hear the rumble of horses' hooves. At such a distance, they sounded to Tejmur more like the purring of a cat than the horrifying rumble of such a horde of mounted men. Murderers, Tejmur thought, and barely human.

At the crest of the hill above Baku, the four warriors took off at a gallop, riding south to join the vast mounted army of the Khan that would soon turn toward the East—and the vast swaths of India and China that would soon lie in ruins at Genghis Khan's feet. Tejmur turned in his saddle to look back at Baku, at what appeared now to be a tan and smoking strip of buildings, small with distance, and not a city at all. It had become just a tiny ruin on the edge of the sea. He could see the Maiden's Tower and the city walls, walls that had proved useless in saving Baku from the Mongol Horde.

Faiq dismounted to examine the mule, and Rostam urged his horse toward Faiq.

"The pigs gave me some of their short swords." Rostam pointed at the mule. "I wish to examine my other possessions. Amin, I think there is at least one bow and a quiver of arrows. Get them. Bring me the bow."

"No." Faiq took a knife from one of the pouches on the mule. He brandished it toward Amin.

Masud produced the Makarov. "Take anything from the mule," he said, "and you are a dead man, Amin."

"Dismount," Tejmur said. "Everyone. Give the horses a rest. Rostam, stay away from the mule. You, too, Amin. Faiq, is that a waterskin the mule is carrying?"

"Water, yes. And bread, old, hard, and dusty—but still bread. I didn't think the barbarians cared much for the taste of bread."

"We all drink, then," Tejmur said. "Only a little. Faiq, help with the water. And the bread—a small piece for each of us."

They all ate a quick and small breakfast.

"Now," Tejmur said, "we go west."

"To Constantinople," Papusza whispered in awe. "Yes."

"Constantinople? Bah! I go to Ardebil," Rostam said. "I take with me my captain, Amin, and my woman. We will take the weapons, which are not much but will serve as a start. For at Ardebil I, Rostam the Great, will raise an army to avenge all Persians for the invasion of these barbarians."

"You take nothing from the mule," Faiq said.

"Genghis Khan has already destroyed Ardebil, just as he destroyed Baku," Tejmur said.

Rostam sneered at Tejmur. "I do not believe you."

Tejmur shrugged. "Go. You will find corpses, burned houses, a few damaged women, and an army of occupation."

Rostam turned to Amin. "He lies. You will come with me. And you," he said to Norin, "for you are my property."

"You go alone," Tejmur said.

"I'll follow Rostam," Amin said.

"What?" Norin demanded. "Why would you do that? He is a terrible man, a weak leader, and a fool."

"I'll have you killed for such words," Rostam growled.

"Norin is right, Amin," Tejmur said. "Why would you go with such a man?"

"I'm a soldier," Amin said. "It is not for me to judge the Shah of Baku." He sighed. "I do what I must."

"You know that I have spoken the truth?" Tejmur said, making eye contact with Amin. "Ardebil has indeed been destroyed. And you will find an army of Mongols there."

"A soldier's job is to follow, not to question the decisions of his leader. And I have long followed Rostam."

"Then," Tejmur said, "do what you must. Faiq, give Amin one of the barbarian swords."

"And the bow," Rostam said, "and that quiver of arrows, and—"

"If Rostam utters another command," Tejmur said to Masud, "put a terrible wound in one of his legs. Let him crawl to Ardebil."

Rostam flushed crimson with rage, but he said nothing. Faiq, his knife ready to strike, handed Amin a short sword.

As Rostam and Amin rode away, Faiq laughed loud and long. "He is a fool to the end," Faiq said. "A greater fool than he will ever know."

"You know something we do not?" Tejmur asked.

"Yes." Faiq patted the mule. "This mule of yours. This wonderful mule."

"What of it?" Papusza asked. "It is just a mule, a beast of burden. Nothing more."

"No." Faiq watched the dust rising from the hooves of the horses as Amin and Rostam grew smaller in the distance. "This mule of Tejmur's carries bags of gold and silver. Tejmur is now richer than Rostam ever was, even in his greediest dreams."

"It appears that the Khan has kept his word," Tejmur said.

"I know nothing of that," Faiq said. "But I do know that Amin serves a fool who owns nothing, while I serve Tejmur, a man as rich as the sultans of Persia. Tejmur, I will call you master from now until forever."

Part Three: Desert Demons

Chapter 23

"You've been quiet a long time, Tejmur," Papusza said. "Longer than I have ever heard you go without speaking. Do you truly find that mule more alluring than the lovely Gypsy woman who rides beside you?"

Jarred out of his reverie, Tejmur took his eyes off the heavily laden mule that Faiq led in his place at the head of their little column, and glanced at Papusza. She was indeed lovely, despite the layer of dust that clung to the sweat coating her face and neck.

"How long have you been riding there next to me?" Tejmur asked.

"Time," Papusza scoffed. "What does it mean, in this desert hell that Faiq has led us into?" She swept an arm at the desert country that stretched as far as the eye could see in every direction.

Tejmur let his eyes wander across the gray desert hills, reddish-brown arroyos, dry rocky creeks, and thorny gray-green shrubs and cacti that had surrounded the party since they followed Faiq south from Baku. Other than themselves and their mounts, the only creatures the companions had seen all day were the lizards and snakes that scurried out from underneath their horses' hooves, and the vultures that circled ominously in the high distance.

"Point taken," Tejmur said. "And to answer your question, I find the lovely Gypsy woman beside me much more alluring than the mule my horse has been following since the early morning."

"In the early morning, Faiq spoke of a trail," Papusza said, her disgust clearly audible, "a trade route he said he knew well that leads through the desert to the Port of Trebizond on the Black Sea. It has been long indeed since I saw any trace of a path beneath the hooves of this tired and thirsty animal I ride on."

"Do you believe Faiq is purposely leading us astray?" Tejmur asked quietly. The thought had occurred to him more than once, as the fierce sun beat down upon them in this desert place.

"To lose us in this hellish wilderness, you mean, and then ride off with your treasure hoard?" There was amusement now in Papusza's voice, and a faint smile crinkled the layer of dust at the corners of her lips. "No. I do not believe that Faiq has the intelligence or the initiative for such a plan. In fact, I begin to question whether he knows north from south, or east from west."

Tejmur felt laughter well up from deep inside him, a welcome spring of well-being and peace that had not flowed in too long a time. He saw Papusza's teeth flash startlingly white in her sunburned face as she laughed along with him; and for a long moment, all was well. But then Tejmur's eyes settled back onto the treasure bags that weighed so heavily on the mule, and on his heart—and he felt the wellspring of humor within him go dry as the desert land that surrounded him.

"I find it difficult to comprehend why you would prefer the company of a beast of burden to the woman you have promised to take to Constantinople," Papusza said softly. "Help me to understand."

"Do you believe in Fate?"

"I am a Gypsy," Papusza said. "Of course I believe in Fate."

"I am not a Gypsy," Tejmur said slowly, gathering his words. "I am a man of science. An engineer. A believer in free will. Evidence. The scientific method. I have spent most of my adult life at work on a way to travel backward and forward through time."

"You have succeeded. Your time window works, when it has a power source to make it function. It saved us from the Soviet invasion. And even before that, it functioned well enough to gather wealth from the distant past. But I must confess that the coins you sent me back in time to recover are like grains of sand in comparison to the fortune that you have been given by that awful man."

"Blood money," Tejmur said. "For the technology to conquer the world, he gave me horses and a few bags of coins."

"Sometimes I do not understand you at all," Papusza said. "You saved our lives by giving Genghis Khan the secret of the fire arrows. If you had not done so, we would all be dead now. And Norin and I would have met the same fate as those two unfortunate women we saw this morning."

"It was the thought of that—of what would happen to you, Papusza, if I chose not to share the secret with Genghis—that led me to give him the power to make fire fly." Tejmur met her beautiful brown eyes. "And I do not regret that choice. But the thought of all those who will die as a result of the choice I made lies heavy on my heart."

"When we sat together beside the Caspian Sea, and you won my heart with your gallantry and kindness, you told me that Genghis Khan would go on to conquer much of the East when he left Baku. That is a fact of history. He did so using the flying fire. That is also a historical fact. Does that not mean that he was fated to do these things? If you had not shared the secret with him, then he would have learned it elsewhere. All things happen because they are meant to happen. Fate will always find a way."

"Perhaps," Tejmur said. He was thinking about his short-lived intention, on the ride out to the oil seep, to shoot the great Genghis Khan dead with the Makarov. If Papusza was right—if the course of history was indeed inevitable—then even if he had chosen to kill the leader of the Mongol Horde, the pistol would have misfired, or the bullet would have gone astray. And Papusza and the rest of their little party would have died for nothing. "I would very much like to believe as you do."

"I believe in you, Tejmur. If you could only see yourself once through my eyes, you would never doubt yourself again."

"Perhaps this is something you can teach me," Tejmur said.

"It will be my pleasure to try," Papusza said. "Certainly, it will make our journey to Constantinople much more interesting."

The cryptic smile Tejmur watched spread slowly across Papusza's face was interesting indeed. He felt his mood lighten, despite the weight of the afternoon sun pressing down upon him, and he felt his thoughts shift away from the horror of Baku toward the promise of Constantinople.

Finally, in the late afternoon, a spot of deep green appeared on the western horizon ahead of them. The intermittent trail Faiq had been leading them along became more solidly visible as the deep green spot grew into a line of trees that curved to intersect the path on which they rode. In the far distance, Tejmur made out green mountains to the north. To the south, the desert stretched away to the horizon. The horses, scenting the water that lay ahead, raised their bowed heads, pricked up their ears, and picked up the pace. Their dispirited walk became a quick-footed trot, then a smooth and easy lope that ended in a lush and shady clearing beside a small river.

The stream ran cold and clear in a rocky bed. The horses waded out into it and buried their heads, taking great gulps and refusing to be led out of the water until they had drunk their fill. The company dismounted in the shallow water; and like the horses, they took a long time slaking the thirst that had been building all day. The taste of the water was crisp and cool, with a hint of mineral that Tejmur guessed came from the rock formation the water flowed across. At length, when they had all drunk as much as they could hold, and Faiq had refilled the waterskin, they led the horses up to a flat space in the shade about six feet above the river.

It was in this broad, smooth patch of delicious shade that they set up camp. While Faiq unloaded the mule and Tejmur unsaddled the horses, the others gathered driftwood from alongside the stream. When a great pile of firewood had at last been deposited at the edge of the open space, and Papusza had started a fire, they all gathered in a semicircle upwind of their little campfire and took stock of the current situation.

"We are low on food," Faiq said. He held up the meager remains of the bread that the Mongols had given them early that morning. "We have one meal left, at best. And there are at least three days of hard riding between our present camp and nearest city that lies on the trade route between here and the Port of Trebizond."

"How long to Trebizond?" Tejmur asked.

"A week, more or less," Faiq said. "But the farther west we ride, the greener and more populated the country becomes. Supplies will be no problem."

"Three days with no food!" Masud exclaimed. "There will be nothing left of us but bones!"

"There must be fish in the river," Papusza said.

"But how to catch them?" Tejmur asked, feeling his empty belly rumble. "We have no hooks, and no fishing line."

"We could make a net," Faiq said. "A casting net. I have seen the fishermen of Baku haul in great loads of fish with such nets."

"But what shall we use to weave it?" Papusza asked. "We have no twine."

"We do have twine," Masud said. "I brought some back with me from the twentieth century. You used some of it outside Baku to tie Tejmur's hands. Remember? I believe that Tejmur kept it. And I have some more." Masud pulled a small ball of twine from one of his pockets and held it up.

"I'm no fisherman," Faiq said. "But it seems to me that a net made from such a small amount of twine would catch no more than minnows."

"Well, it seems to me that even minnows would be better than what we have now," Masud said, his eyes flashing. "It also seems to me that Faiq is less hungry than the rest of us. Maybe, in addition to leading us in circles through this desert hell, he's been raiding our bread supply."

"I have not!" Faiq glared at Masud, his hand straying toward the hilt of his dagger. "I would never steal even a crumb of bread from the stores of my master."

"Peace!" Tejmur said. "I trust Faiq completely, both as a guide and as the custodian of all our supplies. Such as they are. And this squabbling does nothing to solve our food shortage."

"Thank you, my master."

"Perhaps," Norin said softly, "we could gather food from among the plants that surround us."

"There are quite probably a variety of edible plants along the river," Tejmur said. "But unless some of you have specific knowledge of which plants are edible and which are not, then we would be better off going hungry than poisoning ourselves by guessing."

"I have the Makarov," Masud said. "I will try to shoot some game."

"We should save the ammunition," Tejmur said. "We have no idea what we will face on the long ride to Trebizond."

"If I must be hungry," Papusza said, "at least I can be clean. Norin, what do you say to a bath?"

"A bath!" Norin said wistfully. "I cannot remember the last time I felt truly clean."

"Then come with me," Papusza said. "Gentlemen, if you would be so kind as to remain here in camp for a while, Norin and I will walk downstream and wash our bodies and our clothes."

"I still do not understand," Masud said, once the women had disappeared downstream, "why we did not parallel the Caspian and then head south for the Mediterranean coast. Are there not cities along that route with restaurants where we could eat, and inns where we could sleep? And could we not have taken a ship to Constantinople just as easily from there?"

"The Christians have invaded again," Faiq said. "There is fighting in the port cities, and the armies of Islam are on the move. We must continue on to the Black Sea port of Trebizond, which is the seat of the Empire of Trebizond. There, we will take ship for Constantinople."

"I saw green mountains in the distance to the north," Masud persisted. "Why not head that way, instead of pushing on through this hellish desert?"

"The mountains are nearly impassable," Faiq said. "The desert route is the easiest, and best. And as I said before, soon the country will be greener along our present route."

It wasn't long before Papusza and Norin returned, looking refreshed. Their hair and their clothes were damp, and their skin shone clean and fresh in the late afternoon light.

"I could use a bath myself," Tejmur said, rising.

"And I, as well," Masud said.

"I have better things to do than wallow in a river," Faiq said. "There is money to be counted!"

The last thing Tejmur saw as he and Masud headed downstream was the fierce grin on Faiq's face as he began counting the gold and silver.

Chapter 24

"I can smell Faiq from here," Masud grumbled.

"Yes." Tejmur, delighted to be clean after bathing in a river pond, wrinkled his nose as he and Masud approached their camp.

Norin met them with an enthusiastic smile. "The day still has some hours," she said, addressing Masud. "You might begin teaching me ways to inflict injury on men who would harm me. Yes?"

Papusza spoke from behind Norin. "You want to learn to fight?" She laced her words with disapproval and disgust.

"Of course. Masud will teach me." Norin's voice carried a sweetness that seemed to Tejmur to be at odds with the subject she proposed to study. "And I will teach Masud the ways of my world."

"We can start here and now," Masud said. "Plant your feet thus, hold your hands loose, out from your side but not in a threatening way. Rock back on one foot to prepare for the kick. Most men do not expect low-level attacks, so they are quite vulnerable."

"I refuse to watch this," Papusza said. Then she turned to Tejmur. "Come with me."

Papusza took Tejmur's arm and guided him toward Faiq, who sat beside a large, flat shelf of rock where he had sorted the riches from Genghis Khan into a series of stacks. Coins of gold were on one side, coins of silver were on the other, and all the coins in each pile were of the same diameter.

"Tell him to bathe," Papusza whispered.

"Ah, Tejmur the Wealthy." Faiq stood and bowed, his teeth gleaming in a brown and snaggled grin. "I have two bits of good news. The best news is that you are wealthy beyond most men's dreams. Some of these," his hand swept over the rock holding the gold and silver, "are too strange, too foreign for me to assign an absolute value. Others I know well and can count with precision. I will guard this treasure trove with my life, and I will guard you with my life."

"And the other bit of good news you mentioned?" Tejmur asked.

Faiq sniffed the air, the nostrils of his huge nose flaring. Then he pointed in the direction from which the wind blew. "There, upwind, someone is making bread."

"You can smell bread when I cannot?" Papusza demanded. "And

yet you cannot smell . . ." Her voice trailed off and she blushed.

"Gold," Tejmur said. "She means you cannot smell gold."

"I see what you mean," Faiq said, "since even the most precious of metals has no odor. But bread?" Faiq spread his nostrils wide again. "Ah, that is another matter. And my sense of smell is very keen. I sometimes have the illusion that I can smell gold."

"That's not what I meant," Papusza whispered to Tejmur.

"Be still," he turned and whispered back. Then he looked at Faiq. "Who could make bread out here in the desert with no ovens?"

"Nomads. I've traveled with some of them, and I've learned never to trust them. But they know how to survive in the desert. They mix a crude batter for their bread, then bake it on the hot sand."

"You jest," Papusza said.

"Not at all. They bury fresh coals beneath a thin layer of sand. When the sand gets hot, they pour the batter onto it. In a short time, they have bread."

"I've heard of that," Tejmur said. "But of course the bread they make has sand in it."

"Yes." Faiq waved his arms about in excitement. "But it is edible, although with a great grinding of the teeth. When those nomads chew the sand bread, they make terrible crunching sounds. The bread tastes like pond scum, but it is still the stuff of life. I say we hide your hoard, take some tiny bit of it—perhaps a few pieces of silver—and trade those nomads out of some of their sand bread."

"A good plan. Masud, Norin. We now have a way to get food. Faiq, take whatever coins we'll need for trading and hide the rest. Papusza, you and Norin will stay here with Masud. I'll leave him here to protect you."

"Bah!" Faiq said. "Women need no protection. But the gold and silver deserve the security of a trained warrior on guard. Masud, you must kick the kneecaps from any Arabs that approach Tejmur's wealth."

"So, Faiq, your cousin is worthless because she is a woman?" Norin asked. "When I learn the trick of it, yours will be the first kneecap I kick from a leg, and I'll not bother learning to put it back in place."

"Arabs?" Tejmur asked.

"The nomads. I'll bet my mother's teeth that they are desert Arabs. Some are good men and honest traders. But most of them are dangerous, particularly when they have the advantage of numbers."

"Take the Makarov," Masud said, passing the pistol to Tejmur.

Tejmur and Faiq headed upwind in the direction of the scent of bread. It was not long before they caught sight of the nomads and their encampment. Four men in black robes squatted in the undergrowth not far from a small mixed herd of horses and camels.

Faiq said, low and fierce, "Black robes. These men are jackals, more dangerous than the Mongols."

"They have horses, three of them, and two camels," Tejmur whispered. "That means five men. But where is the fifth?"

"Shh!" Faiq whispered, indicating with a subtle hand gesture that Tejmur should keep an eye on the surrounding undergrowth.

Two of the nomads rose and began to tend the animals. The other two still squatted, fumbling around with the desert stove of hot sand. The smell of bread, full of sand or not, was now so strong and so wonderful that Tejmur had trouble keeping focus on the nomads doing the cooking—much less scanning the underbrush for a fifth man. He reached under his shirt and grasped the Makarov, hoping he wouldn't have to use it.

Suddenly, the two cooks came to their feet, their hands dancing over their short swords, though they left them sheathed.

"Bread." Faiq pointed to his mouth. "Trade." He held up a silver coin.

The cooks laughed and seemed to relax, their hands moving away from the hilts of their swords. But Tejmur noticed the other two, approaching from the side, kept a threatening stance.

The nomads spoke to one another in what Tejmur recognized as a variety of Arabic, though he understood only a word here and there. "What are they saying?" he asked.

"They might as well be speaking Greek," Faiq said. He grinned, opened his mouth, and jabbed a finger into it. Then he pointed at the bread cooking on the sand and again held up the silver coin. "I'm offering more than the bread is worth, but we are hungry."

"Offer less."

"Trust me." Faiq continued to wave the coin as the blackrobes jabbered. Judging by Faiq's puzzled expression, it appeared that the carpet merchant understood even less Arabic than Tejmur.

One of the cooks used a stick to scoop up three of the pieces of sand bread, wrapped the bread in the hem of his robe to keep from burning himself, and offered the bread to Faiq. Faiq pointed at the other two chunks of bread still on the sand and again held up the coin. The nomads laughed again, and the other cook picked up the remaining pieces, holding them in a fold of his robe.

Tejmur tried not to think about what might be on the robes being used to hold the bread. He knelt, scooped up some sand, pointed to the bread, and let the sand trickle through his fingers.

"We need to buy flour as well as bread," he said.

One of the blackrobes barked out something and the others laughed.

Tejmur turned to the one who spoke. "Flour," Tejmur repeated. He saw a glimmer of understanding in the man's face, though it was there only for a moment before the perplexed look the man had worn before returned.

The man understood Azeri, Tejmur realized, and didn't want that fact to be known. But why not?

Faiq pointed at the bread, then at a bundle on the ground not far from the little herd of horses and camels. "Flour," he said, speaking loud as a tourist in a foreign land. "Need flour. Will pay. Silver. That okay?"

"Don't shout," Tejmur said.

"Will pay more silver than worth, your flour," Faiq shouted.

The blackrobes chatted more in Arabic, then one of them took a sack from a pack on one of the camels. He held up five fingers. Faiq gestured that he should see the sack. The man handed it to him. He sniffed the contents, made a sour face and held up one finger.

The man held up five.

Faiq sighed in a theatrical way and held up two fingers.

Despite the danger they faced, Tejmur had to struggle to keep from laughing. Faiq, he told himself, might be the worst-smelling man in the desert, but he knew how to drive a bargain—even using only gestures.

The Arab pointed at the bread, still clutched in the robes of the cooks, then pointed at the flour sack and held up four fingers.

Faiq held up three fingers, and the nomads burst into laughter. The one negotiating the deal nodded and reached for the money. Faiq dropped three coins into the man's outstretched hand, then took the flour sack and handed it to Tejmur. Next, Faiq held out the front of his shirt. The two nomads dropped the five lumps of sand bread into the folds of the filthy garment.

As they walked out of the encampment, Tejmur resolved not to tell Papusza about the preferred desert method for carrying hot sand bread. "Their laughter meant we were being cheated," he said. "They deemed their bread and flour worth far less than we paid. But then, we are hungry and they are not."

"Yes," Faiq said, still almost shouting. Then in a wheedling voice he added, "But I did my best. I truly did my best, master. Those men are skillful traders." He lowered his voice to a whisper. "Say nothing else."

When they had put some distance between themselves and the camp of the blackrobes, Faiq said, "That fifth man might be following us, but I doubt it. I also doubt he speaks Azeri, as their leader does."

"It also seemed to me that the leader of the Arabs spoke Azeri. Why would he not deal with us in that language?"

"Those men, they are jackals, as I said. Dangerous."

"Do you think we were in danger back there?"

"No. They are jackals in every way, which means they are cowards. Five against two are not odds such jackals like—at least, not in daylight. The danger comes with darkness, for they are planning an attack on our camp."

Tejmur stopped walking and turned to Faiq in astonishment. "You speak Arabic?"

"But of course." Faiq's cheeks spread into a cunning grin. "I speak many languages, for I have traveled much as a merchant. Pretending ignorance of other tongues is an excellent way to learn enough about your opponents to gain advantages, many advantages. So you and I now know that those jackals will attack us tonight, and I have every confidence you will come up with a plan to defeat them. We should kill them all. Then we will be three horses and two camels richer. Plus all the merchandise they carry, whatever it may be."

"We don't need their animals or their junk." Tejmur regretted his tone when he saw the wounded look on Faiq's face.

"Of course you need nothing from them, for you are richer than a sultan. And I am the luckiest of servants to be allowed to manage some of your wealth. I meant no insult."

"None taken. Nor was I scolding. You are the most cunning merchant between the Caspian and the Black Sea."

Faiq beamed, but only for a moment. "How will you protect us tonight? Those men will come in the dead of night walking on feet that make no noise. They will slit the throats of anyone they take by surprise."

Chapter 25

"It doesn't taste like pond scum." Papusza took another nibble of the sand bread. "The grit is not so good, but it is tolerable. I'll consider it roughage for my system."

"If you weren't so hungry," Norin said, "you would know how terrible this bread is. We all would."

"If I weren't so hungry, I wouldn't eat it at all," Papusza said.

Instead of commenting, Tejmur took another gritty mouthful and tried not to think of the filthy robes the sand bread had been carried in.

"We had a visitor while you were away," Masud said to Tejmur. "I smelled him before I spotted him, spying on us from beyond those rocks."

"The fifth jackal," Faiq said.

"We figured there were five," Tejmur said, "though we saw only four."

"They were planning to attack us even before we traded for the bread and flour," Faiq said. "The man you saw came as a spy to take the measure of our camp and our strength. They will come tonight."

"We'll kill all of them," Masud said.

"You are all talk," Papusza said to Masud. Then she turned to address the whole group. "I know because even as a Russian soldier, he carried a rifle with no bullets, and when his captain ordered the soldiers to kill people in Baku, he refused."

"You ordered Masud to kill Baku citizens?" Faiq turned in surprise to Tejmur.

"Not me," Tejmur said. "Papusza speaks of a time in the distant future."

"You confuse me," Faiq said.

"I confuse myself, sometimes."

"Masud is right, though. We should kill the Arab thieves," Faiq said.

"Can't we frighten them away?" Papusza asked.

"I'd prefer that," Tejmur said. "We have enough flour to make bread for the three days it will take to get across this desert and into the more populated area near the Black Sea. We can avoid nomads, if we are lucky, and not fight anyone."

"And in Trebizond," Faiq said, "Tejmur can hire an entire army to fend off such jackals. If you want an army, that is."

"The question is," Tejmur said, "how to frighten off the nomads without risking our own lives."

"Kill one of them with the Makarov?" Masud suggested. When he saw the look on Papusza's face, he added, "Or maybe wound one of them to make him yell."

"Yes," Norin said. "Or you could kick off his kneecap."

"Those nomads can take much pain without making a sound," Faiq said, "much less running away because of it. It will take more than a leg wound to frighten them into leaving us alone."

"Perhaps we could use words to scare them," Papusza said.

"Words?" Masud asked. "What good are words against swords?"

"Words can be deadly weapons," Tejmur said.

"Yes," Papusza said. "If these desert rats are as superstitious as the rest of the people of this time, we might be able to make them believe that Tejmur has the power of black magic."

"Black magic?" Masud made a face.

"There is a nursery rhyme that children love in Baku," Norin said. "It is about how rocks and swords can bash flesh and cut it, but words will harm no one. But the children who chant that rhyme are wrong, for they have not yet learned that words can hurt worse than swords and clubs."

"Norin is right," Papusza said. "Women know how hurtful words are, though most men seem not to know."

"Do you know of any superstitions that might frighten the blackrobed jackals?" Tejmur asked Faiq.

"Superstitions? No," Faiq said. "But I do know they are much afraid of jinn, as well they should be."

"Jinn?" Papusza said.

"They are sometimes called Genie," Tejmur said. "Magical creatures who are like people in some ways, but who have great power."

"Power for evil," Faiq said. "We are better off not conjuring any desert jinn."

"What other creatures frighten the desert jackals?" Papusza asked.

"Iblis is a most dangerous jinn," Faiq said. "Anyone with any sense will avoid Iblis at all costs."

"Who was this awful she-Genie?" Masud asked, his eyes rounded with false fright.

"He, not she. Do not joke about Iblis," Faiq warned.

"Iblis," Tejmur said. "Of course. He would scare the pants off of anyone who believes in the physical presence of Shaitan."

Faiq dropped his voice to a whisper and looked around. "Do not say that name."

"We have the words we need, it seems," Papusza said.

"Iblis," Norin said, "rebelled against God and became Shaitan, who will never again see heaven. He walks among us, causing much evil and taking vengeance on mankind because of God's banishment. Can we avoid talking of him? If not, we must protect ourselves."

"We will fight with words," Tejmur said with authority. "At least, we will try it."

"If you are determined, I will go along," Masud said. "But only if you promise to keep the Makarov ready. And we still need a plan. A soldier knows even the most powerful weapons are no good without a solid battle plan."

"Darkness comes in mere hours," Tejmur said. "Faiq, my thinking is that the blackrobes will attack in the early morning hours when people are in deepest sleep."

"Not so," Faiq said. "For the jackals are lazy, and they love to loll around in bed when morning comes. They will come into our camp as soon as they think we have bedded down for the night."

"So if we post a watch," Papusza said, "with two of us who talk in loud voices, the murderous desert rats might not come into our camp at all."

"They will come," Faiq said with conviction.

"So we must deal with them," Tejmur said. "I have a plan. It involves all of us learning some words in Arabic. Faiq, can you help us pronounce the words I need?"

Faiq, clearly nervous, nodded gingerly.

"We must seem to move camp up from the water to the base of that low cliff." Tejmur pointed. "And we must hurry. Faiq and Masud, gather firewood and take it to the top edge of the cliff. Build a raging fire in a shallow pit, then cover it with sand, but only enough to stop the flames without quenching the fire in the charcoal. I will make bedrolls near the talus, and you will help me, Norin. We will set up five places for sleep so that the intruders will think all of us have bedded down. Papusza, you are to gather the blackest river mud you can find, enough to cover all our faces and hands."

"And then what?" Papusza asked.

"Then we gather to smear mud on each other, of course. And to practice our magic words with Faiq. Go. All of you. Work fast."

Night came quickly, seemingly hastened along by the frantic preparations of the party for the attack that all knew would come soon. In the trees near the river, where Tejmur was hidden, the darkness was heavy—almost absolute.

When Tejmur heard the first faint rustling of feet moving into the false camp, he hoped his party atop the cliff had also heard the sound. Masud had argued that Tejmur should not hide himself near the bottom of the cliff. "I must be closeby to protect you," Masud had said. But he was a good soldier and followed Tejmur's orders, though he did insist again that Tejmur keep the Makarov ready.

When he heard the first thumping sound of a blackrobe striking a bedroll with his sword, Tejmur chanted in what he hoped was a good approximation of the language of the desert jackals: *"Iblis, Iblis, I conjure you to come."*

On the cliff above, Masud and Faiq chanted in unison, *"I am Iblis, the evil one. I come for vengeance, and I am not alone."*

Norin and Papusza, also on the cliff, chanted, *"We are the followers of Iblis, powerful jinn, more evil than men know."*

"Come to me," Tejmur intoned.

"We come in fire," the four voices at the top of the cliff chanted, *"and we come for human flesh!"* Then they raked the charcoal from the

fire over the cliff.

The results, Tejmur thought, were even more spectacular than he had hoped. The charcoal reignited as it tumbled through the air so that the whole cliff seemed to be covered with an avalanche of fire.

The raiders yelped—no doubt, Tejmur thought, as a result of being pelted with fire. But perhaps worse was their being hit with the words chanted in unison from above:

"*I come, I come, Shaitan once Iblis, I come in the fire of evil and hate.*"

The blackrobes, who had arrived with such stealth, departed with great noise. Tejmur had to struggle not to laugh in triumph. His people on the cliff's edge did as he had instructed them: they remained quiet while he picked his way around the steep slope of the hill and up to the cliff where they waited.

"Papusza?" Tejmur whispered.

"I'm okay. Maybe a small burn on my hand."

"Norin?"

"Yes. We did well."

"Masud?"

"Biting my tongue. I want to laugh out loud."

"Faiq?" Tejmur whispered. Then he called, a little louder, "Faiq?"

"He ran into the night," Masud whispered. "In the middle of our last chant, he ran away."

"He will return," Norin said. "I almost ran away myself. We said such terrible words."

"We will wait here, then. Try to sleep. I'll take the first watch, though I doubt the thieves will return."

"They will never come again into this part of the desert," Norin said. "But I will take the second watch."

"And I the third," Masud and Papusza said in unison, after which Masud graciously deferred to Papusza and offered to watch last.

In the early light of morning, Tejmur awoke with a start. He had slept badly with many sharp pebbles jabbing into his side and legs, and he had dreamed of vague evil—of smoke and pits that smelled of corpses. He sat up.

"Good morning," Masud said. "You awoke in time to see Faiq returning to our camp. There. He comes from the direction of the desert rats who sought to kill us."

Faiq, carrying a bag over one shoulder, climbed the hill. "I have good news," he said.

Tejmur thought the man looked embarrassed.

Norin and Papusza sat up, yawning away sleep. "Faiq," Norin said, "we frightened you with our chants."

"I knew I smelled something," Papusza muttered. She rubbed her nose and scowled at Faiq.

Faiq set the bag on the ground. "I found dates in the camp of the jackals. They fled in such a hurry that they left most of their belongings. I have more flour, better flour than they sold us. And dates. Ah, dates."

"The horses and camels?" Tejmur asked.

"Gone. My guess is that they rode away into the night as fast as their mounts would carry them, and they cared not at all about abandoning their merchandise. We could take it, if we wish."

"No," Tejmur said.

"Of course we do not want their trash. I took the flour and dates only because we paid amply for them. They gave us only moldy flour in their hard-hearted bargaining, and they took too many coins."

"You were afraid," Norin insisted. "And that's all right. I, too, was frightened by the words we uttered."

Faiq hung his head in shame.

"But Faiq," Papusza said, "you taught us those words, and you practiced them with us. The words didn't frighten you when you were teaching us."

"Ah, but they did," Faiq said, looking up at Papusza. "I curbed my fright in the teaching. But in the dark, as you were chanting, didn't you see? In the dark the words conjured jinn all around us. Or so it seemed to me, and I ran. I had no choice. My legs ran."

"Darkness does strange things even to the coolest heads," Tejmur said. "I, too, felt a sharp tingle down my spine when you said your final words and poured the fire down the cliff."

"You?" Papusza said in awe. "You were frightened?"

Tejmur nodded.

"Then hell," Masud said. "I'll also admit to being frightened by the chanting and the darkness. But only a little."

Part Four: Cities on the Sea

Chapter 26

Tejmur caught sight of the city of Trebizond from above as the party descended the steep trail that crossed the high pass over the mountains separating Trebizond from the tableland they had been riding through for the last day and a half. Like an iron crown cupped in a gray rock fist, and nestled at the edge of a sapphire blanket that stretched to the horizon, the city was the loveliest sight Tejmur had seen since falling through his time window into the past.

"The port of Trebizond at last," he said, turning to smile at Papusza who rode behind him on the narrow trail. "Our gateway to the Black Sea. It won't be long until we sail into the Golden Horn and enter the brightest gem of the Medieval world: the city of Constantinople."

"Why is it so cool here?" Papusza asked. "The temperature dropped several degrees as soon as we could see the water."

"The Black Sea is a heat sink," Tejmur said. "Its water is quite deep, and it takes on the heat from the air above it, cooling the atmosphere."

"I have never understood why they call this body of water the Black Sea," Papusza said. "In my experience, it has always been this same lovely shade of blue."

"There is a simple scientific explanation. The Black Sea was so named because the lack of oxygen in the water inhibits the development of microorganisms, making the sea appear black."

"But I thought that ancient Greeks had named it!" The frown wrinkling Papusza's face expressed her disdain for Tejmur's logical answer.

"So they did."

"What did the ancient Greeks know of microorganisms? I think that you do not know what you are talking about," she snapped.

Puzzled and a little hurt by the vehemence of Papusza's response to what he considered a simple scientific fact, Tejmur turned and led the way down the pass. He had lived enough life to know when to leave well enough alone. The trusty dun horse that had carried him so nobly and ably across the desert, and through the heavily forested hills on the far side of the mountain range they had just crossed, flicked his ears and dipped his head—as though agreeing with Tejmur's decision not to argue with Papusza.

We are all tired, the horse seemed to be saying. Focus on the view. The Mongol pony that Tejmur had started calling Ming after Ming Antu, the great Mongolian astronomer, had proved its intelligence again and again over the course of their long ride from Baku. Tejmur patted the horse's neck and thought, once again, about how hard it would be to sell Ming when they got to Trebizond. He had never owned a horse before, and he was finding—to his immense surprise—that he truly enjoyed it. For Tejmur, Ming had become more than a mode of transportation. He thought of Ming as a friend.

"Let's not think about what comes after we reach the city," Tejmur whispered. He leaned into Ming's neck and rubbed his sweaty coat. "Let's just enjoy the cool and the beauty on our last ride together."

The city spread out before them as they descended. Laid out in three levels, Trebizond was surrounded by high crenellated walls of gray rock flanked by two steep ravines. The lower level was girded by moats. Formidable indeed, Tejmur thought. Even from this distance he could make out three towers in the upper part of the city; the domes of churches in the middle level, one of which looked to be covered in gold leaf; and on the far side of the lowest level, the Black Sea stretching beautiful and blue to the far horizon with its vastness interrupted only by a gray rock seawall that protected the harbor.

By the time they approached the great gate that led into the lower level on the western side of the city, the sun hung low over the darkening sea; and even the sure-footed Mongol horses were stumbling with fatigue. They rode through the heavily fortified gate, passed through the tunnel that led through the massive western wall, and found themselves in a big open area that stretched all the way to the harbor wall. The city walls were lined with brightly colored merchants' stalls, and the broad open space near the harbor held a vast marketplace filled with merchants hawking goods in a myriad of languages—selling food; weapons; tools; all types of trade goods; and silk, linen, and woolen fabric. But silk predominated. Vibrant shades of silk cloth fluttered everywhere in the stiff sea breeze. And the smell of roasting meat and exotic spices filled the air, highlighting the poignancy of the emptiness in Tejmur's belly.

Tejmur nudged Ming forward down one of the broad aisles that separated the merchants' stalls. The aisle ahead of him was crowded with pedestrians dressed in the colorful costumes of a dozen lands. Tejmur had never ridden through crowded streets; but Ming knew what to do, moving slowly along and allowing the people on foot time to make way before him.

Trusting Ming to guide them through the crowd, Tejmur looked back to check on the rest of his party. Seeing them strung out in single-file behind him, he nodded to indicate that they should keep moving forward. Then he turned his eyes back to the crowd—and suddenly felt a hand take hold of his leg.

Tejmur jerked back, instinctively, and felt Ming shy underneath him and then prance a nervous circle around the clinging boy. Once he had regained his balance, Tejmur looked down into the eyes of the dark-haired boy who managed to keep hold of his leg even as Ming shied and pranced. The boy's eyes were wide with fear, but determined. He fixed Tejmur with a fierce gaze and spewed forth a string of sentences in a language Tejmur did not understand.

Tejmur reigned Ming in, not wanting to drag the boy under the horse's hooves; and as Ming came to a stop, the boy switched to another language and spewed forth another string of sentences. The language was familiar—Italian, Tejmur realized—but he only caught a word or two.

Then the boy switched to Azeri. "Master!" he said. "Whatever it is that you seek, I can help you. Food, lodging, pleasure. All of these are here for you. And I can guide you. The best only for you. Let me guide you, master!"

Tejmur found himself smiling at the boy, who still clung to his calf. "What is your name, boy?"

"Alexis, master. After Alexis the First, the Great Comnenus, Emperor of the Romans, he who rules over the Empire of Trebizond from the height of the palace in the Upper Citadel."

"Well, Alexis," Tejmur said, feeling his smile broaden, "I do indeed find myself in need of food and lodging—"

But before he could finish his sentence, Tejmur was cut off by a crowd of boys who looked very much like Alexis and who descended upon Tejmur and Ming—taking hold of Tejmur's legs, his saddle, even Ming's long black mane—and crying "Master, master, let me guide you. Not him. Not him. Choose me!"

Then the confused throng around Tejmur became a melee as, with the sounds of cursing and of leather striking flesh, Faiq came plunging forward on his horse. "Bastards! Whoresons! Bloodsuckers! Back! Back!" Faiq punctuated each syllable by striking a wide-eyed boy with a leather strap that he swung wildly as his horse plunged among them.

Momentarily frozen, all Tejmur could do was stare in horror at the sight of a grown man beating children about the head and neck and leaving a trail of red welts on the upturned faces of the boys, who scattered. But when Faiq turned the whip on Alexis—who gamely kept hold of Tejmur's calf despite Faiq's cursing and beating—Tejmur felt himself snap. Setting his feet in the stirrups, he leaned out and snatched the leather strap out of Faiq's hand, only keeping himself from bringing the strap down into Faiq's shocked face by force of will.

"Enough!" Tejmur shouted. "Faiq. Enough of this."

"But—"

"Silence! As long as you choose to follow me, we will have no more of this. You shame me." Tejmur felt his eyes boring into Faiq's—eyes as wide all of a sudden as those of the boys he had just been beating. "You shame all of us. I will have no more of this, or you will ride with me no longer."

Reigning his mount to a halt, Faiq lowered his head in submission. "It shall be as you say, master."

"Good." Tejmur took a deep breath and looked back into the face of the boy, Alexis, who clung to his leg like a life raft in a violent sea. "You may guide us," said Tejmur, "to a place of lodging. Take us to the best inn you know, with the cleanest beds and the finest food. I will reward you richly."

"Thank you, master," Alexis said. "You have chosen wisely, for I am the best guide in the city. There are no fine inns such as you seek in the lower town. We must go to the middle town to find the comforts you seek."

"How far?"

"Not far. We must cross the lower town and pass through the gate to the middle level. The inn you seek lies just inside, near the Church of the Panaghia Chrysokephalos."

"Lead on, then. We will follow," Tejmur said to the boy. Then he turned to address the rest of the party, whose faces were filled with a mix of fatigue and shock. "This boy knows an excellent inn on the middle level of the city. Stay close. It will not be long before we can all eat and bathe and rest."

Alexis led them slowly through the open marketplace and into an area of narrow streets lined with shops and cheap-looking inns, pausing when the crowd was too thick to ride through. At length, they passed through another heavily fortified gate into the middle level of the city.

The contrast between the lower town and the middle town was marked. The streets were wider and less crowded, and the shops lining the streets were fancier than those on the lower level. It was not long before they rode past the glorious gold-domed church that Tejmur had caught sight of from the top of the pass. In the late afternoon sun, the golden dome glowed as though it were lit from within.

"Alexis," Tejmur called, as they rode past the towering Byzantine church. "What is the name of this cathedral?"

"This is the Church of the Panaghia Chrysokephalos, master. It is the glory of Trebizond. Only the Hagia Sophia in Constantinople outshines it, they say. But I would not know. I have never been to Constantinople."

"And the inn you lead us to, it is near here?"

"Very near, master. Follow me. We will arrive in a mere moment."

True to his word, Alexis led them through an ornate wooden gate that arched its graceful way through the middle of a beautiful carved stone façade and into a cobbled courtyard. A central fountain plashed and played in the middle of a wide open space flanked by Roman arches that divided the courtyard from the inn proper.

"Tell the innkeeper we will need three rooms," Tejmur said to Alexis, "and livery for five horses and a mule. Go quickly, for we are tired and hungry."

"It is done, master." Alexis bowed and disappeared into an archway on the far side of the courtyard.

Tejmur dismounted, his legs unsteady from the long ride down the pass and through the city. Around him the rest of the party dismounted also, stretching their legs and backs in the silence that comes from near exhaustion.

"Will this do?" Tejmur asked Papusza.

"It is lovely." She waved an arm at the fountain, the arches, the polished-looking cobbles of the courtyard. "The only thing that could make it any better would be a long, hot bath."

"We'll see what we can do." Tejmur wondered if he sounded as tired as he felt. He turned to loosen the cinch on Ming's saddle. But just then, he felt Papusza take his arm and turn him to face her.

"I appreciate what you did earlier, defending those boys against Faiq." Her eyes were lit with an inner fire that seemed to transcend the fatigue of the long ride. "And I am sorry for being so cross with you this morning about how the Black Sea got its name."

"Both were nothing," Tejmur said. The fire in Papusza's eyes reminded him of the sun in the golden dome of the Church of the Panaghia Chrysokephalos, and he smiled at the thought. "What matters now is making you comfortable."

"You asked for three rooms. What sleeping arrangements did you envision?"

"I had thought that Masud and I could share a room, and you and Norin. If Faiq refuses to bathe again, as I am sure he will do, he will need a room of his own."

"I concur," Papusza said, smiling a weary smile, "on all counts. But I disagree about your defending those boys being nothing. It is moments like those that make me look forward with great anticipation to our entrance into Constantinople."

To his surprise, she leaned forward and kissed him long and deeply, and with an intensity that left him short of breath as she turned to loosen the cinch on her own saddle.

Chapter 27

Tejmur sank a bit deeper into the bronze tub and felt the hot, spice-scented water ease the ache in his saddle-weary muscles all the way from his toes to the base of his jaw. He tried to remember the last time he had felt this relaxed, drew a blank, and gave up. Instead of sifting through the distant past—or rather, he reminded himself, the distant future—he silently congratulated himself on the way he had handled the last couple of hours.

He had managed to recover sufficiently from the unexpected and delicious feel of Papusza's mouth against his own just in time to confront the owner of The Lion's Head Inn, whom Alexis had just led into the courtyard. Without hesitation, and in his most authoritative tone, Tejmur ordered the innkeeper to prepare hot baths in his three best rooms, to bring clean clothes to be put on after the baths, and to bring heaping portions of the specialty of the house to each room immediately after the party was dressed.

The innkeeper—a fat middle-aged man with pasty skin, grayish-blonde hair, and green eyes set deep into fleshy pouches in his face—hesitated, looking askance at the dirty clothes and scruffy equipage of the party. Tejmur scowled, reached into a pocket, and took out a handful of gold coins. Then he crossed the fat man's palm with precious metal.

The innkeeper smiled and bowed low. Then he strode away, clapping his hands and shouting a flurry of orders in an unfamiliar tongue..

Suddenly, the courtyard was abuzz with activity. Male and female servants scurried back and forth unloading horses; leading the animals to the fountain to drink; and guiding the party across the courtyard, beneath the lovely Roman arches, and into high-ceilinged rooms that were as spacious as they were well-appointed. Servants brought bronze tubs to the rooms and poured steaming water into the tubs, while other servants brought clothes. It was all done with a great deal of smiling and bowing.

Tejmur dipped his head under the water, holding his breath and feeling the hot water wash the soap from his hair. When he broke the surface again, he grinned an impish grin. Despite his socialist leanings, Tejmur was coming to appreciate the great usefulness of minted precious metals. As a means to an end, there were not many more effective tools than a handful of gold pieces.

He looked around the room that he and Masud shared. The floor was covered with a beautiful Byzantine mosaic of lions' heads, their mouths open to roar. The heavy door, which looked to have been carved from a single piece of oak, had scenes of lion hunting engraved into four separate panels. An intricate filigree of brass divided the panels, and the hinges were of brass also, so that the door gleamed in the lamplight. Two brass-filigreed wardrobes, also carved with lion-hunting scenes, flanked the door. Against each of the three remaining walls sat a big wooden bed covered with richly colored woven fabric. In the center of the room, a low table with no chairs sat in the middle of a blue rug. It was by far the nicest room Tejmur had ever bathed in. He took another deep breath, savoring the solitude that Masud's post-bath visit to Norin had provided. The much-needed time alone felt almost as good as the bath.

Finally, feeling waterlogged and half-starved, Tejmur climbed out of the bronze tub, dried himself with one of the plush towels the servants had brought, then put on the clothes that had been laid out: a knee-length gray tunic of wool with long sleeves, brownish-gray leggings of wool that reached to mid thigh, and a pair of leather sandals. The clothes fit well enough, but felt strange—almost as though he was wearing a dress. The first order of business for tomorrow would be to find a clothing shop that sold pants.

But the awkward feel of the clothes faded with the entrance of Masud, followed by servants bearing trays heaped with food. The smell was wonderful, and Tejmur wasted no time digging into the spicy roasted lamb, tabouli, fried plantains, and heavy wheat bread that the servants set down on the table. Tejmur and Masud sat on the rug, ate food enough for a half-dozen hungry travelers, and washed it all down with a carafe of spicy red wine.

"For the first time," Masud said at last, when both had eaten as much as they could hold, "I feel at home in the past."

"This place is an excellent way station on our journey to Constantinople," Tejmur answered. "But it is merely a means to an end, not an end in itself."

"Why bother with going to Constantinople?" Masud asked. "I like it here."

"Because I promised Papusza to take her there." Tejmur eased back onto an elbow to accommodate the vast amount of food that was settling now, in a most satisfying way, in his belly. "And besides, I must repair my time window."

"Back in Baku, you said that you needed a bar of copper to fix your time machine. It seems to me that in a rich trade city like Trebizond, there would be copper enough to do the job. You could open your window here."

"I suppose so," Tejmur said. "But still, I promised to take Papusza to Constantinople. And when we return to the future, Constantinople will have become Istanbul. They are not the same."

"What will Trebizond be, in the future?"

"The city of Trabzon, in modern Turkey. And my promise to Papusza aside, Trabzon will not suit our needs as well as Istanbul."

"I don't understand."

"Think, Masud. If we go back through the time window now, we will find ourselves in a small provincial city in Turkey. We will be aliens, foreigners in the country illegally, and without passports. Indeed, with no papers of any kind—and with a great load of ancient coins. What do you think will happen if we are stopped by the police?"

"I hadn't thought of that."

"Think of it now. Istanbul, on the other hand, is a modern metropolis that stretches onto two continents. As such, it is a hub of trade and travel. It contains a vast black market in which we can sell ancient coins without any awkward questions, and then use the proceeds of the sale to buy new identities for all of us. With our new passports, and the papers establishing our new identities, we will be free."

"But couldn't we go back and forth, once the window is working?"

"What do you mean?"

"If you could find the supplies you need here to get your time machine working, couldn't we go forward to Trabzon and buy supplies? A modern battery for your window, for example, and ammunition for the Makarov. Hell, we could buy guns for us all. Wouldn't that make things safer, and easier, on our trip to Constantinople?"

Tejmur sat bolt upright, despite the protest of his belly. "I hadn't thought of that," he said.

"Think of it now." Masud's half-grin was full of mischief. "As for me, I think I will go say goodnight to Norin."

"Masud," Tejmur said, as Masud started for the door. "Have you thought about what you are going to do with Norin?"

"To tell the truth, for the past few days I have thought of almost nothing else." Masud's mischievous grin seemed now to fill his entire face. "And I believe that Norin has been thinking those same thoughts."

"I've noticed," Tejmur said. "And I agree that Norin feels the same way about you. But that's not what I meant. When we go back to the future—to our own time, I mean—what will you and Norin do then?"

The grin disappeared from Masud's face. "I don't know. That is a thing I have been thinking about also." Then he walked out the door.

Left alone again, Tejmur began to formulate a plan for repairing the time window. Masud was right. With a little ingenuity, it should be possible to find the items needed for the job in this hub of trade. In fact, with a bit of luck, he might be able to make a much more powerful battery here in resource-rich Trebizond than the cruder type he'd envisioned back in Baku.

First, Tejmur would need a piece of copper, which should be easy enough. Any metalworking shop would have it. But he would also need a potato to boil, and that was a problem. Potatoes came from the Americas, so they wouldn't be available in Asia Minor for centuries. Thinking hard about a substitute, Tejmur let his eyes wander across the remains of his and Masud's meal that still lay on the table in front of him—and found the fried plantains. Of course, he thought. He could use plantains instead of a potato to generate a flow of electrons.

All that remained was a piece of zinc. And as with the potato, Tejmur thought, zinc would be a problem. Zinc was a metal that was difficult to produce without modern methods. It would not come into common use for another several hundred years. Tejmur studied the contents of the room, racking his brain for a solution. Then he looked at the filigree on the door and the wardrobes, and he had his answer.

"Brass!" he shouted, then jumped up from the rug and rushed to the door to make sure it was true.

Sure enough, it was brass all right. And that, Tejmur knew, meant zinc. Zinc had been used, but not recognized, in ancient times. The brass of this period was made directly from copper and calamine—which was a kind of zinc ore. In an imprecise process, metalworkers heated calamine in a furnace such that it would give off zinc vapors, which soaked into the accompanying copper. Zinc metal was a by-product of the reaction. He should be able to get what he needed from the condensation at the bottom of any furnace used to make brass.

Someone pounded on the door, shattering Tejmur's moment of solitidue—and his train of thought.

"Yes?" he said with more than a little irritation.

"Master?" he heard. "Master, are you all right?"

Tejmur opened the door to find Faiq standing outside, a look of what appeared to be genuine concern on his face. "Of course," Tejmur snapped. "Why wouldn't I be?"

"I heard you shout. I was worried that you might need assistance."

It occurred to Tejmur that there was something different about Faiq. Then it hit him. Faiq was actually clean, and he wore clean clothes.

"Faiq," Tejmur said with an involuntary smile, "you bathed."

"Yes," Faiq said, and his look of concern turned to disgust. "Papusza insisted on it. But it is not a practice that I plan to adopt."

"As you wish," Temjur said, and made to close the door. "Good night."

"Master, wait! I have something to tell you, and a favor to ask."

"Quickly then."

"First, I would like to apologize for making you angry this afternoon when we rode into the city. I would never have struck those boys if I had known you would disapprove."

"Now you know. What about the favor?"

"Have you inquired about the prices of any of the things—the very many things—that you have been ordering from this pig of a thief of an innkeeper?"

"I have not."

"Oh, my master. This innkeeper will charge you exorbitantly. He will do his best to take every piece of gold and silver that you own."

"I have enough coins to cover a hundred such stays as ours. We have wealth to spare, Faiq. More than enough to live as we wish. You said so yourself."

"I said no such thing. Nor would I ever do so. More than enough wealth? It goes against the will of God. Are you not familiar with the parable of the talents?"

"I am. But I am also reminded that greed is a serious sin."

"Please, my master. Humor me. Let me go and speak with the innkeeper about price."

"All right, Faiq. If it will make you happy."

"Thank you, master."

Faiq disappeared almost before he finished his sentence, and Tejmur shut the door. He turned his attention to a long-delayed inspection of the beds. How long had it been, he wondered, since he had slept in one? But in all too short a time, Faiq was back. This time, Faiq opened the door while he was still knocking and barged into the room.

"Come right in," Tejmur said, too sleepy now to be irritated. He had just finished testing the ticking in the mattresses. To his delight, all three of the mattresses in their room were filled with feathers. This would be his first night sleeping in a feather bed, and he was eager to begin it.

"I have good news," Faiq said. "The owner is a thief, but an honorable one. His prices are steep, but not exorbitant. And there is security at the inn. Armed guards are stationed in the courtyard from dark to dawn. If needed, the owner has offered to present a letter of recommendation from the keeper of the Middle Fortress. I believe that almost everything is going well."

"Why almost?"

"The boy, Alexis, still lingers. He says that you promised to reward him richly, and that the money I gave him does not fulfill this promise. The boy, I am afraid, is a much less honorable thief than the innkeeper."

"How much does he want?"

"A gold coin like the ones you gave the innkeeper."

"How much did you give him?"

"A smaller silver coin."

"Give him what he asked for, and bring him to me," Tejmur said. "And hurry. I have never slept on a feather mattress, and I am most eager to do so."

Moments later, Faiq ushered Alexis into room. The boy held a gold piece in his left hand, and rubbed his belly with his right. His eyes were fastened onto the pile of leftovers on the table.

"Have you eaten, Alexis?" Tejmur asked, suppressing a smile.

"I have not. The keeper of the inn insisted that you had not ordered food for me."

"And rightly so," Faiq said, indignant. "You have just been paid enough to buy a dozen such meals. A hundred."

"Alexis, go ahead and have whatever you like. You can eat while we talk."

In an instant, the boy was leaning over the table and stuffing food into his mouth with both hands.

"Sit down, and slow down," Tejmur said. "No one is going to take it from you."

Alexis sat down, but kept stuffing food into his mouth.

Tejmur shook his head. "I have work for both of you for tomorrow. Very important work. Alexis, you will take Masud and me shopping for supplies in the morning. We will need to find a smithy that makes brass and a food stall that sells plantains. Faiq, you will take the women shopping for clothes and travel gear. Alexis will recommend shops that sell clothing and travel items. And Faiq, one of the innkeeper's servants can direct you to the shops."

"But master," Faiq said. "Why send me with the women?"

"Because, Faiq," Tejmur lowered his voice as if telling a secret, "I am entrusting you with all of the bargaining. Except for the clothes that Papusza and Norin select, you will have final authority over all that is purchased. And for everything that is bought, you will have the final say about the price that we pay."

Faiq smiled broadly, and bowed. "I will not disappoint you."

Chapter 28

Tejmur, standing with Masud and Alexis in the street outside the inn, felt certain the day would bring good fortune. Surely the city contained the makings of a battery with enough power—especially when combined with the smaller battery that operated the eyepiece—to open his time window. He looked at the lower town on the hill below the inn, at the rooftops stretching to the edge of the Black Sea. Then he turned and looked up the hill.

"I would like to start in the upper town," he said to Alexis.

"The gate will be closed to us," Alexis said. "Only the royal ones and those who serve them go there."

"Gold will not unlock the gate?" Masud asked.

"Perhaps, but offering a bribe to the wrong guard can get even a rich merchant like you put to the sword."

"Before leaving this wonderful city I would much like to see that palace." Tejmur pointed at the beautiful Byzantine castle that rose over the upper wall.

"As would I," Alexis said. "The Comneni live there in the castle keep and in those three towers. I have seen the royal ones only at a distance, for they move about with armed guards. And they seldom visit what they must see as the rabble below them. Rabble such as us. I mean no insult, only to tell of the high and mighty there in the upper town."

"I have always heard," Masud said, "that rich capitalists believe themselves to be better than commoners. Do you resent the Comneni, Alexis?"

"Resent?" The question seemed to astound the boy. "No more than I would resent the sun for sinking into the west at night or the sea for being wet."

"We go below, then," Tejmur said.

"In the markets nearby, here in the middle town, we will find the plantains you want. But the metalworkers you seek are in the lower town."

"The metal first, then," Tejmur said.

"This way, to the gate." As they moved through the streets, Alexis kept up a running commentary about Trebizond. "There," he pointed, "set high into the cliff on the eastern edge of the city, is the monastery of Saint Eugene. And there, as I said yesterday, is the magnificent Church of the Panaghia Chrysokephalos where we crown the emperors of Trebizond."

"Such astounding wealth," Masud said. "Who would have thought priests here in the dark ages would control so much?"

"Do you resent the wealthy priests?" Tejmur asked.

"Why should I?" Masud laughed. "Their wealth harms me not. It would be like resenting the sun for being hot."

"Well said," Alexis declared, then ducked his head as if fearing to give offense. "Here in the middle town are other traders, some from Georgia who speak a language difficult for me, and there are the Italians. I know their language, but they are harsh and unkind."

The chatter of the boy kept Tejmur full of the sense of well-being he had found in Trebizond. He was content to let the boy rattle on as they descended the hill and went down through the vast wooden gate manned by bored-looking guards armed with swords and pikes.

In the lower town the streets narrowed, edged by brick and stone walls. The people they passed wore coarse wool, simple and cheap, and they eyed Masud and Tejmur with only mild interest.

"Even the poor here seem prosperous," Masud said.

"This is a fine city," Tejmur said. "A safe city, and one I shall be sorry to leave. But Constantinople is surely even more beautiful and wealthy."

"The lower town," Alexis said, "is safe enough, if you are careful. Here, close to the docks, are bad men enough. One of them is following us even now."

"What?" Masud's hand went inside his tunic. No doubt, Tejmur thought, to the butt of the Makarov.

"He is a man I know something about," Alexis said. "A coward he is, but dangerous enough because he carries reports on traveling merchants to men who would rob them. We are in no danger now, but we must watch ourselves when we leave the city for Constantinople."

"We?" Tejmur asked, amused.

"But of course you will want my services as a guide as you leave the city. And you will be glad to have me along in Constantinople."

"Enough of that for now," Tejmur said. "Take me to the men who work in metal."

"Such men live in these houses." Alexis swept his hand toward the walls beside them. "One of their forges is there, beyond the next crossing of streets. The smoke there, you can see it. And you will soon feel the heat of the furnace."

"Take me to a furnace not in use today," Tejmur said.

Alexis led the way to a building with a short brick smokestack, one that produced no smoke. The metalworkers in the shop eyed Tejmur with amusement when he offered them a silver coin to allow him to scrape slag from the bottom of the furnace. The foreman took Tejmur's coin and handed him an iron bar.

In minutes, Tejmur had a flat piece of disreputable-looking gray material in hand. He inspected it with elaborate care, feeling his excitement rise. Then he purchased a small spike of copper, something the foreman clearly regarded as scrap to be thrown into the vat for melting.

"Now," Tejmur said, "we return to the inn. On the way we will purchase plantains."

"You will make a battery with fruit, slag, and a copper nail?" Masud asked.

"Absolutely. Any schoolboy can make a battery from a potato that is powerful enough to light a low-watt bulb. Boiling the potatoes increases the power tenfold. There won't be potatoes in Asia for several centuries. But I should be able to do the same thing with a boiled plantain or two."

"And you're willing to risk your life stepping through a time window powered by such a contraption?"

"Of course," Tejmur said. "All the window does is create a threshold, like the opening to a tunnel. Then the window makes contact with the master chronoton, which actually bores the tunnel through time between the two parallel hours it is set for. The master chronoton draws energy—a great deal of energy indeed—from the main power plant in Baku. So all we need from the plantains is enough power to work the window. The key is the electrolytes contained in the juice of the plantains. When I attach the copper and zinc electrodes to the—"

Masud shook his head and held up his hand to stop Tejmur from going into further detail. "I believe you. But the ingredients for your battery strike me as something a medieval magician might assemble so he could magic lead into gold."

"Is that how you are so rich?" Alexis asked, round-eyed. "This thing you call a battery, then, is the philosopher's stone that makes base metal into gold?"

"It is impossible to turn lead into gold," Tejmur said.

"Must they be large plantains?" Alexis asked, obviously disappointed with Tejmur's answer.

"Large is good. Yes."

Back at the inn, after a brief stop at a fruit stall on the middle level of the city, Tejmur summoned the innkeeper. "I want your cook to boil these," Tejmur said. He handed the innkeeper two big plantains.

"Fried would be better, and drizzled with fresh honey," the innkeeper said. "Then topped with sweet spices." The portly man's eyes became moist with pleasure as he envisioned the dish.

"Just boiled. Make sure the cook does not peel the plantains, and that they are cooked through—but not boiled into mush."

"Not peeled? This is a custom of your country?"

"Not peeled. I want firm plantains. Cooked, but firm. And I want them brought to my room right away."

When Tejmur pressed three silver coins into Alexis's hand, the boy said, "You pay too much for today's simple service." He put the coins into a pocket. "But I will not insult you by refusing your generosity." He grinned and tilted his head in a comical way. "I will wait there, just outside the door to the inn, in case you need me later."

In his room, Tejmur put the furnace slag on a table. "That's fairly pure zinc," he told Masud. "But of course the metal workers haven't the slightest idea what it is, nor will they figure it out for many hundreds of years. The workers in brass make it by accident. I need a nail carved from this zinc."

Masud tapped on the metal with his knife. "A nail?"

"A spike, then, like a nail the length of your finger."

After scraping to locate the best spot, Masud began cutting. "This works, but it's tough going."

"The iron in that blade is harder than zinc, but not by much. You'll dull your blade, but you can get us a spike."

When a servant brought the boiled plantains, Tejmur had all the materials assembled. He poked half the length of the zinc spike into one of the boiled plantains, then did the same thing with the copper spike. He slid the second fruit onto the other half of both spikes, leaving a centimeter's worth of bare metal between the two pieces of fruit. Next he assembled his time window. Then he connected the wires from the small battery on the eyepiece to the two spikes and to the window, and peered through the back metal frame.

"Darkness," he said.

"The banana battery doesn't work," Masud said, his voice laced with disappointment. "I knew it."

"It works, I think. In our own time, the place we are standing might be covered with centuries of rubble and dirt, so I would see no light through the time window. We need to go to a higher place. Carry the plantains, and I'll take the rest."

It struck Tejmur as comical that Masud walked beside him with such prissy care to keep from pulling the wiring loose. Here is a warrior, Tejmur told himself, fierce enough to kick a man's kneecaps off in hand-to-hand fighting—and he looks so fastidious and funny in the tender way he carries two boiled bananas connected by a pair of metal spikes.

After setting up again in a little courtyard just above the inn, and powering up the time window, Tejmur peered once more through the black metal frame. This time, he saw traffic moving down a modern street and pedestrians thronging a concrete sidewalk beside the asphalt road.

"It works!" He could barely control the excitement in his voice. "The picture is completely clear, which tells me that I have good power from the combination of the smaller battery and the plantains—enough to carry us back into our own time."

"If you're sure this thing is safe, let's go right now," Masud said. "I'll leap through, have a good look around, and return immediately."

"If you leap through now, you'll be run over by one of those cars that seem to be moving half-in and half-out of the frame," Tejmur said thoughtfully. "It looks as though the time window has opened about a meter above the street. But even a glimpse of our home time is comforting after all we've been through to get the window working again. Besides, even if the time window opened directly onto the sidewalk, you would startle people by appearing so suddenly."

"It would be funny, not dangerous." Masud threw his head back and laughed. "It would be a good stunt, and much fun to see the shock on the faces of those around me. Move the window over a couple of meters. I'll leap through, wave my arms about, make hideous faces, make the ladies wet their panties—and then, just before they start fainting left and right, I'll tell them that I'm part of a traveling circus. I'll say that I'm the king of magic tricks, a master of the art of disappearing. Then I'll leap back through the window."

Tejmur enjoyed Masud's childish enthusiasm. "They would look at the way you are dressed, and they would believe you. If the Turks understood your Azeri, that is. But what if one of the men decided you were some sort of threat and pulled out a gun to shoot you?"

Chapter 29

"In modern Turkey," Masud said, "the government doesn't allow its citizens to carry guns. The police would arrest anyone caught with a pistol."

"A knife, then. What if you frightened someone into coming at you with a knife?"

"I would kick his legs from under him." Masud laughed. "But of course, you're right. It's just that I so long to taste the clean, wet air of my own time, to touch a woman in modern clothing, to see the sky streaked with vapor trails of airliners."

"Thinking of returning has made you into a poet."

"I didn't realize how much I missed the future." Masud grinned. "The present—whatever you want to call our own time. Anyway, I'm homesick. But just a glimpse, Tejmur, just a glimpse, and perhaps I would be ready to return to these Dark Ages and travel with Norin and you to Constantinople."

"I guess I could find a store with the eyepiece, one where I could buy some batteries so you won't have to carry a pair of giant bananas around."

"A store. Of course. I could buy ammunition for the Makarov. We can make a fast trip of it, one that will get what we need and satisfy my desire to see home for just a few moments."

"Even a short return could prove dangerous," Tejmur warned.

"How?"

"I don't know," Tejmur said, disassembling the time window and placing it into the carrying pouch with the eyepiece. "But I do know we have been surprised much since using the window, and those surprises have almost gotten us killed."

Back at the inn, Tejmur and Masud found Alexis sprawled, half-lying and half-leaning against the outside wall, half-asleep. He came to his feet immediately.

"What would you like, master? A tour of the city? A closer look at the monastery of Saint Eugene?"

"Lead us to someplace quiet," Tejmur said, "maybe to a building that has been here for many years and will likely endure into the future."

Alexis grinned. "We go this way then. There are many such places in the city. The side of the Church of the Panaghia Chrysokephalos is quiet enough, though often people crowd around the front where there is a small marketplace."

People glanced at them as they made their way through the narrow streets. Most simply cut their eyes toward them, though several children stared openly at Masud, and most people looked amused. One child pointed and laughed.

"And what could be so funny?" Masud demanded.

"Have you forgotten that you carry a pair of cooked bananas connected by a pair of metal spikes?" Tejmur chuckled. "And there are stringy-looking wires hanging from them. You are quite the amusing sight."

"So they think me worthy of their laughter, do they? Wait until I vanish before their eyes, then come jumping back as out of nowhere. You will have batteries when we return, so I can throw plantains in the face of anyone who dares laugh."

"We must do all our travel through the window with great discretion," Tejmur said. "We have no idea how people will react in either time to the sight of us popping into, and out of, thin air."

When they neared the church, Tejmur reconnected the eyepiece to its small battery and looked through. He moved about the open area outside the church, tilting and panning the eyepiece like a motion picture camera, until he found what he was looking for.

"This is good, Masud. Up the street there," he pointed, "is a small shop. The sign on the front is in English, no doubt written by someone new to that language. It says *Sweetness and Groceries*, so I suppose the shopkeeper sells food and perhaps candy."

"What, master? Where?" Alexis looked confused.

"Ignore him," Masud said. "He often speaks in riddles that only he can understand."

"And, ah, yes. There, across the street from Sweetness and Groceries, I see what passes for a hardware store in the distant future."

"Batteries," Masud said.

"Exactly. A couple of big ones for the time window, and a smaller backup battery for the eyepiece. Alexis, find us that quiet spot where there are few people."

"This way, master." Alexis led them to a small side street not much wider than an alley.

Tejmur looked again into the eyepiece. "Perfect," he said. This same place will still be there, uncluttered by the debris of centuries, and no one is in sight now or then." He took the metal parts of the window from the pouch strapped to his waist, telescoped them to their full length, and began connecting the wires from the control box. Then he wired the battery from the eyepiece and the plantain battery into the time window and took a deep breath.

Alexis stared, open-mouthed.

"This is going to be difficult to manage," Temjur said to Masud. Then he turned to Alexis. "We will need your help. You must stand here and hold this corner of my window."

"Window?"

"Another riddle," Masud said.

"This is a trick," Tejmur said. "A clever trick. Masud and I, and all we carry, will seem to disappear. Then I will reach back to take the frame of what I call a window, and it will also disappear. It is very important that you keep holding the frame, no matter what happens, until I reach back through and take it from you. Do you understand?"

"Yes master." Tejmur heard the skepticism in Alexis's voice and knew the boy didn't believe him. "What shall I do after you have vanished with your window?"

"Please wait for us over there. We should return soon. But do not be alarmed if we are gone for what seems a long time. Are you ready?"

"Yes."

"Good. Now hold the corner here to keep the window from falling over. This will take only a moment." Tejmur fingered the switch on the box.

Masud hunkered down, holding the plantains with great care, and duck-walked through the window. As he followed with the smaller battery, Tejmur heard Alexis gasp.

On the other side, Tejmur felt a great pressure in his ears—as though they had just become plugged with wax. As he grabbed the frame of the window and pulled it through after them, he yawned fast. Then he felt a kind of click in his inner ears, and the sounds of the modern world came flooding in.

Tejmur looked around the alley and found Masud beside him, grinning.

"Look. Normal people." Masud pointed to the street at the end of the alley. Then his grin faded into a look of confusion. "Why is my voice so odd?"

"Air pressure," Tejmur said. "It isn't your voice, it's your inner ears. There must be a low pressure area in the atmosphere here in our time, so it feels like you would when you descend suddenly in an airplane. Yawn to equalize the pressure in your head, and your hearing will return to normal."

"The air," Masud said. "It stinks of car exhaust, of garbage, of asphalt, and of chemicals."

"Welcome back to the modern world." Tejmur dismantled the window, and started to stow all of their equipment into his carrying case.

"It seems someone just paved this alley," Masud said, wrinkling his nose in disgust. "Look at the knees of my tunic. I got asphalt on them when I came through the time window. There's no way to get this mess off my clothing. And look. I'm still holding these silly boiled bananas. Can I throw them away now?"

"It would be wise to wait until we have batteries. Hand me the zinc and copper spikes."

Masud pretended to examine the bananas with elaborate care. "Boiled fruit kicked us ahead in time by almost eight hundred years."

"Not just boiled fruit."

"I know, I know. You did it with the magic of science. And, and . . . boiled fruit." Masud grinned in a comical way. "This world of ours is dirty, and it stinks. But it is home, even here in this city on the Black Sea. Sort of home."

When they emerged from the alley, several men turned to stare. Two pointed and laughed.

"It's our clothes," Tejmur said.

"Look what this world did to our great city walls." Masud spoke with disgust. "What a waste."

Part of the wall around the lower town stood crumbling below them. Tejmur felt his heart sink at the sight. What had been a marvelous structure built by the ancients was now only fifty meters or so long. Streets cut the wall, and it crumbled into rubble here and there. He saw other pieces of the wall loosely stitched across the hill below them like the hem of a tattered garment. When he turned toward the upper town, Tejur saw the same kind of careless damage to the higher wall.

"Disgusting," he said. "The Turks tore apart the walls so they could better pollute the city with the exhaust from their cars and trucks."

"The hardware store." Masud pointed. "Let's get the batteries. I'm ready to go back now. And I'm not carrying these boiled plantains into that shop." He set the pieces of boiled fruit down at the foot of the steps that led up into the shop.

In the store, a clerk standing behind a glass-topped counter spoke to them in Turkish. Tejmur winced. Azeri and Turkish had common roots, but the languages were different enough, Tejmur knew, to cause some confusion.

"Can you understand Azeri? Tejmur asked.

The clerk held his palm out and tilted it back and forth. "Little. Much no."

"Batteries," Tejmur said. He hoped the word in Azeri and Turkish was close to the same, though it might be pronounced somewhat differently.

The man frowned. He wore clothing that made him look like a modern European, except for a white knit skullcap—one that declared him to be Haji, a man who had made the pilgrimage to Mecca. He shook his head.

Tejmur pointed to a display of batteries behind the counter.

The man said something else, then placed batteries of several sizes on the counter. Tejmur selected a large one, that would fit the time window, and held up two fingers. The clerk produced another battery of the size Tejmur had indicated. Then Tejmur repeated the process with a smaller battery for the eyepiece.

"Now for the difficult part," Tejmur muttered. He put several silver coins on the counter. "Will you take some ancient coins? They are worth much to collectors, and even the silver in them is worth more than the price of these batteries." Tejmur hoped that the clerk had caught enough of the words to make out his meaning.

Clearly astonished, the clerk picked up one of the coins, eyed it with skepticism, and dropped it onto the counter. He shook his head.

"Fake," he proclaimed.

"No. Genuine," Tejmur said. "Perhaps you will recognize gold?"

The clerk scowled. "Gold good, but you no have."

Tejmur put a single gold coin on the counter. The clerk picked it up, bit it, and examined what his teeth had done. He nodded.

"He's robbing us blind," Masud said. "For that gold piece we should get a whole bucket of batteries. How about some ammunition?" He raised his voice. "Bullets for a Makarov. Bullets!"

"Shouting doesn't help," Tejmur said. The man isn't deaf—he simply doesn't understand your words."

"I'll use sign language, then." Masud pulled the Makarov from inside his clothing and laid it on the counter. "Bullets." He tapped the pistol. "Makarov bullets."

The clerk, clearly startled, stepped back.

"He still doesn't understand," Tejmur said.

Masud broke open the Makarov and jacked out a shell. "Bullets, man, bullets." He held up the shell and pointed to the shelves behind the clerk.

A look of understanding came over the clerk's face. "I no have," he said. "But friend have. I call, yes? He bring box. For you. Two golds."

The clerk took a cell phone from a pocket, flipped it open.

"One gold." Masud held up a single finger.

The clerk's face hardened, and he closed the phone. "Two."

"Two, then." Tejmur placed a second gold coin on the counter.

The clerk scooped up the coins, opened his cell phone, and punched the keypad.

"He's robbing us," Masud growled.

"It doesn't matter," Tejmur said.

The clerk muttered into the phone, snapped it closed, and smiled. It was a fake smile, Tejmur realized—an avaricious smile, one that left the clerk's eyes frowning.

"Is there anything else in this store we might need back in the thirteenth century?" Tejmur asked.

Masud looked around, then picked up a couple of cigarette lighters. "These." He set them on the counter.

"One more gold," the clerk said.

"No more gold." Next, Masud picked up a couple of tubes of Superglue and added them to the pile. He looked around the counter for a moment, then expanded his search to the front part of the store. "Duct tape. Do you have duct tape?"

Tejmur heard a distant siren.

The clerk looked alarmed, held up a single finger, and said, "One minute." Then he stepped through a door into what looked to be a supply room behind the counter.

The siren grew louder. "That rat!" Tejmur said. "He didn't call a friend about bullets. He called the police. We're in serious trouble."

Chapter 30

A police car screeched to a halt in front of the store, its lights flashing angry blue and red, and two uniformed men got out. They were both holding pistols.

"Serious trouble?" Masud reloaded the Makarov and knelt behind the counter, pointing the weapon at the front door. "Your talent for understatement may rival your engineering expertise."

"Maybe," Tejmur said. "But then again, it may be that we can talk our way out of this. Put the pistol away, and come back around to this side of the counter. When the police come in, look surprised, maybe even outraged."

Masud made the weapon vanish inside his clothing, and walked around the counter to stand next to Tejmur. "What do you have in mind?" Masud asked.

"Just follow my lead."

The first policeman to the door stepped on one of the boiled plantains and fell, his arms flailing. He gripped the door handle and pulled himself to his feet, his face crimson with embarrassment. The other policeman laughed, which seemed to infuriate the crimson-faced cop. Then the two came into the store pointing pistols and barking commands. Most of the words meant nothing to Tejmur; but he understood a few, and certainly he understood their intent. *Put your hands on the counter* was clearly what they were saying.

"We are simple carnival workers." Tejmur dragged the words out, hoping his slow pronunciation of Azeri would communicate something of his meaning to the police, who no doubt spoke only Turkish. "We are magicians, tricksters who create illusions to entertain people." He put his hands on the counter.

The first policeman spoke a string of words that contained the words *search* and *pistol*.

"He wants to search you," Masud said.

"I'll allow that," Tejmur said. "But we can't let him search you."

While the second policeman covered them with his pistol, the first policeman holstered his weapon and patted Tejmur down. He pulled the pouch of Tejmur's coins from a pocket, and emptied it on the counter.

"Gold," the policeman said, his voice full of awe. "Silver."
"You want it?" Tejmur asked. He gestured that the man should pocket the coins. "It is yours."
"All?" the policeman asked.
"All." Tejmur felt relief wash over him.
"You," the second policeman said to Masud, then said something that included the word *search*. He moved toward Masud, pistol in hand.

Masud smiled, and moved as if to put his hands on the counter. Then he turned in sudden fury, slammed a fist into the policeman's throat, punched him in the stomach, and snatched the pistol out of the man's hand as he fell.

The first policeman fumbled with his holster, trying to draw his weapon, then became still when Masud put the barrel of the fallen policeman's pistol into his face.

"Hands," Masud said, smiling. "Counter."

The fallen policeman lay on the floor clutching his throat and making terrible sounds. It looked to Tejmur as though the man was choking to death.

"Will he die?" Tejmur asked.

"Maybe not." Masud relieved the first policeman of his pistol, belt, and holster. "Take this gun. Please. Take it now."

Tejmur took the gun from Masud, who still held the second policeman's weapon. The second policeman now seemed to be winning his struggle to get air.

"What do we do with these men?" Tejmur asked.

"The back room," Masud said. "Quickly. We'll lock them in the backroom where that bastard clerk went to hide."

Tejmur helped the fallen policeman to his feet and shoved him behind the counter. Masud twisted the first policeman's arm behind his back and hustled the surprised-looking cop toward the back of the store.

In the stockroom they found the clerk cowering behind a chair. Masud flung the first policeman to the floor. He rolled once, seemingly stunned. But then he pulled a pistol from his boot, pointed it at Tejmur, and fired.

Tejmur felt a burning pain sting the left side of his face.

Masud fired twice, and the first policeman became still. "Two pistols. The silly man carries two pistols. We will take them both." He nudged the man with a toe.

"Dead?" Tejmur asked. He felt the warm trickle of blood down his neck.

"No. He plays at being dead so I will put no more bullets into him."

"We need to leave. The gunfire will attract more police." Tejmur looked at the pistol in his hand, then pointed it at the clerk. "Stand up. Take off your clothes."

The clerk looked confused and frightened. "No understand."

"Explain it to him," Tejmur told Masud.

With a broad grin, Masud thrust a pistol into the clerk's face. The man blanched white, stood, and began removing his clothes.

"Can you fit into the clothes of one of the police?" Tejmur asked.

"That one," Masud pointed to the one still rubbing his throat, "is about my size. I can wear his uniform. But his feet. Look. They are tiny. Ah, but the other one. His feet are large, as is proper for cops."

"Hurry them." Tejmur began taking off the clothes he had gotten from the innkeeper.

Masud waved the pistol barrel in circles to indicate hurrying. The clerk and the policeman understood.

Dressed as a store clerk now, Tejmur rummaged through the supply room and found a couple of rolls of gray duct tape. "Here is that duct tape you were looking for," he said. "Help me tie these men and gag them."

Masud seemed to be enjoying himself. "We'll put a sock in their mouths," he said, "and the duct tape will hold it in. I saw a movie once where some bad men had to have their mouths stuffed with their own socks. It looked disgusting. I'm sure these policemen have terrible socks, full of holes and stinking worse than the alley where we crawled through the time window."

"I think I hear another siren," Tejmur said.

Masud pulled the boots from the wounded policeman, who groaned and burbled. "He isn't hurt that bad," Masud said. "I think I'll bind his hands and feet with the tape, and tape a sock into his mouth."

On their way out, Tejmur took the chair the clerk had cowered behind and jammed it under the door handle to the storeroom. "Take large sacks, there," he pointed under the counter. "Put the pistols and gun belts, the batteries, the lighters, some of that Superglue, and the duct tape into the sacks. When we leave, we'll just be two customers carrying our purchases."

"A customer and a cop," Masud said. "And the boots aren't a bad fit. Too wide, but good enough."

Outside a small crowd milled around across the street. Tejmur put a hand over his left ear to cover the blood from his bullet wound. He smiled what he hoped was a reassuring smile. Then he and Masud, paper sacks in their arms, headed for the alley beside the Church of the Panaghia Chrysokephalos. It seemed to Tejmur that some in the crowd eyed them with suspicion. Sure enough, several crowdmembers began fingering cell phones.

The siren that Tejmur had heard faintly sounded much closer now. "We need to hurry," Tejmur said. "But not run."

Three men went into the hardware shop, and in seconds they returned to the door shouting and pointing toward Tejmur and Masud. Half a dozen men from the crowd followed them.

"I think," Masud said, glancing back, "that we need to run now."

They ran, and the men behind them chased after, shouting words Tejmur did not understand. But their intent seemed clear enough. The siren was getting very close now, and the men from the crowd were right on their heels.

When they reached the alley, Temur began assembling the window with shaking hands. "I hope these batteries work."

The men reached the alley and started in. "I'll keep them back," Masud said. He waved the Makarov at them, but they didn't stop. "Maybe I take one fast shot over their heads. Is that good?"

Tejmur worked fast, assembling the frame and snapping one of the big batteries into the black box. "One shot. Don't hit anyone."

Masud fired the shot, and the men ran back. A police car, siren wailing, screeched to a stop beside the men. A uniformed policeman jumped out of the car, crouched behind it, and peered over. He shouted something and waved his pistol.

"Go through the window," Tejmur said. "Quick."

"One more shot first," Masud said, and fired a bullet into the squad car. Then he knelt and rolled, vanishing into the window.

A shout of surprise came from men watching from behind the police car, and the officer fired a shot. Tejmur heard the bullet rip into one of the sacks from the hardware store. He held the corner of the window, grabbed the sacks, and thrust them through. Then he scrambled through after Masud, gripping the handle on the window frame as he did so.

The rods collapsed about him in the tiny street beside the Church of the Panaghia Chrysokephalos. He yawned to equalize the air pressure in his ears and flipped off the power switch while Masud rummaged through the hardware store sacks.

Alexis stood plastered against the church wall, eyes rounded, his hand over his mouth. "The noise," Alexis said. "That terrible smell that came from the magic hole you ripped in the air, your bloody ear, your clothes—"

"He clipped your ear," Masud said. "It looks like you'll never wear an earring on your left ear—anyway, not on the earlobe. It's gone." He turned to Alexis. "You're right that the smell of that other world is terrible. And we changed clothes there, though I'm not fond of the stinky ones I now wear. That pig of a policeman either never bathed, or he never washed his shirt."

"You are great magicians."

"That wasn't magic. That was science." Tejmur touched his ear, winced, and looked at the blood on his hand. He picked up the window's edges, telescoped them down, and breathed deep. "I smell the sea, the desert wind, this wonderful city before the people of our own time ruined it."

"We have three more pistols," Masud said, "along with two belts of ammunition and holsters. The Superglue was a great idea. It can be used to stanch the bleeding from serious wounds, although I don't think that you need it for your ear. And the duct tape? What can it not be used for? I can repair anything with duct tape. Ah, and batteries. Batteries enough to open the window dozens of times without ever hooking it up to another cursed banana."

"You want to go back?" Tejmur heard the surprise in his voice.

"No, no, no. The police would clap me into a Turkish prison. If we go back, it must be far from here. Constantinople, maybe."

"Yes. But we still have a long trip, no doubt one fraught with danger."

"But we have guns," Masud said. "Bullets. And of course, duct tape. We will prevail."

"You're going to Constantinople now?" Alexis asked. "Take me. I know the way. I know the people. I am the best of guides."

"No," Masud said.

"Maybe," Tejmur said.

"That man who followed us yesterday?" Alexis said. "He is back, lurking around in front of the church, pretending not to be interested in finding us. But he keeps looking down this street. He means mischief. I can find a way to avoid the men who sent him, for they wish to rob you and maybe kill you. You must take me with you, you must."

"The boy might be right," Masud said.

"We'll discuss it later with the women in our group," Tejmur said. "But for now, let's head back to the inn."

Chapter 31

Papusza and Norin did not return to the Lion's Head Inn until almost sunset. They walked through the Roman arch and into the cobbled courtyard followed by Faiq, who was followed in turn by a half-dozen servants laden with the day's purchases.

"It looks as though you had a successful shopping trip," Tejmur said, as Papusza and Norin approached the fountain's edge where Tejmur and Masud sat on a blue lion's head rug. Both Tejmur and Masud had bathed and changed out of the clothes they had stolen in the twentieth century. Tejmur had treated his wounded ear. And they were enjoying a carafe of spicy red wine, a plate of fried squid, and the play of the late afternoon sun on the dome of the great church.

"Successful is too weak a word to describe it." Masud laughed. "Is there anything left in the shops on the middle level?"

"Only our rejects," Papusza said. "We found much to buy. There is beautiful and fashionable clothing for Norin and me, and of course jewelry to complement the rich garments that will soon grace our lovely forms. For the men we have stylish tunics of two types, along with trousers and soft boots. We have also bought trunks to pack our new wardrobes into."

"We would love to see some of those purchases gracing your lovely forms." Tejmur squinted at Papusza through a haze of red wine and the late afternoon light reflected off the great dome. She was indeed lovely. "Would you model them for us? We will reward you with wine and calamari."

"Please." Masud looked at Norin. "Model for us."

"Very well," Papusza said.

"It would please me greatly," Norin said.

Faiq excused himself, saying he had arrangements to make, including the safe storage of the purchases. He started after the servants who had continued to the guestrooms with their burdens. But suddenly he stopped, looked around the courtyard, and scowled. "Where is that master thief who so cleverly disguises himself as a boy?"

"Alexis?" Tejmur asked. "He's no thief. He did us great service today as our guide through the city."

"He will no doubt wish to be rewarded in gold," Faiq grumbled. "But where has he got to, my master? There is something about that boy which misgives my merchant's heart."

"Come to think of it, I haven't seen Alexis since Masud and I had our baths. Masud, do you know what's become of Alexis?"

"I haven't seen him either," Masud said. "And it's not like Alexis to miss a chance to eat."

"I saw him in the street," Papusza said, "as we returned to the inn. He seemed to have another customer, someone to guide around the city."

"A merchant?" Faiq asked.

"Perhaps," Papusza said. "Though this man was heavily armed. He wore a sword, and several daggers dangled from his belt. He had black up-turned whiskers and shifty eyes set close together."

"I think he was a seaman," Norin said. "I noticed the up-turned whiskers but not the eyes."

"Alexis?" Tejmur called. Getting no answer, he tried again. "Alexis!"

Instead of the boy, one of the inn servants came scurrying across the courtyard with another carafe of red wine. When the young woman turned to leave, Masud caught the hem of her ankle-length wrapping.

"Have you seen the boy who led us here?" Masud asked. "Answer me, woman."

"Please, sir, release me. I have done nothing." The fear in the woman's voice matched the tightness of her mouth and her wide, rolling dark brown eyes. "Please!"

"Let her go, Masud," Tejmur said. "We've had trouble enough for one day."

"As you wish." Masud released the woman, who hurried across the courtyard and out of sight.

"I will seek the boy in our rooms, master," Faiq said. "What should I do with him if I find him?"

"Tell him there is calamari in the courtyard," Tejmur said. "That should send him here at a dead run."

Papusza and Norin followed Faiq to the guestrooms. By the time the women returned, the carafe of wine was mostly empty. The sun sat atop the western mountains so that it illuminated only the topmost portion of the church dome, forming a golden halo of such breathtaking beauty that it struck Tejmur speechless. Everything in the courtyard was tinted gold: the water plashing in the fountain, the graceful Roman arches, the ornate and opulent clothing that Papusza and Norin wore.

Papusza and Norin glided across the cobblestones and through the golden light reflecting off the dome of the Church of the Panaghia Chrysokephalos as though the courtyard and the dome and the golden glow had been created only to accentuate their beauty. Both women were dressed in ankle-length wraps of sheer silk. Over the longer silk wraps, they wore semi-circular knee-length overgarments fastened at the right shoulder and elaborately brocaded with intricate and beautiful patterns. The longer undergarments were white, the shorter overgarments brightly colored—Papusza's was deep red, Norin's sky blue—

and the brocade was woven with golden thread that picked up the light filling the courtyard.

"The sheer wraps are called *tunicas*," Papusza said. "They hug the form, and the feel of the silk against the skin is like the touch of a cloud."

"Delicate and lovely," Tejmur said, and "Gorgeous," Masud said.

"The shorter, heavier cloak is called a *chlamys*. The brocade is made with cloth of gold. And the brooches that fasten the cloaks over our shoulders are made of gold as well."

"Incredible," Tejmur said. "But you said that you had bought other jewelry also. Come closer, and show it to us."

The women made a slow circle around the table. Both Papusza and Norin wore rings of gold on each hand, and each ring was graced with a precious or semiprecious stone. "Red rubies, purple amethyst, and blue topaz," Papusza said.

"I have never owned jewelry before," Norin said, fluttering her fingers at Masud and smiling down into his eyes. "Nor have I ever felt the touch of such fine silk as this against my skin."

"Get used to it," Masud said.

"Opulence in dress is fun, I suppose," Tejmur said. "But I fear it may attract thieves. When we go about in public with such fine clothing and jewelry, we should be like that man with up-turned whiskers, heavily armed."

"Our clean city in the ancient past has a good heart," Masud said. "We are safe enough." He took one of the hands that Norin had extended and drew her down beside him. "Servant," he called over his shoulder. "More wine. And two more glasses."

Papusza settled onto the rug beside Tejmur, who stared dumbstruck at the woman he hardly recognized, and yet felt as though he had known his whole life.

"Have you no reaction?" Papusza held up a hand to show her rings.

"Not one that I would share with any ears except those of the goddess beside me," Tejmur said. He leaned close and whispered into Papusza's ear. "You are Aphrodite. And your presence outshines the light of the golden dome."

"Aphrodite?" Papusza's voice was just above a whisper. "I am afraid that my knowledge of Greek gods is small. Perhaps you could enlighten me. Who was the consort of the Goddess of Love?"

"There were many. But she was said to be greatly enamored of a mortal man, a Trojan prince named Anchises. She fell in love with him on Mount Ida, which lies in modern Turkey, not far from where we sit."

"She was enamored, you say. But did they consummate their love?"

"Indeed. Their son was Aeneas, who survived the Trojan War and founded Rome."

"And I suppose that this Anchises must have been gloriously attired, to catch the Goddess of Love's attention. In a tunica, perhaps, and a dalmatica, and trousers made of the finest wool?"

"When they met and fell in love, Anchises was attired like the simple shepherd that he was."

"A pity," Papusza said, pulling away from Tejmur with a coy smile. "What will we do with the glorious clothing that Norin and I bought for you this afternoon?" Then her coy smile twisted into a look of surprise and alarm. "But you are wounded! What has happened to your ear?"

Tejmur winced as Papusza touched the place where his left earlobe had once been. "I'm afraid that our trip back to our own time had some complications—"

"He was shot by a Turkish cop," Masud interrupted.

"Shot?"

"It's nothing," Tejmur said. "A flesh wound." He had forgotten that Masud was even there. Now both Norin and Papusza were staring at the side of his face. "Really. It's nothing. I've cleaned it with soap, and rinsed it with what the innkeeper called Aqua Vitae, an alcoholic beverage strong enough to kill bacteria. So there is no danger of infection. And of course, the wine has helped a great deal with the pain."

"But . . . you said *complications*. Were you injured in some other way?"

"We were not," Masud said. "But our enterprise may have been. In the future, Tejmur and I are both wanted men."

"What does that mean?" Papusza narrowed her eyes at Masud. "Wanted for what?"

"I shot the cop who shot Tejmur."

"You shot a policeman? But why? What happened? Did you shoot anyone else?"

"It's a long story," Tejmur said. "Suffice it to say, for now, that we killed no one, that we returned with batteries for the time window, and that we also gleaned some other items that should be most useful here in the past. But I'm afraid that a return to our own time is now impossible, at least in this part of our own modern Turkey."

"Our own Turkey?" Masud scoffed. "What makes that awful sty any more ours than the lovely place where we sit now? You and Papusza must do what you wish. But as for me, I feel disinclined to return again to the twentieth century." He stroked the side of Norin's face. "I prefer to stay here."

"Be that as it may," Tejmur said. "Those of us who do wish to return must go first to Constantinople. We can move into the future again much more safely from there. In modern day Istanbul, we will be faces in a vast crowd. And there will be a modern day black market to supply us with new identities and new travel papers."

"Then I see no real problem," Papusza said. "Certainly, as long as your injury is as slight as you say, I see nothing worth spoiling the rest of this lovely evening. Are there any other issues of which I should be aware?"

"None I know of," Tejmur replied. "Besides the fact that, as Masud has already pointed out, I will never wear an earring in my left ear."

"Then tonight, I would very much like to see Anchises in the clothes that Norin and I have bought for him. And tomorrow, we will begin making arrangements to move on. I want to see the proud city of Constantinople in its ancient glory." Papusza looked deeply into Tejmur's eyes. "I want you to keep your promise."

"There is nothing in either century that I want more," Tejmur said. "But be aware that the danger of our journey to the future was nothing compared to the danger of a journey by ship across the Black Sea."

"What sort of dangers do you speak of?" Norin asked.

"Storms and pirates," Tejmur answered. "And the vast uncertainty of open water in a wooden ship powered only by the wind and oars."

Chapter 32

After a torchlit dinner in the courtyard of seafood, tabouli, and fried plantains—and several more carafes of red wine—Tejmur and Masud headed back to their room to try on the clothes that Papusza and Norin had bought. The two men were under strict orders from Papusza to don the new outfits and to model them for the women in the same way that the women had modeled for the men.

"After all, fair is fair," Papusza had said. "We may be living in the ancient past, but in our little corner of that past, the women and the men live on equal terms."

"Let's get this over with," Masud grumbled as he and Tejmur walked through the brass-inlaid door of their guestroom. "I want to spend some time with Norin. Alone."

"I understand," Tejmur said. "Perhaps tonight's sleeping arrangements could be—"

"At last, my master," Faiq interrupted, as Tejmur and Masud

entered the room. "I have been waiting for you."

"Obviously," Masud said.

"We missed you at dinner," Tejmur said. "And we missed Alexis as well. Have you seen no sign of him, then?"

"As for myself, I was too busy making arrangements to sit down for a formal meal. And as for that master thief who so cleverly disguises himself as a boy, I have seen no sign of him. His absence is a great blessing, and one that I hope with all of my merchant's heart will continue."

"Still no sign of Alexis?" Ignoring Faiq's gibe, Tejmur directed his next question to Masud. "What should we do?"

"Put on these new clothes as quickly as possible," Masud said, "in hopes of taking them off again just as fast." Masud's eyes twinkled with a combination of wine and anticipation. "But for that last, I think Norin and I would prefer a room of our own."

"Not a problem," Tejmur said. "As I was saying before I was interrupted, you and Norin can have this room tonight. I'll bunk with Faiq."

"It would be an honor, my master," Faiq said. "But first, allow me to show you the results of the first set of arrangements that I have made." He pointed Tejmur to an ornately carved wooden trunk sitting at the foot of the bed that Tejmur had slept in the night before. "This first set of arrangements has been made to ensure your comfort, and the proper deference due to you in your new place in society. I hope you will be pleased."

"What about my comfort and deference?" Masud asked.

"Your trunk is over there." Faiq pointed Masud to a smaller and less ornate trunk at the foot of the other bed. Then Faiq turned back to Tejmur. "For you, my master, I have purchased a pair of tunicas, knee-length and long-sleeved and tight-fitting. And a dalmatica, which is waist-length with long open sleeves. All are made of silk, and the dalmatica is interwoven with cloth of gold. I have also purchased several pairs of trousers made of finest wool, and a pair of boots of the very finest quality."

Tejmur opened the trunk and changed into the new clothes, which were surprisingly light and easy to slip into. Then he walked a slow circle around the room, getting the feel of the clothes he would be wearing for who knew how long.

"The trousers feel almost like modern pants," Tejmur said. "And the boots are soft and well-made." He fingered the dalmatica, which was deep red in color, thickly-woven, and stiff with the gold brocade. "The coat is a bit flashy for my taste, but it fits perfectly. You have done well, Faiq."

"Thank you, my master. Now you look like a rich and powerful merchant instead of a seedy beggar."

"I look too rich for safety. Masud, you and I should arm ourselves. This outfit will easily hide one of the police pistols we brought back."

"Why hide them? People here will have no idea what we have strapped on our waists if we wear a gun belt."

"I'll know. And Papusza." Tejmur took a pistol from one of the sacks, checked it for ammunition, and tucked it into his tunic. "You do the same."

"If you want." Masud shrugged. "I'll also put the cop's boot pistol into my own boot—though I won't need it given that my outfit isn't nearly so fancy as yours. Faiq, why doesn't my dalmatica have cloth of gold?" Masud's tone made it clear that he was less than pleased.

"Because you are not a rich merchant," Faiq answered. "You are a soldier."

"So?"

"Here in Trebizond, and even moreso in Constantinople, the clothes a person wears indicate the rank of their wearer." Faiq's tone was impatient, as though he were addressing a simpleton or an unruly child. "You will notice that I have also purchased a new wardrobe. I have even bathed, a practice I despise, but that I will have to get used to."

"You will if you're going to sleep in a room with me," Tejmur said. He looked more closely at Faiq, who was indeed dressed in new clothes: a white silk tunica, a deep green dalmatica that was much less richly brocaded than Tejmur's own, a pair of woolen trousers, and a pair of leather boots. "You look good, Faiq. We all do."

"Excellent. Then allow me to draw your attention to the items I have placed on your beds."

Tejmur and Masud both checked their beds. On each lay a short sword and a matching dagger with bronze, jewel-inlaid hilts. On Tejmur's bed was also a large hat made of felt with a broad brim and interwoven gold threads decorating the top.

"But this is fantastic," Masud said, drawing the sword and giving it a couple of practice passes. "It fits my hand perfectly. Faiq, I must admit that I am genuinely impressed. You have done well."

Tejmur put on the hat. "This is too fancy, but it will block the sun." He picked up his sword and awkwardly drew it from its bronze sheath. "I'm armed with a better weapon than a sword. What am I supposed to do with this?"

"Your magic weapon is good, and you should carry it," Faiq said. "The sword is for looks. You must wear it always, my master. No one of your class goes unarmed, except in the presence of the emperor."

"Thank you," Tejmur said, "for everything you have done. But what is all of this?" He pointed to several bolts of what looked like raw silk that were lying in a corner.

"I was hoping you would ask, my master." Faiq's face became animated, and he waved his arms about. "These are a portion, a very small portion, of the results of my second set of arrangements."

"What do you mean?" Tejmur felt suddenly wary despite the haze of wine that still clouded his perception.

"At one of the shops we visited this afternoon, I saw a man I knew. A man I did much business with, when I was a merchant in Baku. After talking with this man, both in the afternoon at his shop and this evening while the rest of you ate in the courtyard, I have concluded my second set of arrangements. This second set of arrangements will result in the vast increase of your wealth, my master. And a place for us all to live and sell our wares in Constantinople."

"What?" Tejmur asked, aghast. "What you have you done?"

"I have bought a shipload of raw silk." Faiq beamed, despite the look of horror that Tejmur could feel crease his own face.

"For what?" Tejmur asked. "What have you bought it for?"

"For transport to Constantinople. And for resale, of course. I was able to bargain for a most excellent price."

Feeling his legs suddenly unsteady underneath him, Tejmur sat on the bed. But when he saw Masud advancing on Faiq, sword in hand, Tejmur sprang to his feet again. "Masud, no!" he shouted. "Put that away."

Masud did not sheath the sword. But he stopped his advance and glared at Faiq. "What gives you the right to spend all of our money on a pile of colored cloth?"

"I did not spend all of our money. As I said before, I was able to bargain for an excellent price. And I was only following the instructions of my master, who put me in charge of all bargaining."

"I should take this sword you bought and run you through right—"

"Masud," Tejmur interrupted, "put the sword away. Now." To his great surprise, Tejmur found himself laughing. He sat back down on the edge of the bed. "Let's all have a seat and talk about this. Sit down, Masud. Faiq, take a seat on the rug."

"Yes, my master," Faiq said, and "Whatever you say," Masud said.

"It seems that Faiq has taken what I did indeed tell him about his power of bargaining earlier quite literally." The laughter that had quieted for a moment returned as a rueful chuckle. "You said that you got a good deal. How much gold and silver do we have left?"

"Not much," Faiq said. "Enough to pay for our stay here in Trebizond, to carry us through to Constantinople, and to allow us to set up shop."

"And the silk you bought, is this it?" Tejmur nodded at the bolts of cloth in the corner.

"Only a tiny portion, my master. Enough to show you that the silk is of the highest possible quality. The rest is at the warehouse of my friend Ahmad. The shipment will be loaded onto a cargo boat tomorrow morning for passage to Constantinople."

"So, you trust this man?" Tejmur asked. "Ahmad, you called him?"

"I know this man. As I said, I have done business with him in Baku."

"Is he honest?" Tejmur asked.

"He would cheat his own mother out of her last meal."

"And yet you gave him almost all of our money!" Masud broke in.

"It is better to do business with the thief that you know," Faiq said, "than with the merchant whose tactics are unfamiliar."

"Answer me this," Tejmur said. "Why should I not just demand my money back right now, and let someone else lug that load of silk across the Black Sea?"

"Because you are going to abandon me, my master," Faiq said, his voice matter-of-fact, but with a mournful edge that was unmistakable. "You have made that clear. And when you go, wherever it is that you are going, I will have nothing. You took my old life. You owe me a new life."

Tejmur sat quiet for a long moment.

"As much as I hate to admit it," Masud said, "Faiq has a point."

"Yes," Tejmur said, "yes he does. What do you propose, Faiq?"

"We will take the shipment of silk that I have purchased to Constantinople. We will set up a business there, buying raw silk from the merchant friend I have here in Trebizond, reselling most on the open market and tailoring the rest to suit the needs of the rich new merchant class that has taken control of Constantinople. This way, I have a new life, and you get your money back—plus a great deal of interest."

"But how will we get the silk to Constantinople? And how will we get there ourselves?" Tejmur asked.

"Why, in the only way possible," Faiq said. "Which brings me to my third set off arrangements. I have chartered a ship, a trading galley that flies the Venetian flag, bound for Constantinople. It's a fast boat with many oarsmen. This third set of arrangements will transport ourselves and our wares to the great city, and help us to set up our business there. The silk will be loaded in the morning. We board ship and depart for Constantinople tomorrow afternoon."

Tejmur sat for another long moment, too stunned to speak. Then another slow chuckle worked its way out of him, followed by a long bellylaugh. "Faiq," he said at last, "I like it. But I must talk this over with Papusza. If you will excuse me."

Tejmur walked out into the courtyard, grateful for the breath of cool air that came courtesy of the sea breeze he heard rustling through the trees. He heard Masud's soft footsteps behind him. The two men approached the fountain together, where they were greeted by a whistle from the table they had left earlier.

"Anchises returns in a more proper attire," Papusza said. "And who is this tall and handsome shepherd who walks beside him? Model for us, brave Trojans."

"At your service." Tejmur took off the felt hat with its interwoven gold threads, waved it as part of what he hoped was a fancy bow, and put the hat back on. "But, alas, we didn't come only to model."

"We came with news," Masud said. He took a seat at Norin's side.

"What news?" Papusza asked.

"In addition to the clothing we are all wearing," Tejmur said, "Faiq has purchased a shipload of silk with most of our remaining gold and silver."

"You're joking, of course," Papusza said.

"He is completely serious," Masud said. "As am I, as I try to decide whether to thank Faiq or to kill him."

"Nobody is going to kill Faiq," Tejmur said. "And it does sound as though thanks may be in order. Faiq insists that he has made a fantastic deal—a deal that includes passage for the silk and ourselves to Constantinople, and still leaves us resources enough to make the voyage in comfort and to get a business set up when we arrive. But I wanted to get your approval, Papusza, before I agreed."

Papusza stood a bit unsteadily—whether because of the wine or the weight of the news, Tejmur was unsure. But her beauty in the torchlit courtyard was perhaps the most certain thing Tejmur had ever known. "Why ask me?" she asked, her eyes rounded in surprise.

"For two reasons," Tejmur answered, "only one of which I'm prepared to state in the company of others. That reason is simply that the coins belong to all of us, not just to me alone."

"Very well then, I will reply to the first reason and save the second for a more appropriate time and place." Papusza smiled at Tejmur. "I believe that we should trust Faiq. The worst that can happen is that we lose our money. And with the time window, as has already been proved, we can always make more." She turned to Masud and Norin. "Besides, I am coming to believe more and more that it will not be only Faiq who will be starting a new life when we get to Constantinople."

"Then it is agreed," Tejmur said. "We leave tomorrow. But there is one other issue related to our departure that we should all decide on together: Alexis."

"What about him?" Masud asked. "It seems that he has disappeared."

"I have a feeling that he will be back in the morning," Tejmur said, "if not before then. And he has asked to accompany us on our voyage. This is not a decision that I am willing to make alone, as it will affect all of us. What do all of you think?"

"Alexis is most welcome," Papusza said without hesitation.

"I agree," Masud said. "Bring him along. If we ever see him again, that is."

"I agree with Masud," Norin said. "And I appreciate being asked. As with the jewelry and the touch of the finest silk, it is not something that I am used to."

"It is decided then," Tejmur said. "Four against one, Faiq having cast his no vote already. He has distrusted that boy from the first. If we see Alexis before we board the ship, he comes to Constantinople with us when we leave tomorrow."

Chapter 33

Tejmur tilted his fancy hat and looked at the play of afternoon sun on the Church of the Panaghia Chrysokephalos, knowing it was the last time he would enjoy the beauty of the city. He stood in a moment of indecision beside the shop where Norin and Papusza wanted to spend more time before boarding the galley for Constantinople.

"Masud and I should inspect the ship one more time," Tejmur said.

"We won't be long," Papusza said.

"I'll stay to bargain for them," Faiq said. He tapped the sword at his side and said with some swagger, "and to guard them from rogues."

"We have no need for guards," Papusza said, "not here in Trebizond."

"Spend little," Tejmur said. He drew Alexis aside and whispered, "Stand there, across the street and away from Faiq and the women. Report to me immediately if there is trouble of any sort."

Alexis had appeared again that morning outside the inn, hungry as ever. Once he had eaten his fill from the remains of the company's vast final breakfast at the Lion's Head Inn, Tejmur told Alexis of the decision that the boy could join the company on the trip to Constantinople. He was properly thankful—though Tejmur found it strange that Alexis wasn't visibly excited by the news.

But among the upscale shops of the middle town, in the afternoon sun, Alexis seemed much the same as he had on the day the company had ridden into Trebizond. "I will watch and report," Alexis said. "You can count on me."

"I should stay with the women," Masud said.

"No need." Tejmur gestured toward the gate to the lower part of the city. "I want you to assess the crew of the merchant galley. When I was on the ship this morning, I thought the crew too scant. And I worry about pirates."

After their short trip down to the harbor, the ship captain, who called himself Marco Bruto, assured Tejmur and Masud that he had "the best, most noble crew of oarsmen ever to ply the Black Sea."

"But I count only fifty men," Masud said. "Exactly as many as the number of oar ports. In a battle, we will be outmanned in the event the combat becomes hand-to-hand."

"I hire only the strongest men," Marco Bruto said, "the best oarsmen. There are no galley slaves on this ship. And all of these men are excellent archers in case we are attacked at sea. Any one of them could put an arrow through the eye of a seagull in flight."

Tejmur accepted Captain Bruto's reasoning, but he believed the captain worried more about saving money on wages than about hiring a crew of oarsmen and warriors large enough to fend off a serious attack by Black Sea pirates.

When he and Masud emerged from inspecting the small but comfortable berths below deck, Tejmur saw Papusza, Faiq, and Alexis on the wharf, coming toward the galley. But something was wrong.

Faiq stumbled and dragged his feet while Papusza held him up on one side and Alexis struggled with his other side. And where, Tejmur wondered, was Norin?

"Masud!" Tejmur called. "Come quickly."

"They cut him," Papusza called out. "He bleeds."

Masud and Tejmur carried Faiq across the gangplank and laid him on the deck of the merchant galley. Faiq's eyes rolled back, and he breathed in shallow gulps.

"He has lost a lot of blood," Tejmur said. "He's going into shock."

"Where is Norin?" Masud demanded.

"Taken." Papusza knelt beside Faiq and began loosening his clothing where he bled on both arms and the side of his chest.

"For ransom," Alexis said.

Masud pulled the Makarov from his belt. "Which way did they go?" he demanded.

"Toward the ships," Papusza said.

"They are pirates." Alexis pointed. "They are in that ship, there. The one that is casting off."

Tejmur, after looking at Faiq's wounds, glanced up and saw a ship some hundred meters away, its sails unfurling and oars frothing the sea. Many oars.

Masud ran down the pier and along the dock toward the departing ship.

"Captain Bruto," Tejmur said, "bring cloth for washing the wounds. And do you have any of the liquor the locals call Aqua Vitae?"

"Liquor?" the captain turned toward the door to the lower deck. "Of course, we carry a small stock for the journey. Why?"

"Let me worry about why. Just get a bottle up here," Tejmur said. "Hurry."

Masud ran out onto another pier and began firing the Makarov at the ship that held Norin. Tejmur saw the splashes of bullets hitting the water.

"It's no use!" Tejmur called.

Masud must have realized the futility of his actions, for he ran back to the pier where the merchant galley was docked.

"This is not a cheap way to get drunk." Captain Marco Bruto set a jug down next to Faiq. Beside it, he placed some rags.

Papusza picked up the jug, tilted it, and poured lavish amounts of the Aqua Vitae onto Faiq's arm and into the deep gash across his ribs.

"What a waste of my good liquor!" the captain sputtered. "Your man will never recover from a chest wound of that depth. If he does not bleed out, the wound will fester. Better to save the liquor for the captain's table."

"Faiq will live," Tejmur said, "if he hasn't lost too much blood."

Faiq grunted, and his eyes fluttered open. "Stings," he said. "Stings."

"The liquor has washed away the evils of your wounds," Tejmur said. "Don't move. I'll be right back." He went to his quarters below the raised afterdeck, found one of the tubes of Superglue they had brought back from twentieth-century Trabzon, and returned to the main deck just as Masud came puffing back on board.

"Push off!" Masud demanded of the captain. "Push off and catch that ship."

Captain Bruto looked at Masud as if he were a simpleton. "Look at that galley," the captain said. "There are twenty-five men at the oars on each side, the same as our ship. Now look how the galley scuds high in the water. That ship carries no cargo, while we waddle deep from a full load. Our oarsmen must work twice as hard to go half as fast. We will never catch them."

"We must," Masud said.

"We will," Tejmur said. "I promise you that. But not today. We'll find out where they are headed before we cast off. Right now, I must tend to Faiq."

"I know where they are going," Alexis said.

Startled, Tejmur turned to the boy. He had forgotten about Alexis. The boy leaned against the mast, his clothes bloody, his face animated, excited—much more so than when Tejmur told him he could go to Constantinople.

"Where?" Masud demanded. "Where are they taking Norin?"

"To Constantinople."

"Not . . . true," Faiq croaked through clenched teeth.

Tejmur turned back to the wounded man. "Listen to me," Tejmur said. "I have to seal these wounds, and I need you to cooperate. You must not move while I do this."

"Not move? With Papusza pouring . . . liquid fire into my cuts?" Faiq paused to breathe in shallow gasps, and then continued. "I doubt I can . . . be still. Did they tell you . . . that I killed four of the rogues? Four. Where is my sword?"

"How do you know they're going to Constantinople?" Masud took Alexis's arm and nearly lifted him from the deck.

"Easy on the boy," Tejmur warned.

"Are you going to sew up the wounds?" Papusza asked. "The cut on his rib cage is long and deep, and will be difficult to stitch—if not impossible. But we must try. Do you have thread and a needle?"

"One of the pirates told me," Alexis said. "He even told me where he would take Norin for the ransom. He said that I should tell you."

"There's too much going on," Tejmur said. "Captain Bruto, cast off and get us moving. Papusza, use those liquor-soaked rags to put direct pressure on that chest cut. Masud, let the boy go. He'll talk without your jerking his arm out of socket."

"That man, the one who took Norin," Alexis said, "is a pirate who calls himself Leo the Wild Isaurian."

"I know of him," Captain Bruto said. "He is a fierce and merciless pirate, and he sometimes takes rich people for ransom."

"Are you still here?" Tejmur said, a note of irritation in his voice. "I told you to cast off. We must get moving toward Constantinople."

"Now!" Masud barked, his voice a threat.

The captain shouted orders, and the ship began to move as Tejmur treated Faiq's wounds. The gash on the ribs was the first concern. As Papusza had said, it was deep.

"When I tell you," Tejmur said to Papusza, "pull the rags off the top half of the wound and press the lips of the cut together. Ready? Now." He squeezed a line of the Superglue deep into the cut and along the edges, working down the seam of the wound as Papusza pressed the lips of slashed flesh together. "Damn it, Faiq, don't move!" Tejmur barked, feeling Faiq start to squirm. Tejmur used his knees to keep Faiq still while the glue set. "Now we'll do the same with the bottom half of the wound. Ready? Now." Tejmur again squeezed the Superglue into the bottom of the cut and along the edges, as Papusza pressed the sides into a tight seam that the glue sealed.

"I never thought that a wound could be sealed in this way," Papusza said.

"It looks to be working perfectly," Tejmur said. "There is no leakage at all."

"It feels . . . strange," Faiq murmured. "Is it magic?"

"Of a sort," Tejmur said. Once Faiq's chest wound was sealed tight, Tejmur turned to the shallower cuts on Faiq's arm, dotting them with Superglue and pressing the lips of sliced flesh together. "Be still," Tejmur warned. "You will open the wounds again if you move, and you cannot afford to lose any more blood."

"Must I lie like this . . . for days?" Faiq's voice had become a querulous whine.

"You will be able to get up." Tejmur felt for tackiness on Faiq's skin. "Not yet. But soon."

"Four. Maybe five. I sliced them . . .with my sword and they lay . . . dead at my feet. Where is my sword?"

"Where is Faiq's sword?" Tejmur asked Papusza.

"But how did the pirate know that we were going to Constantinople?" Masud broke in.

"Half the city knows," Alexis said. "Your man there caused a big stir, throwing his gold around in every shop in the middle town. And such a large purchase of silk attracts attention."

"You say this man . . . the Wild Isaurian . . . talked to you?" Faiq said. "I don't believe it."

"Be still," Tejmur said.

"Did the pirate talk to Alexis?" Masud asked Papusza.

"I don't know. It all happened so fast—swords flashing, blood, Norin screaming. She kicked one of the men, I saw that, and he went down holding his knee. Maybe Alexis talked with one of the men, though I had no idea they were pirates."

"She kicked his kneecap," Masud said. "Yes!" Then he turned to Alexis. "Where will they meet us with Norin to make the exchange for the ransom?"

"On the steps of Hagia Sophia." Alexis looked pleased with himself.

Tejmur looked closely at the boy, and didn't much like what he saw. There was a cunning twinge to the boy's smile, a bit of triumph—of

164

superiority—in his brows and eyes that made him look older than his years.

Masud must have seen it, too. "You know something else," he said. "And you'd better tell it, and tell it now."

A look of false innocence and fake outrage crossed the boy's face. "But I know nothing."

"I'll throw you overboard, and let you swim back to the docks. If the sharks don't get you. Tell me the truth now, or you will never see Constantinople."

The shrewd look returned to the boy's face. "I know the ransom amount."

"And I'll bet you get a cut of it." Masud grabbed Alexis's arm again.

"Can I move now?" Faiq asked. "I'm feeling better, and I wish to laugh."

"Do not move. And don't laugh!" Tejmur said. "Laughing will jerk your sides, which is the worst kind of movement."

"What is this ransom that you claim to know?" Papusza asked.

"Tejmur must bring his hat full of gold coins. The big hat he wears now, the one you bought for him yesterday." Alexis looked pleased with himself.

"Impossible," Faiq said. "And now I no longer wish to laugh."

"There's something more," Masud said. "Something important about Norin that you're not telling." He grabbed Alexis, took two quick steps to the side of the ship, flipped the boy upside down, and dangled him by one leg over the rail. "Tejmur, may I drop him into the sea?"

"No," Papusza said.

"Yes," Tejmur said, "but only if he doesn't tell us all he knows. And, Papusza, Masud is right. The little scamp knows something. It's written all over his face."

"I will count to three, then into the drink you go," Masud said. "One, two—"

"The pirate's base," Alexis said, his voice shaking. "I know where to find the pirate's base."

"I don't believe him," Faiq said. "Toss him overboard like the garbage he is."

"I don't believe him, either," Tejmur said. "Alright, Masud, toss him—"

"Wait! On a hill," Alexis stammered. "On a hill at the mouth of the Bosporus. A treeless hill that overlooks the place where the Bosporous drinks the Black Sea. Please! I am telling the truth!"

"Maybe I do believe him," Tejmur said. "Back into the boat with him, Masud. For now."

Chapter 34

By the time their ship had cleared the harbor, the pirate galley was lost from sight. Tejmur stood on the raised foredeck of the Venetian trading galley that Faiq had chartered, staring ahead into the empty waves that seemed to stretch into infinity along the rocky gray Black Sea coast. Occasional gusts of wind kicked up spray that chilled his skin and then dried. The unfamiliar rise and fall of the prow churned his belly. Next to Tejmur, Masud leaned as far over the wooden railing as gravity and the bucking of the galley would allow, as though trying to push the ship ahead faster by force of will.

"I have failed her," Masud said through clenched teeth. "I should never have left Norin alone."

"No," Tejmur said. "It was I who failed Norin. You wanted to stay with her and Papusza. I was the one who decided that it was more important for you to inspect the ship and its crew than to protect our party. The blame is mine alone."

"Isn't there an easy way to get Norin back?" Masud asked. "With the window, I mean. Reset the timer so we can step back to the hour when the pirates attacked, and I will shoot every last mother's son of them."

"I would reset the window if I could," Tejmur said. "If you have come to know me at all, then you must believe that. But there are three problems. First, I can only reset the time window with the help of the master chronoton, which is in my lab in twentieth-century Baku. Second, even if we were in Baku, I could only tunnel through to a parallel hour—a moment in the past when the current of time has looped very close to the moment that we are in. The barrier between two such parallel hours is very thin, and little power is required to penetrate it. If I had infinite power, I could take us anywhere. But this is not the case. I found two such parallel hours back in my lab in Baku, and I set the time window to open onto them. The window is locked between the time we knew back in our own world and the year 1221, which is when we are now. Third, and perhaps most importantly, I don't know whether it's possible to undo something that has already been done. Our gift of flying fire to Genghis Khan is an example. The history books say that Genghis Khan discovered the technology for the fire that flies on the campaign during which he conquered Baku—the same campaign during which he met us."

"So what you're saying is that we made history even before we were born?"

"It certainly looks that way," Tejmur said. "But to paraphrase a great philosopher: the only thing I know for sure is that I don't know."

"Then we do what we must in the here and now," Masud said. "That boy had some role in this." His face darkened. "He has not told all he knows."

"Faiq was right about Alexis from the beginning. He warned us, and I failed to see the wisdom in his merchant's instincts. I have failed Norin, not once, but twice."

"Listen to me." Masud turned his gaze away from the empty horizon ahead of them and met Tejmur's eyes. "Neither of us has failed her yet. Not completely. I will get Norin back, or I will die trying. I will torture, kill, steal, lie. Anything, to get her back safely. For me, there is no middle way."

"I understand." Tejmur narrowed his eyes into Masud's earnest gaze, then looked away into the rolling waves. "And for myself, I am with you. But remember that I am also responsible for the safety of Papusza and Faiq, and for their continued well-being."

"What does that mean?"

"It means that we must be very careful not to let a desire for revenge dictate our strategy or our tactics. The aim is to get Norin back, safe and sound. And with as little human cost on our side as possible. It means that we'll have to use the resources which we do have wisely and well. It means that torturing and killing are less desirable than saving and surviving. Are we agreed?"

For a long time, Masud was silent. The only sound was the wind and the crash of the ship as the raised prow rose and fell in the waves.

"We are agreed," Masud said at last. "What do you have in mind?"

"Honestly?" Tejmur turned back to Masud, his lips clenched into a grim smile. "Nothing. At least, not yet. You and I will have to work together to maximize the resources we currently possess. And those resources are not inconsiderable."

Masud smiled grimly back at Tejmur, and patted the pistol at his waist. "Modern weapons are chief among them."

"True," Tejmur said, patting his own waist. "But as you discovered when the pirate galley pulled away from Trebizond, the power of your Makarov and our police pistols is limited. We must also employ our Medieval resources." Tejmur waved an arm at the galley upon whose raised foredeck they stood. "For example, this ship."

The galley stretched about thirty-five meters, Tejmur guessed, from stem to stern. Raised platforms dominated the fore and aft sections, and banks of oars—currently shipped—lined the port and starboard sides. The ship was about eight meters wide, with the metal outriggers for the oars making it seem wider. Eight or ten of the oarsmen, currently idled because of the shipped oars, scurried about the main deck and in the rigging. Since they had cleared the harbor and caught the sea breeze, the ship's progress had been maintained solely by the square sail rigged from the single mast amidships.

"But the captain said we could never run the pirates down," Masud said.

"True," Tejmur replied. "But we know where they are going. And when we get there, this ship—a combination merchant and war galley—will pack quite a punch."

"We're undermanned. When we reach the pirate stronghold, we'll be hopelessly outnumbered."

"A pitched battle won't save Norin anyway," Tejmur said. "A lightning raid by a small party will serve our purposes much better. And for such a raid, we'll need a diversion. And a way to discourage, or disable, pursuit."

"How can this undermanned ship, a ship without modern cannons, help with any of that?"

"By using this." Tejmur leaned out over the railing, and pointed down at a metal tube that projected beyond the hull, just beneath the spur of the raised foredeck.

"But what is it?" Masud asked. "It looks like a cannon. But cannons haven't been invented yet."

"Greek fire," Tejmur said. "A kind of Medieval napalm. The weapon is fired, I believe, by a pump that is housed directly beneath the platform on which we stand."

"A flamethrower?"

"Exactly. And in an age of wood, a flamethrower is the perfect tool for creating diversions, and for disabling pursuit."

"I see many possibilities." Masud's smile turned fierce, almost frightening. "And our lightning raid, as you called it?"

"For that, we will need more information," Tejmur said. "And as you have said, the boy has not told all he knows."

"Perhaps a little of this Greek fire could persuade him."

"I won't torture a child, Masud. Not even a child like Alexis."

"Then how—"

"We will bide our time, treat him well, and keep the fact that we know he has not been completely honest with us a secret. Good treatment and the prospect of a new life in Constantinople might be enough to induce him to tell us the rest."

"And if they are not?"

"Then we will see. Perhaps the threat of torture, combined with complete surprise, might be enough to get the truth out of him."

"Maybe," Masud said, all trace of a smile disappearing now from his face. "But if it is not, be aware that I will stop at nothing to save Norin. Nothing. Is that clear?"

"Why don't we save that question for the moment when it becomes necessary to ask?" Tejmur did his best to make his tone gentle, soothing—although in his heart, he was horrified. "Can we at least agree on that?"

"Agreed," Masud said. "For now."

"Excellent. Since now, I believe, it is dinnertime. And that will give us a chance to speak with the captain and his officers about the possibilities of Greek fire."

As Faiq had informed Tejmur prior to their departure, Tejmur's chartering of the galley afforded him and a guest the privilege of dining at the captain's table. Accordingly, when the dinner bell rang, Tejmur and Papusza were escorted by a crewman to the officers' table in a tiny cabin beneath the raised rear deck. Masud, Faiq, and Alexis ate with the crew.

Captain Marco Bruto and his first mate, introduced as Michelangelo Antonini, were the only other diners at the captain's table besides Tejmur and Papusza. The four were served by a cabin boy who looked to be about Alexis's age, with dark hair and eerie greenish-blue eyes that caught Papusza's attention.

"But what lovely eyes you have," she said, as the boy served them a delicious light red wine in heavy-bottomed bronze cups. "What is your name, boy with the lovely eyes?"

"Gino," the boy said, his sun-bronzed cheeks coloring until they were almost the same shade as the wine.

"Well, Gino," Pasusza said, "thank you for the wine."

"It pleases me to . . . to serve you," the boy stammered, "milady."

"You must forgive the boy's embarrassment," Captain Marco Bruto laughed. "He is not used to the presence of great ladies such as yourself aboard the *Santa Barbara*."

"Santa Barbara?" Papusza smiled at the boy, then looked at the captain. "Who is she?"

"This ship, lady, is the *Santa Barbara*," the captain said. "And a great lady she has proved to be for all who have journeyed in her."

"Santa Barbara," the first mate broke in, "is the patron saint of all those who work with fire, or who fear lightning and storms."

"How appropriate," Tejmur said, "for a ship such as this one, equipped with Greek fire."

"You saw the firing tube, then?" The captain narrowed his eyes at Tejmur.

"Of course. And a welcome sight it was for a man on a mission to raid a pirate stronghold and recover a lost member of his party."

"What do you know about Greek fire?" Captain Bruto asked.

"Only that you can fire a stream of burning liquid, at pressure, from the tube in the front of your ship. I have no more than a vague idea of its range, or its effectiveness against ground forces or structures."

"Its precise range, and the composition of the *liquid fire* as you call it, are secret. But I can tell you that its effectiveness against inland structures is virtually zero. It is designed for fighting against other ships. But I speak too freely, for even talking about the weapon is forbidden lest it fall into the wrong hands. I must ask you to speak no more to me of Greek fire."

"Perhaps we can talk about it only in general terms? I have an idea for its use with arrows—"

"You must give me your word that you will speak no more to me about the Greek fire."

"Not after tonight, but—"

"Your word. I must have it." The captain's voice took on a commanding tone. "Or I turn this ship around and drop you and your party back in Trebizond."

"Then I give my word. No more about Greek fire." Tejmur nodded. "So any attack on the pirate stronghold itself must be made by men on foot."

"By your men," the captain said. "Not mine. I will not risk my crew in such a ground attack. Not for any price. I have only enough men to operate my ship and protect her cargo. Any loss of life in such a raid would leave the *Santa Barbara* vulnerable."

"But what about—"

"Again, respectfully, I must repeat that a ground attack by my men is out of the question. I will not risk my ship to recover your lost woman." Here the captain glanced at Papusza. "I am sorry, lovely lady."

Gino returned bearing a tray of smoked and salted fish, and a bowl of the same tabouli dish that the party had eaten at The Lion's Head Inn. For a while, all activity centered on the food and the wine. Tejmur was surprisingly hungry, and the fish and tabouli were savory indeed. In addition to calming the fire of hunger in Tejmur's belly, the meal offered a welcome break in the conversation, which had grown too tense for Tejmur's comfort. He decided the best policy for enlisting Captain Bruto's aid was a waiting game—a game that could be much influenced by the charm of the lovely Papusza, who had obviously caught the captain's eye.

"I have a question for you," Papusza said to the captain at last. "One that does not involve your secret fire or raids on fortresses."

"It would be my pleasure to answer such a beautiful lady as yourself to the best of my poor ability," the captain said.

"I don't understand why they call this body of water the Black Sea. It is such a lovely blue. Tejmur here says the sea got its name because of a lack of oxygen that keeps bacteria from growing. I do not believe that he is correct."

"Bacteria?" the captain said. He looked to his first mate, who shrugged.

"Bacteria," Tejmur said, "are tiny creatures that live in the water, and in food."

"There are no such creatures in this food, I assure you," the captain answered.

"Of course," Tejmur said. "I meant no offense. The dinner was excellent. As is the wine."

"I agree," Papusza said. "Thank you very much, Captain Bruto, for the delicious meal and the fine company."

"It pleases me to serve you, milady. As for the name of this body of water, I have heard that the Black Sea is so named because of the intense fogs."

"Fogs? We have seen nothing but clear weather."

"I assure you, milady, thick banks of fog are most common on the Black Sea. They are a grave danger to navigation. When they develop over the water, they absorb all light, making the sea appear black. Hence the name, Black Sea."

"Thank you, Captain. I like your answer much better than the one I received from Tejmur."

"I am most happy to have pleased you," the captain said. "But I am afraid that Michelangelo and I have duties we must now attend to. I will have Gino escort you to your quarters. Until tomorrow, milady. Gino!"

The cabin boy led Tejmur and Papusza down a cramped passageway to a tiny cabin just a few feet away from the officers' mess. When the boy made as if to leave, Tejmur stopped him.

"Wait," Tejmur said. "These are the lady's quarters. Where is the cabin that has been assigned to my bodyguard and me?"

"I'm afraid I don't . . . well, understand, sir," Gino stammered. "Your bodyguard will sleep in the other guest cabin with the wounded man and the boy. This is the arrangement that the lady ordered."

"But what about . . ." Tejmur let the sentence trail off as he glanced inside the half-open cabin door and saw Papusza in the lantern light, unwrapping her silk tunica to reveal the silken curves of her skin. Beside the narrow bed, he saw the trunk containing his belongings sitting next to an intricately-worked trunk that must be Papusza's.

"Come inside," Papusza said in a low and sultry voice, "and shut the door behind you. There has been a change of plan."

Chapter 35

When he saw the treeless hill at the mouth of the Bosporus looming in the evening mist, Tejmur told Captain Marco Bruto to order silence among the crew—and to immediately reverse course. "Get the ship into that fogbank behind us as soon as possible."

The captain did as he ordered, then asked, "Why reverse our course?"

"When I attack Leo at his pirate base, I'd like it to be a surprise."

"As I have said before, I won't risk my men in such an enterprise."

"You won't have to. When I said that I plan to attack Leo, I meant just that. Only myself and my bodyguard Masud, and perhaps my man Faiq, will enter the pirate stronghold."

The captain took in this information with a quiet shake of his head.

Clearly, the man thought Tejmur was crazy. And maybe, Tejmur found himself thinking, maybe the captain is right.

"The ship is headed for the fogbank, as you requested," Captain Bruto said. "Is there anything else?"

"Have one of your men fetch Masud, Papusza, and Faiq. Have him bring them to the foredeck, once the boat has entered the fogbank. Have him bring along a lantern and some writing utensils," Tejmur said. "We have much planning to do. And Captain?"

"Yes?"

"I need you to be there, too."

Tejmur watched the fogbank as the boat headed silently toward it. The captain had been right about the Black Sea's fogs. The water did indeed turn black as the *Santa Barbara* slipped into the thick mist. It seemed as though the boat was standing still as the mist rippled around and across the ship. The only sound was the slip of the oars and the creak of the ship's timbers.

The trip along the coast of the Black Sea had been uneventful. When there was a fair wind, the ship proceeded under sail. When the sail went slack, the oarsmen took their benches—and the ship's progress slowed to a crawl. On the final day, this day, the winds had died again and huge banks of fog appeared. Captain Bruto had warned Tejmur that such fogs often crouched on the sea close to the Bosporus, and that the sea became still as wet glass.

The damp air chilled his skin as Tejmur stood at the rail and looked out into the fog. The time had come, he knew, to redeem the many mistakes he had made since falling into the past.

Among his many failures since fleeing the Soviet invasion of Baku, these few days—and nights—with Papusza gleamed in Tejmur's memory like the golden dome of the Church of the Panaghia Chrysokephalos in Trebizond. Tejmur regarded that first night aboard ship as a series of miracles, the first being his bravery in not running as soon as he looked through the cabin door to find her waiting for him. The next miracle was the night itself, the tenderness of it and the warmth of Papusza, and her passion. Finally there was the next morning, when he awoke feeling that the world was good; that Papusza, lying in his arms, was exactly where she should be; that he had done something huge, and hugely right. It was a conviction she somehow brought to him each night.

The days had been another matter. He watched the boat cut through the dark waters and worried about the fate of Norin, and his role in her being taken back in Trebizond. Had he left Masud there, the pirates would lie scattered in the street, cut down by pistol fire, and Norin would be safe. But that was only one mistake among many. He feared his gravest error had been letting Genghis Khan live when he had the Makarov in his hand and the power to put a bullet in the brain of the Medieval world's worst mass murderer. That is, if it was indeed possible to change the past.

Tejmur found his thoughts returning to that moment again and again: point-blank range, nine-millimeter pistol, one of the foulest mass murderers who had ever lived. Genghis Khan had killed ninety percent of the people he encountered in his raids around the Caspian. And then there were the millions of people who died in the loins of the dead: all the descendants of the murdered people who would never be born. Their shades almost seemed to be visible in the mist, and Tejmur told himself they were condemning him for letting the murderer live. Among those faces, Tejmur saw the two women in Baku that Genghis Khan had offered him in Rostam's gloomy tent—the woman with gray-blue eyes who mumbled a plea for help and the other woman, her sister. And Tejmur had refused the Khan's offer. If he had accepted, would they have lived?

Tejmur had tried pardoning himself for not accepting the gift of the women, and for not killing the killer, by telling himself that he didn't understand the nature of time, and that he might not have been able to change the past even if he had tried. But it was difficult for Tejmur to truly believe this. He remembered what Papusza had said, back in the desert, about Fate—that all lives were predestined to run their exact, preset courses. If this were true, it would imply the existence of some force that regulated the flow of time, and that controlled the course of events. Such a force might absolve him of guilt, but its existence would strip Tejmur of free will. And free will was a principle that Tejmur's engineer's mind was unable to let go of without proof. The time window was the perfect tool for obtaining such proof. And Tejmur promised himself that if they did indeed free Norin, and they reached Constantinople safely, he would find a way to prove—or disprove—whether it was possible to alter the course of history.

Time . . . Norin . . . the attack on the pirates. As Tejmur headed toward the conference he had called on the foredeck, all those elements swirled around in his mind like the fog around the *Santa Barbara*. They were going to have to come up with some kind of strategy that would get Norin out of the pirate stronghold—and Tejmur and Masud, and perhaps Faiq, along with her—and back to the ship, without getting everyone killed in the process. Right now, he had no time to brood on his guilt. Now was a time to make choices. He chose to love Papusza, and to accept her tenderness. As for the rest? He would have to make it up as he went. But his thoughts kept circling back to the time window. If they were going to succeed, they would have to do so through trickery of some kind. Brute force would not do.

Tejmur found Papusza, Masud, Faiq, and Captain Marco Bruto waiting on the raised foredeck, just as he had asked. A small lantern hung from the rigging, throwing a ring of light around them and on the campaign table that had been set up directly beneath the lantern.

"I need a plan for rescuing Norin," Tejmur said. "And I need your help making the plan." He sat down, cross legged, at the table and motioned for the others to join him.

"We must dock somewhere safe," Masud said, "and we need to do it tonight. That will be tricky since we don't know the shore, and the currents of the Bosporus will sweep our ship through the channel down to Constantinople."

"So we need someone who knows the waters," Tejmur said. "Captain?"

"The waters, yes," the captain said. "I know them. On the left at the mouth of the Bosporus, below the hill, there is a dock beside a small fishing village of maybe thirty people. Someone with wealth has built a small fortress above the fishermen's shacks, higher on the hill."

"It isn't a fisherman's village," Masud said. "It's a pirate village, and no doubt Leo the Wild Isaurian lives in the fortress. We need to know something about that fortress if we are going to have a chance to rescue Norin."

"I have never seen it except when passing," the captain said.

"I know someone who has seen it," Faiq said. "I'll be right back."

He returned dragging Alexis by the collar. "Master Tejmur," Alexis pleaded, "Make him leave me alone. He abuses me. He has never liked me."

"For good reason," Faiq said. "You must tell us what you know about the fortress of the pirate Leo."

"But I know nothing. I've never been there, never seen it."

"Masud," Tejmur said, "throw the rascal overboard."

"But he will drown this far out from shore!" Papusza said.

"That's the idea." Masud snapped up Alexis with ease and stepped to the railing where he dangled Alexis by both ankles over the dark water.

"I know some, I know some," Alexis wailed.

Masud let go of the boy's ankles, then snatched him out of the air as he fell. Tejmur heard the boy scream with real fear, and Papusza made as if to go to Alexis's rescue. But Tejmur held her back.

"Some about what?" Masud asked grimly.

"Some about the pirate's lair. I've heard tales. Some might be helpful to you. Please, master! Bring me back aboard, and I will tell you."

"Tell now," Masud said, "and I might bring you back on board, depending on the level of detail I hear in your story."

"Leo the Wild Isaurian built his lair in the shape of a caravanserai. It has a heavy oak door that opens onto a wide hallway that circles the building—between the outer walls and the inner rooms—and another hall that leads to a central courtyard. The outer walls are stone and brick without windows. But windows do open from the outer hallway to the courtyard."

"It would take a small army to penetrate it," Captain Bruto said. "And as I told you before, my men are not going ashore."

"The job I have for you and your men does not involve going ashore," Tejmur said to the captain. Then he walked over to the rail and looked down into Alexis's face. "And you know all of this how?"

"I've heard rumors only, master. I swear. I know nothing for certain about the pirate."

"Is there a guard posted outside the door?" Tejmur asked.

"No. Yes. I—"

"If one from the small village below knocks on the door," Masud interrupted, "will it open?"

"Yes. Maybe." Alexis squirmed.

"He's lying," Papusza said. "Although it breaks my heart to say so."

"Yes," Faiq said. "The door to a caravanserai always has a tiny window that the doorkeeper can open to see who knocks."

"Like the one where we stayed in Baku," Tejmur said.

"Precisely," Faiq said.

"Once we are inside, where do we go to find Leo?" Masud asked.

"I don't know exactly. I only know that Leo's rooms are in the very center, off the courtyard. I have heard that his rooms are full of treasures, that rich silks hang on the walls, and that Leo has a bed of oak with silk pillows, though his guards must sleep on straw spread on stone floors."

"Such detail," Faiq said.

"That's all I know," Alexis said. "And it is all rumor, reported to me by rogues and thieves who have worked with Leo the Wild Isaurian. Perhaps none of what I've said is true. Perhaps the king of pirates sleeps in a straw shack on the cold ground."

"Shall I toss him into the sea?" Masud asked.

"Not now." Tejmur turned to hide his relieved smile in the shadows. "Let him back aboard. And Alexis, go below."

After Alexis had left, Faiq laughed, clutched his ribs, and grunted. The captain chuckled, as did Papusza.

"No more," Tejmur said. "For now, no more laughter. We have grim business to plan. Tomorrow in the early and dark hours we will spill blood, and people will die. We will make our move upon the pirates shortly before dawn when people sleep best, and a dangerous raid it will be. But I believe, upon hearing of Leo's inner courtyard from Alexis, that I have hit upon a plan that should ensure little of the blood spilled will be ours."

"This heavy fog drifts toward the Bosporus," Captain Bruto said. "You will find it difficult to see anything even as the sun rises."

"Good," Tejmur said. "No one on shore will expect an attack to come out of a thick, dark fog."

Chapter 36

Masud slipped over the side into the shallow water near the shore and pulled the prow of the tiny wooden rowboat—piloted by the first mate of the *Santa Barbara*, Michelangelo Antonini—up onto the rocky beach. Tejmur and Faiq clambered out onto the slippery mix of rock and sand that was wet from the heavy fog, and Masud pushed the boat back into deeper water. In moments, the boat had disappeared into the darkness, leaving the three of them alone.

Tejmur followed Masud and relied on sound to guide him, for it was impossible to see much. The crunch of Masud's boots and the muffled stumbling of Faiq helped him focus each step toward the fishing village that served as a base for the pirate band of Leo the Wild Isaurian. For the first time Tejmur was grateful for Faiq's dislike of bathing. His smell, bad as it was, helped Tejmur know the direction to walk in, as did the slap of tiny waves onto the rocky beach and the occasional curse from Faiq when he stumbled over an uneven patch of ground. Would the pirates also smell Faiq? Tejmur wondered. It seemed unlikely, for they were a smelly group themselves.

Tejmur's awkwardness in the dark was made worse by the burden he carried: a loaded pistol, a sword, a dagger, and a bag full of supplies for the raid. Faiq and Masud carried only their weapons.

Masud moved in complete silence—a result of years of training for such raids as these, Tejmur guessed. He found himself envying Masud's silent and confident manner and his easy grace. Tejmur had neither of these things. Fear sat cold as a wave-washed rock in his belly, and his legs felt like soggy pieces of driftwood that had been washed up by the Black Sea. Although this was not Tejmur's first time to engage in a death struggle against other men, it was the first time he had ever sought out an enemy on an unfriendly shore, in such darkness and uncertainty, and with the fates of so many people depending on his ability to think quickly and accurately.

The raiding party crossed a low rise, and the faint glow of lanterns from the fishing village came into sight. Torches burned on poles set at regular intervals along the wooden docks, casting an eerie glow over low buildings bunched up against the docks on the landward side—and on the two wooden piers jutting out from the rocky coastline into the sea. A galley that Tejmur guessed was the one which had outdistanced them at Trebizond rode high in the water at the end of the closest pier. In the torchlight, two dark figures moved about on the docks. Despite the chill in the air, Tejmur felt himself start to sweat. Beside him, he could hear Faiq's rapid, shallow breathing. It sounded as though Faiq's belly carried the same rock of fear as Tejmur's.

"Tejmur, give me one of the rolls of duct tape." Masud's whisper was so close to Tejmur's ear that he could feel Masud's warm, even breathing. "Quickly."

Fumbling in the bag for a roll of the tape, Tejmur felt the time window's metal rods cold against his fingers, and he felt the bandages and the tube of Superglue. Then he located a roll of duct tape at the bottom of the bag and handed it to Masud.

"Good," Masud said. "You two stay here. Those guards are mine.

Do nothing. And say nothing, no matter what you see. I will wave one of those torches when I'm ready for you to come."

"What if the torch never waves?" Tejmur asked, wishing his own voice sounded as self-assured as Masud's.

"Then I will be dead, and Norin's rescue will fall solely upon you. We must not fail her again."

With that, Masud was gone. He seemed to vanish into the fog and the jagged shadows below the low rise where Tejmur and Faiq hunkered down. Tejmur strained his eyes, trying to make out a hint of movement that would mark Masud's passing—but there was nothing.

"I would not wish to be one of those guards," Faiq whispered.

"Shh!" Tejmur admonished, then added: "Neither would I."

Tejmur watched the two guards as they continued to make slow rounds around the docks. Every couple of rounds or so, each man walked out onto one of the piers; the two of them met again, after a couple of minutes, under one of the torches on the docks. Time seemed to draw out, and Tejmur found himself wondering if something might have happened to Masud. If Masud was dead, or captured, then the entire responsibility for the rescue mission would fall on Tejmur and Faiq. Tejmur felt the rock in his belly turn into a glob of ice. Without Masud, Tejmur doubted they were up to the challenge.

Then came a round where only one of the guards returned to the rendezvous point.

"Hah!" Faiq whispered fiercely. "Masud must have taken him—"

"Shh," Tejmur admonished Faiq again. But Faiq was right. Just as Tejmur interrupted Faiq, there came a flash of shadow, and the second guard disappeared from the torchlight.

Masud, Tejmur knew, had taken them both. But it was a long time before a lone dark figure appeared in the torchlight. He removed the torch from the pole above him, bobbed it once, and set it back. Then he disappeared again into the darkness.

"I would not wish to be one of those guards," Faiq whispered again.

This time, Tejmur did not quiet him. "I only hope . . ." Tejmur began, but let the sentence trail off. "Come on."

As he and Faiq hurried to the spot where they had last seen Masud, Tejmur found himself dreading what he would find there. Back on the galley, Masud had said he would stop at nothing to get Norin back. Tejmur understood what that meant—Masud's desire for vengeance was a part of the reason Tejmur had sent Masud to take out the guards. But Tejmur desired no such revenge for himself. He hoped that death for the guards had come quickly.

The docks at the edge of the torchlight were spattered with blood.

Long streaks of smeared blood told Tejmur that Masud had dragged both of the guards into a dark space between two dry-docked galleys, where the ships had been pulled up onto ramps parallel to the piers. As he and Faiq closed in on the spot where Masud knelt over one of the bodies, Tejmur heard the squelch of blood under his boots, and the air smelled like a slaughterhouse.

The dim flicker of torchlight turned the scene into a nightmare. Both dead men were naked, their hands and feet duct-taped. Both had been castrated, and their throats had been slit.

Masud rose quickly, turned, and looked hard at Tejmur. "I have information," Masud whispered. "Norin is being kept in the private chambers of the pirate Leo. And it appears that Alexis told the truth about the layout of the stronghold."

Tejmur felt his gorge rise, making it difficult to speak. Masud's face was streaked with blood, and yet his voice was calm: matter-of-fact.

"Masud," Tejmur blurted out, "these men have been tortured."

"Only one was tortured," Masud said. "The other has simply been mutilated. There is a difference." Then Masud continued in his matter-of-fact tone: "The first man did not wish to tell me what I needed to know. The second man saw what I did to the first, so he was much more cooperative. And now you must assemble the time window, Tejmur, while I dispose of this garbage. Move quickly. If our presence is discovered, Leo may move Norin—or worse."

It felt to Tejmur as though he stood outside himself, watching events unfold. He saw his hands open the bag, remove the time window, and begin its assembly. He saw Masud and Faiq drag the tortured and mutilated bodies of the guards deep beneath one of the dry-docked ships where darkness was total. While Tejmur squinted through the flickering torchlight of his here-and-now past and across nearly eight hundred years into the moonlight of what had once been the present moment, Masud and Faiq began stepping off the distance between the shoreline and the pirate fortress.

Through the time window, Tejmur saw the same hill that Masud and Faiq now walked slowly up. On the hill through the window, a full moon illuminated the barren hilltop. There was no sign of habitation, except for what appeared to be a highway guardrail that ran along the brow of the hill. Tejmur breathed a sigh of relief, and a strange, back-inside-himself sort of feeling rushed through him. He felt his brain reconnect with his hands and felt his thought process start to work again. They might, he told himself, actually have a chance to rescue Norin.

"There's more light on the other side of the window," Tejmur said to Masud, when Masud and Faiq came trotting back down the hill. "There's no fog, and the sky begins to streak from the coming sun."

"Excellent," Masud said. "Let's go."

"Masud, you hold up this corner of the window," Tejmur said. "Faiq, you go through first."

"What . . . what will I feel?" Faiq stammered. "When I step into the magic window, what will happen to me?"

"Nothing at all," Tejmur said. "It will be just like walking through a door, though your ears might feel a bit strange from a shift in air pressure. Faiq, you must trust me. We can't do this without you."

"Air pressure? I don't understand, but I do trust you." Faiq took a deep breath, and stepped through the window.

"Now you," Tejmur said, handing his bag of supplies to Masud. "But when you step through, move quickly to the side. I'll be right behind you."

Masud stepped through the window, with Tejmur right on his heels. As he passed through the frame, Tejmur caught hold of the handle and dragged the time window with him into the twentieth century—where he staggered over the cowering body of Faiq and fell in a heap.

"Damn it, Faiq," Tejmur sputtered, struggling to disentangle himself from the smelly merchant and gather the time window at the same time. "What's the matter with you?"

Faiq didn't answer. Instead, he lay on the ground and moaned.

"Faiq," Masud said. "Stop acting like a woman and get up."

"Ohh . . ." Faiq moaned. "My ears popped so loud. And I smell brimstone, and the moon suddenly drank up all the fog. Your cursed magic has carried us all into hell."

"The air pressure is only a slight bit different, and that's not brimstone," Tejmur said. "It's not even magic. It's technology. The fruits of science. There is a highway close by, and the city of Istanbul—which is called Constantinople in the time that we came from—lies very near here. Cities in this future time stink with many foul odors."

"Magic. Technology. What's the difference? Hell is hell."

"Tejmur's magic can carry us back again," Masud said. "But first, we must locate the heart of Leo's stronghold. The sooner we find it, the sooner you can get back to your proper time."

"So you can really get us back again?" Faiq asked in a quavering voice, sitting up at last.

"Of course," Tejmur said, and sighed. "I am a great magician, as you yourself have said. Now get up, and let's step off the distance from the shore to Leo's outer walls. It doesn't look as though the level of the land has changed much. We should be able to locate Leo's inner courtyard, just as we planned."

Masud walked to the waterline, then began taking quick, measured steps up the hill. Tejmur refolded the time window and put it back into the supply bag. Then he hauled Faiq to his feet and followed Masud to the top of the hill.

On the brow of the hill overlooking the Black Sea, a metal guardrail stretched into the distance as far as the eye could see. On the far side of the guardrail, asphalt glittered in the moonlight and the smell of tar rose into the air.

"What kind of magic is this?" Faiq asked. Instead of frightened, he seemed fascinated. "It looks like a pool of water, but it is shaped like a river."

"This is a modern highway," Tejmur answered. "And it is not made of water, it's made of stone and gravel and something called tar. In this place, wheeled carts are made of metal—like this railing—and they don't need horses or oxen to pull them. These carts run very fast, on highways like these."

"More magic." Faiq leaned over the guardrail to put a finger on the surface of the highway. Then he swept a hand along the smoothness of its surface. "Will we see one of these metal carts?"

"Let's hope not," Masud said. "It looks as though the heart of Leo's stronghold lies in the middle of this twentieth-century road."

"We should hurry, then. Where is the spot where the walls begin?" Tejmur asked.

Masud took five quick steps back from the guardrail. "Here," he said.

"Faiq," Tejmur said, "we're counting on you. We need your merchant's instincts, and your experience with caravanserais, to guide us to the place to set up the time window. Alexis said that the stronghold is laid out like a caravanserai. Based on your experience, how far will it be from the outer wall to the inner courtyard?"

The merchant stood beside Masud, then started taking quick, measured paces toward the road. He hesitated a moment at the guardrail, then stepped over and continued until he stood in the far lane of the highway, almost on the shoulder of the road.

"Here," Faiq said. "The courtyard would be here."

"Tejmur," Masud said, "open the window."

"I should look through the eyepiece first, and get the lay of the land. We don't know what we'll find on the other side. They may have raised or lowered the level of the ground to make this highway. And Faiq's instincts may be less than precise."

"And if a cargo truck comes along while you're fiddling around with the eyepiece? Or a police car? Or a group of tourists in search of a scenic overlook?"

"Point taken," Tejmur said. He stepped over the guardrail, crossed the highway, then opened his bag on the shoulder of the road and began to assemble the time window. As he powered up, Masud and Faiq gathered next to him, and they all looked back through into the past.

About half a meter below them, what could only be the inner courtyard of Leo's stronghold flickered in torchlight. Two men armed with swords tended a pair of horses. Stacked boxes and piled bags filled the corner of the courtyard that was visible behind the two men.

"Can they see or hear us?" Masud whispered into Tejmur's ear.

"As I've told you before, the window works in only one direction at a time."

"Perfect," Masud said. He pulled the policeman's pistol from his belt, checked to make sure it was properly loaded, then did the same thing with the Makarov. "Check your pistol," he said to Tejmur. "You're about to be using it. And you, Faiq, draw your sword."

"What do you plan to do?" Tejmur asked.

"Shoot those two guards down like the dogs they are, to begin with. If the pirates can't hear our gunshots, we can kill both guards and still maintain the element of surprise. As soon as those two men are down, we rush through the window just like we did on our way here."

"Will my ears explode with pain as they did the last time?" Faiq asked.

"You'll probably feel some discomfort," Tejmur said. "Just swallow hard as you go through."

"Your ears will be the least of your worries, Faiq," Masud said. Then he turned to Tejmur. "Too bad your window opens only to one spot in the future. If you could calibrate it to go anywhere, then we could have some real fun. We could save Norin from the pirates, escape to a later time, then tinker with the timing of the window by twenty minutes or so—enough to get us back to the pirates' time just before we wake them up with gunfire. That would be grand. We could listen to ourselves kill the rogues, and at the same time give ourselves a head start back to the boat."

"Masud," Tejmur said, "remember what I told you back on the *Santa Barbara*. We must not let a desire for revenge dictate our strategy or our tactics. The aim is to get Norin back safe and sound."

"You're right. Our purpose is to rescue Norin. But if a large number of pirates have to be killed in the process, it will make me very happy. When we make this jump, Faiq, you will go through the window like the angry lion who killed four pirates back in Trebizond—and not a frightened lamb. Those are the men who sliced you up and left you for dead. Remember that."

"What about me?" Tejmur asked.

"You and Faiq will hold the courtyard and reassemble the time window. You've got six shots in that pistol. Make them count. After that, you'll have to use your sword. Remember, though, that these men are trained swordsmen. Better to use the pistol as long as you can."

"And you?" Faiq asked. "What will you do?"

"If what Alexis said was true, Leo's private rooms will be just off the courtyard. I'll kill any guards that may be posted, gut Leo, and bring Norin back to the time window. We'll have to get back through the window in a hurry. Once the shooting starts, the courtyard will fill up with pirates very quickly. You've got to have the time window ready to go. Is everyone clear on his mission?"

"Clear," Tejmur said, and "Clear," Faiq said.

Masud nodded, raised the Makarov, and took aim through the window. "When the second man falls," he said, "we go through." Then he squeezed the trigger, and the Makarov spat fire into the night.

Chapter 37

Even as Tejmur saw the first man fall, the Makarov spat fire again. The second man jerked back and crumpled. Then Masud, Faiq, and Tejmur rushed through the time window and into the stronghold of Leo the Wild Isaurian.

Tejmur grabbed a corner of the frame and pulled the window through after him, managing somehow to keep his feet despite the half-meter drop and the wild careening of the horses that seemed to have gone mad at the sudden appearance of the raiding party. Masud was already sprinting across the courtyard. As Tejmur gathered the pieces of the time window back together, he saw Masud fling open the heavy wooden door that, according to the description of Alexis, opened onto the private chambers of Leo the Wild Isaurian. Masud held the Makarov in one hand and the policeman's pistol in the other as he burst into the corridor on the far side of the door. Tejmur saw Masud raise the Makarov, and heard two shots ring out. Then Masud disappeared down the corridor.

In the courtyard, the horses screamed and bucked their way toward the main gate that Alexis had said faced the docks. Tejmur knew that it was through this gateway that Leo's reinforcements would soon arrive. He did his best to ignore the horses, steeling himself against the noise and the mad plunging of the animals as he took one of the crates from the corner and carried it to the space just outside the corridor Masud had disappeared into. They needed a barricade that he and Faiq could shelter behind, and over which he could fire the pistol, while waiting for Masud's return. That is, Tejmur thought, if Masud somehow managed to kill the guards and Leo, rescue Norin, and get back to the courtyard in one piece.

"What happens if Masud doesn't come back?" Faiq asked, seeming to have read Tejmur's mind.

"He'll be back. Now help me with this. We need to stack these boxes and bags into a barrier thick enough to stop arrow fire. Move!"

More quickly than Tejmur thought possible, he and Faiq set up a wall of boxes and bags. The horses stopped their screaming and bucking, and pricked their ears up—their attention focused on something beyond the gate. Leo's reinforcements, Tejmur figured. It was only a matter of time before the courtyard would be full of pirates. He used the precious seconds to reassemble the time window, making sure that all was in order before the inevitable melee ensued.

Almost as soon as he had the time window reassembled, Tejmur heard heavy footsteps approaching the front gate. "Faiq," he whispered fiercely. "Hold this."

Faiq took hold of the time window's frame while Tejmur crouched behind the barricade, leveling the pistol at the entryway from which the pirates would emerge when they entered the courtyard.

Not more than a couple of seconds later, two men burst into the courtyard and charged the barricade, swords drawn. Tejmur aimed the pistol at the first man and squeezed the trigger. The pistol bucked, and the first man went down. Then Tejmur leveled the pistol at the other man and squeezed off another shot. The second man tumbled over headfirst and rolled, coming to rest not two feet away. The first man Tejmur had shot lay quiet, unmoving. Dead. But the second man curled into a ball and started to moan. Tejmur looked over the barricade at the wounded man, who had both hands locked across his midsection.

"You have pierced his stomach and intestines," Faiq said, laughing in a way that made Tejmur's belly churn. "He will die slowly, and with much agony."

Two more pirates burst into the courtyard, one with a drawn sword and one wielding a crossbow that he leveled at Tejmur.

Tejmur aimed and fired. The crossbowman went down. The other man kept coming, though, charging at the barricade and swinging his sword. Without pausing to think, Tejmur thrust the pistol into the man's face and fired, point-blank. Blood and brains exploded in the torchlight, and the man went down.

"Well done, Master!" Faiq shouted. "The whore's son never knew what hit him."

Instead of replying, Tejmur leaned over the barricade and vomited onto the cobblestones, the bile from his stomach mixing with the blood from the man he had just killed. The stench of blood and vomit filled the courtyard, and Tejmur's nausea seemed to fill his entire body. But despite the feeling in his belly and the taste in his mouth, some tiny corner of Tejmur's brain registered the fact that he had only two bullets left in the policeman's pistol. They were running out of time. That same corner of Tejmur's brain pondered the irony of the situation—running out of time while standing next to a device that could bridge centuries in the blink of an eye. The man who had made the greatest scientific discovery of the late twentieth century was about to die in a Medieval courtyard at the hands of pirates. He checked the window, flipped the switch on the black box, and looked through at the moonlit landscape half a meter higher than the ground on which he stood.

Footsteps pounding toward the front gate brought his whole focus back into the here and now. From the sound of it, there were many more than two pirates headed their way. Very many more. Tejmur took the deepest breath of his life, and leveled the pistol at the main gate.

Just then, Masud burst back into the courtyard. In his arms was a figure wrapped in a silken sheet that must be Norin.

"I've got her!" Masud shouted, heading toward the open time window without slowing down. "Let's go."

"Masud!" Tejmur somehow managed to shout back. "Jump up, up!" Then to Faiq: "Go, Faiq. And remember to jump as you go through."

Masud jumped through the time window with Norin in his arms. Tejmur caught hold of the handle on the frame, and Faiq leapt through the window in turn. Finally, Tejmur gathered himself, snatched up the supply bag, started through . . . and felt a heavy impact in his left shoulder.

Tejmur managed to drag the frame after him as he plunged upward and outward, and felt a wave of pain ripple down his left arm and through his whole body as he hit the ground. He rolled across the asphalt in the early light of dawn, his mind racing to take stock of the situation.

Masud stood on the shoulder of the road with Norin in his arms, shouting something at Faiq that Tejmur couldn't quite catch. Faiq knelt in the middle of the road, running his hands over the smooth asphalt. A wooden shaft fletched with what looked to Tejmur, strangely, like chicken feathers protruded from his own left shoulder.

"Faiq! Tejmur," Masud shouted. "Get the hell out of the road."

Tejmur became aware of a dazzling light that seemed to be getting brighter and brighter. A rushing noise growing into a roar accompanied the light. He saw Faiq stare into the dazzling glare, eyes wide with a mix of wonder and fear.

"Aiyee!" Tejmur heard a woman's horrified voice exclaim. "A demon."

"No," Faiq said, as wonder won out over fear on this face. "It is not a demon. It is a metal carriage that runs without horses. Is it not beautiful?"

Then Tejmur felt a strong hand haul him out of the road and saw Masud's other strong hand do the same to Faiq. The sound of a blasting horn was immediately followed by a roar and a rush of air, and they were all on the shoulder of the road watching the red taillights of what looked like a cargo truck fading into the distance.

"Ah, what could I sell such a metal beast for when we reach Constantinople?" Faiq's voice held a dreamy quality, as if he had seen a vision of heaven. "The rich Byzantines would pay almost anything . . ."

Suddenly, despite the pain in his shoulder and the realization that he and Faiq—after surviving a raid on a pirate stronghold—had very nearly been killed by a truck, Tejmur felt himself laugh. He had an image in his mind of Faiq on a vast car lot, vending high-dollar luxury vehicles to Byzantine nobles. Faiq, Tejmur realized, would build an empire if he could import cars from the future into the Byzantine past.

Masud, Tejmur saw, was not laughing. "Are you delirious?" Masud asked. "An arrow has pierced your shoulder. Perhaps it has sent you into a strange kind of shock."

"I'm not delirious." Tejmur felt the laugh slowly die out of him as the pain in his shoulder grew. "And I'm well aware that I have an arrow in my shoulder. Did the arrowhead go all the way through?"

"Yes," Masud said. "I'm going to break off the arrowhead, and remove the shaft. Do you hear me?"

"No," Tejmur said. The image of Faiq's Byzantine car lot was replaced suddenly by a picture of his own arrow-free shoulder spurting blood. "If you pull out the arrow now, I'll lose too much blood. We'll have to wait until we're back on the ship."

"I agree with Tejmur," Faiq said. "We must get to the ship as quickly as possible."

"What do you know about military tactics?" Masud growled at Faiq. "If I had not pulled you out of the road, you would be a hood ornament right now."

"If Tejmur and I had not held off those pirates," Faiq answered, "you and Norin would both be in Leo the pirate's hands."

At the mention of Norin, Tejmur glanced at her. She was sitting up now, still partially wrapped in the sheet with her bare breasts showing in the moonlight. There were bruises on her face, and one of her eyes was swollen almost shut. She stared blankly down the highway in the direction that the cargo truck had disappeared. He tried not to think of what Norin must have gone through, in the hands of the pirates.

"Faiq is right," Tejmur said. "Look at Norin, Masud. She is not in a good way. We have to get her back to the *Santa Barbara*. She needs calm and quiet."

Masud pulled the sheet back up around Norin's shoulders, then looked at Tejmur. "Very well. Let us—"

"Wait," Tejmur interrupted, as a terrible thought struck him. "What about the time window? Where is it?"

"The truck did not hit it. The window is here, lying next to you, on the side of the road."

The wave of relief that swept over Tejmur was so intense that for a long moment it drowned out the pain from his shoulder. "Faiq," he said, "gather up all of the metal pieces on the highway and put them into my bag. Masud, gather up Norin. Let's go."

They made their halting way back to the seaside, with Faiq supporting Tejmur and Masud carrying the seemingly catatonic Norin. When they reached the beach, Masud set Norin down gently and Tejmur talked him through setting up the time window. Then Tejmur hit the power. The darker, earlier morning of the pirate docks on the Medieval shoreline winked into view through the metal frame.

"Masud," Tejmur said, taking hold of the handle attached to the frame, "you carry Norin. Faiq, carry the bag. I'll come through last, and haul the time window through after me. Go!"

Tejmur watched the rest of the party step back through window. Then he lunged after them, dragging the window with him into the past. As he twisted his shoulder to pull the window through, the pain that shot through his body was unbelievable—worse than anything he had felt in his life—and he saw the world go white, then black, as pain filled his consciousness. He reached deep into himself, tapping into a well of strength and resolve that he hadn't been sure until that moment was even there . . . and the world blinked back into focus.

The *Santa Barbara* rode low in the water at the end of the nearest pier. The pirate galley on the far pier was in flames, and the far pier with it. Tejmur heard shouts from the *Santa Barbara*, and shouts coming from the direction of the pirate stronghold. For a long moment, everything was confusion. Then he remembered that Captain Bruto had been instructed to set the pirate ship afire when he heard false claps of thunder—the sound they had heard when Masud chased after the pirate galley leaving Trebizond. It was clear that Captain Bruto had done his job well.

Flames leaped into the sky, lighting the docks and the hillside between Leo's fortress and the waiting *Santa Barbara*. Tejmur knew that the pirates must have seen the flames. It would be only moments before Leo's men, who had been drawn to the stronghold by the sound of gunfire, overran the docks. And yet, Tejmur could not seem to find it in himself to move.

"Gather up the time window and get aboard the ship!" Masud shouted, breaking Tejmur's reverie. "Tejmur, can you carry the bag?"

"I think so."

"Good. Faiq, take Norin. Get aboard."

Tejmur's left shoulder was numb now, as were his left arm and hand. With his right hand, he frantically recovered the pieces of the time window and stuffed them into the bag. Faiq gathered Norin into his arms. In the eerie glow of the flames, Tejmur saw a gangplank being lowered onto the near pier.

"Go now!" Masud shouted. "Onto the ship, all of you." He knelt, raised the Makarov, and began firing into the mass of pirates that was charging now down the hill.

Fire spat twice from the mouth of the Makarov, and Tejmur saw two of the frontrunners go down. The rest of the pirates slowed, then scattered—except for one man with an upturned beard who kept coming on, shouting at the others to follow him. The Makarov spat fire again, and the pirate with the upturned beard went down.

"Damn it, Tejmur," Masud shouted, turning to face Tejmur for a moment. "Go!"

"You come, too."

The pirate with the upturned beard was back on his feet now, limping toward the shelter of the dry-docked galleys and shouting at the rest of the men.

"That man with the upturned beard is Leo," Masud said. "He managed to escape me in the fortress. But I won't leave this dock until he is dead."

About a dozen men emerged from behind the dry-docked galleys—spurred on, no doubt, by Leo the Wild Isaurian—and charged headlong at Masud and Tejmur. As Masud leveled the Makarov, there came a high, whistling moan and a volley of arrows from seaward whined overhead and plunged into the charging pirates. A few of them fell. The rest ducked back into the cover of the dry-docked ships. But they were much closer now.

"Their next charge will reach us," Masud said calmly. "Then the fighting will be hand-to-hand."

"Masud," Tejmur said. "Norin needs you. Perhaps more than anyone has ever needed you in your entire life. Vengeance or Norin,"

Temjur said, surprised to hear his voice sound as calm as Masud's. "The choice is yours. But you must choose now."

Masud hesitated for what seemed to Tejmur like an eternity. Then he caught Tejmur's good arm, and the two of them made their way toward the gangplank.

At the end of the pier, strong hands pulled Tejmur and Masud onto the deck of the galley. As the gangplank was hauled back aboard, Tejmur heard Captain Bruto yelling for the oarsmen to get back onto their benches and row for their lives.

The deck cleared of everyone but the raiding party and the stricken-faced Papusza—who stood next to Tejmur and stared at the arrow protruding from his shoulder, her face a mix of sympathy and horror. She seemed to be trying to speak.

"I'll be all right," Tejmur said, meeting her eyes and trying to sound more sure than he felt. "We'll get the arrow out once we're clear." He reached his good arm in her direction, and Papusza folded her body against his, bearing him gently to the deck.

"What on earth am I going to do with you?" she choked out. "And what on earth would I do without you?"

Tejmur's only answer was to catch hold of Papusza's hand with his good hand, and squeeze. He felt her return the pressure—and knew for the first time that everything really was going to be all right. Then he looked up to see the first mate, Michelangelo Antonini, standing over him and Papusza. Beside the first mate, Alexis slouched like a convicted criminal. His hands were bound behind his back.

"The oarsmen caught him trying to escape," Michelangelo said, answering Tejmur's unspoken question.

"Damn."

"This boy has broken my heart," Papusza whispered. "I don't know what to do with him anymore."

"I know what to do with him," Faiq barked from his place at the railing. "Give him to me."

"What do you have in mind?" Tejmur asked.

"An appropriate punishment for a master thief and traitor, who traded on our friendship and trust."

"As I said before, I'll not stand for the torture of a child," Tejmur said.

"Do not worry, master," Faiq said. "What I have in mind will not harm the boy permanently. In fact, it might even do him some good."

"You won't tell me what it is?" Tejmur asked.

"I prefer to make it a surprise," Faiq said with a sly grin. "Both for you, and for the boy."

"Very well. As long as you do not to beat him, or harm him in any permanent way."

While they talked, the *Santa Barbara* made its slow way out into open water. Then the ship finally began to pick up speed—pulled by the oarsmen, Tejmur knew, into the current of the Bosporus. Behind them, the glow from the burning pirate galley was slowly fading into the early morning twilight. Masud sat at the railing, holding Norin on his lap. Papusza sat holding Tejmur's good hand.

Faiq stood beside Alexis, chuckling ominously to himself. "It looks like we're safe," Faiq said to the scowling boy. "Too bad for you."

"We aren't out of danger yet." Michelangelo stared behind them into the fading glow of the fire. "You are forgetting those other two boats dry-docked on logs in the pirate village. They will quickly be rolled into the water and launched. And Leo the Wild Isaurian still lives."

Chapter 38

As the sun emerged from a heavy cloud over the Black Sea, Tejmur glanced at the banks of the Bosporus and marveled at how they seemed to fly by. But he gave most of his attention to Papusza and her tending of his wound. She removed the arrow with a skill he didn't know she possessed.

"It missed the artery." She pulled the now-featherless shaft all the way through his shoulder. "Your muscles will pain you much, but you will heal. You must. That's a formal command, Tejmur, and a statement of faith in my ability to keep the wound clean."

"Norin," Tejmur said, his breath coming in shallow gulps from the pain. "Where is Norin?"

"Below deck," Masud said.

Captain Bruto knelt beside Tejmur. "The pirates," he said in a grim tone, "are gaining on us. They have more oarsmen, and they carry no cargo."

"They launched their ships from dry dock so quickly?" Tejmur marveled.

"They are pirates. They always keep their boats a finger's width from the water. One of them will soon pull beside us, and they will attempt to board."

"Masud," Tejmur said, "Faiq. Lift me to the side of the ship. I will use one of the pistols. Captain, I know a way to make fire fly on the backs of arrows. Tell men to bring a bolt of the silk from below so we can shred it for the weapons."

"No," Papusza said. "You will remain where you are while I dress your wound."

"Shred silk," Faiq wailed. "Shred? Shred?"

"Tejmur is delirious," Captain Bruto said to Masud. "We cannot fight pirates with strips of silk and mythical arrows flying with fire. I must prepare the ship, for the vessels of the Wild Isaurian will soon seek to draw alongside us."

Tejmur struggled to sit up, and Papusza pushed him back down with little effort. "Your archers," Tejmur gasped. "They can drop fire all over the pirate ships. A little silk, torn into stips and wrapped around the arrows, then dipped into your vat of fluid for Greek fire—"

"Restrain him," Captain Bruto snapped to Papusza. "Tejmur, friend, you will not speak thus." The captain leaned close and growled in an angry voice, "You promised not to speak of the . . . the special fire."

"Cooking fat, then." Tejmur tried again to sit up, but he knew he lacked the strength. "Cooking fat, arrows, and silk can stop the pirates . . ." Tejmur heard his own voice trail off as he realized how like a madman he must sound to the captain.

"The pirates' arrows will soon come," Faiq said. "We must take you below deck, master."

"No. I forbid it. I must stay on the deck. My pistol, Papusza, where is my pistol?"

"I have it," Masud said. "And I'll use it, though my guess is that the captain knows what he is doing in his preparations to meet the pirate ship. The arrows of his crew saved our lives, remember, as we boarded back at the pirates' den. We shouldn't underestimate the power of their primitive weapons."

"If you stay where you are when the arrows come," Faiq said, "Papusza will have many more to pull from your body."

"There." Masud pointed to the port side of the ship. "The pirates will attack us from that side. We will drag him there, below the shields of the oarsmen. That will almost be safe."

"Almost safe?" Papusza said. "That isn't good enough."

"Perhaps almost safe is as good as anyone ever gets in this dangerous past," Tejmur said.

"Or in the dangerous future," Masud said. "Or anytime in the war-torn world of human beings."

Tejmur could see, but not well, between the shields of the two oarsmen beside him. The eastern shore of the Bosporus, so crowded with buildings in his own time, was just barren rocks. The wide channel washed between the port side of the *Santa Barbara* and the shore, for

Captain Bruto kept the starboard side of the boat close to the other shoreline so the two pirate ships couldn't attack from both sides at once.

Before Tejmur saw the ship, he heard the shouts from its crew.

"They taunt us," Faiq said.

"They want to terrorize us," Tejmur said. "But this crew will not be easily frightened."

As the pirates came closer, their boat driven by superior numbers of oarsmen, Tejmur could smell them. The east wind washed the rank odors of the ship and its pirate crew across the deck of the *Santa Barbara*. The air stank of unwashed bodies, rancid oil, garlic, and dirty hair.

"Phew," Papusza said. "They'll gag us to death with the stench of their filth."

"Stench?" Faiq looked puzzled.

"Arrows!" shouted one of the oarsmen near Tejmur. The men on the left side of the ship hunkered closer to their wall of shields while the men on the other side made a great banging sound as they swung their shields around. The arrows clattered onto the deck, some falling close to Tejmur's feet.

The oarsmen answered with a volley of their own arrows. Tejmur hoped some of them had found their targets on the pirate ship, though he heard no sounds of pain—only the continued taunting of the pirate crew that had now become a terrible song:

We will disembowel you,
We will slit your throats,
We will have your tongues for lunch,
We will chop off your genitals,
We will turn the sea red with your blood,
We will drape our whores in your clothing.

"Masud," Tejmur said, "do you see anyone with an upturned beard? If you do, shoot him."

"Leo must be on the other ship. But I might be able to nail a couple of those who think their shields make them safe."

"Do it."

"This," Masud said to the oarsman beside him, "will sound like thunder, and fire will spit from the end of my weapon. But it will not harm you."

The oarsman kept rowing, though he leaned aside while Masud aimed through the small space between two of the round wooden shields that lined the railing. The Makarov barked, and a man on the other ship cried out in surprise and pain.

"We should have stockpiled arrows dipped in cooking fat," Tejmur said. "It would be so easy to burn that ship with flying fire."

At a command from the captain, all of the oarsman ceased rowing and dug their oars into the water. The pirate ship shot past. When it was a few yards ahead of them, the men on the starboard side of the *Santa Barbara* pulled hard so the bow of the ship came close to the rear of the pirate ship.

At another command from the captain, fire belched from the *Santa Barbara*, engulfing the entire stern of the pirate ship. The oarsmen on the *Santa Barbara* shouted and set their oars aside. Then they stood and began raining arrows onto the pirates, who ran about the deck of their ship in confusion.

Tejmur winced in surprise at the intensity of the heat. Soon many of the pirate crew were leaping overboard, their clothes ablaze. Others, struck by the arrows from the *Santa Barbara*, crumpled to the deck of the pirate ship to be consumed in flame.

"Napalm," Masud said in awe.

"Something very like it," Tejmur said. "Greek fire. The pirates are doomed."

It surprised Tejmur that the flammable material in Greek fire burned with such furious intensity. Globs of the stuff skittered in blue-white flame across the surface of the Bosporus, though most of it clung in burning masses to the pirate ship.

Some of the *Santa Barbara*'s oarsmen returned to rowing while the others crowded the railing, shooting arrows at the men who had abandoned the pirate ship and were swimming for the *Santa Barbara*. Tejmur could hear the fear and the agony of the men in the water as arrows found them, and he recoiled at the smell of charred hair and burning flesh.

"This is all so brutal," Papusza said.

Faiq clapped his hands, grinning fiercely. "Yes," he said. "Yes."

"Brutality is the nature of battle," Masud said "no matter what the time in which it occurs. It is the great shame of our kind that we take such delight in it. But I must admit that I myself have never felt so alive as in those moments when blood was being spilled and death was nearest."

The burning ship spun around and around now, a flaming mass caught in the current and out of control. Corpses bobbed in the water around the stricken ship, some still on fire and others completely blackened.

"I see Leo the Wild Isaurian!" Masud shouted, suddenly excited. "He is turning his ship around."

"The man isn't completely stupid," Tejmur said.

"But look," Masud said. "Leo's men are casting anchors. That makes no sense."

"Yes, it does," Tejmur said. "He's not casting those anchors to the bottom. He's using them to run against the surface current, back to his lair on the Black Sea. I'll explain later."

Tejmur had read about the twin currents on the Bosporus. The current on the surface always ran from the Black Sea to the Sea of Marmara on the Mediterranean. It was a fairly warm current. But some twenty meters down another current, a cold and strong one, ran the other direction. Ancient mariners had learned they could lower anchors into that current, and it would drag their boats toward the Black Sea.

"The pirate runs in defeat," Faiq said. "But I fear we have not seen the last of him."

"But we have," Tejmur said. "At least, for today."

"And what if we must return to the Black Sea in a quest for more silk?"

"That could be a problem," Tejmur admitted. "But for now, we go to the fabulous city of Constantinople. Indeed, we are almost there. It will not be long before we sail into the Golden Horn."

Chapter 39

As the massive walls of Constantinople came into view on the western shore of the Bosporus, Tejmur almost forgot the pain in his shoulder. They had come so far, and seen so much death and suffering. But the sight of Constantinople raised his spirits, and his hopes that everything might work out after all. He stared in awe from the chair Captain Bruto had provided for him on the forecastle.

"Istanbul." Papusza squeezed his hand. "Always the magic city for me."

"Yes," Tejmur said. "Byzantium and Constantinople and Istanbul. A magical place for so many centuries. Look! Do you see it? There in the distance, the Hagia Sophia, for a thousand years the largest building in the world, and the most magnificent."

The vast golden dome of the cathedral gave back the morning light with a shimmer of brilliance that reminded Tejmur of the Church of the Panaghia Chrysokephalos, though the Hagia Sophia stood taller and more glorious.

"Such beauty," Papusza whispered. "Tejmur, you have kept your promise."

It seemed impossible, but it was true. "The beauty of the city is as nothing compared to the beauty of the woman beside me," Tejmur said, taking Papusza's hand with his good right hand. "And keeping the promise I made to you was the wisest and best thing I've ever done."

Papusza's eyes shone into Tejmur's like the dome of the Hagia Sophia in the strong morning light. "I never wish to return to Baku with its drab Soviet-era buildings that look as if they have been dipped in acid and spattered with filth," she said. "I wish to make my life here, in this city and in this time, with you."

"I will make my home anywhere, and anywhen," Tejmur answered, "as long as you are there and then."

Masud stood beside Norin, who looked gaunt and drawn. Her face was bruised, her left eye swollen almost shut, her skin an unhealthy white. But even Norin smiled at the sight of the city.

"We will make our home here also, Masud," she said softly, "you and I."

"Yes," he said in a tone that suggested to Tejmur a finality, an affirmation that he knew he would make Constantinople his home.

"You could return to the Istanbul of the future, Masud, and live like a king with such gold as Faiq's merchant instincts will soon make for us in this rich past."

"They would hunt me down. The Turks, for what we did in Trabzon. And the Russians also, for deserting Gorby's army. So no to Istanbul and yes to Constantinople and to Norin."

"Master," Faiq said, "I think that the time has come for me to punish that master thief and traitor who so cleverly disguised himself as a boy and a friend. I fear he will sneak ashore in Constantinople, where he will flourish in thievery and villainy."

"Bring Alexis to me, then, and tell us your idea of punishment." Tejmur had no intention of letting Faiq torture the boy, though it was certain Alexis deserved some sort of redress for his actions.

By the time Faiq returned with the boy, the *Santa Barbara* had reached the edge of the city's wall along the west side of the Bosporus, and the lesser part of the city that lay on the eastern bank loomed near. Captain Bruto approached with two oarsmen beside him. The oarsmen carried a short, thick log.

"What is this?" Tejmur asked Captain Bruto.

"Faiq wanted something that this rascal Alexis could use to stay afloat during the final part of his journey. I'm providing wood that would otherwise be used by our cook."

"So, Faiq," Tejmur said, "you plan to toss the thieving boy into the Bosporus?"

Alexis yelped. He tried to squirm away, but Faiq held the boy's arm in a firm grip.

"He will drown me, master," the boy said. "Please do not let him."

"No one will drown you," Tejmur said. "Faiq, is that your punishment? To set the boy adrift with only a log to cling to?"

"Yes. But there is more. Boy, remove your trousers."

"You plan to make the boy a castrato, then?" Captain Bruto said, seeming to take a much greater interest in the proceedings. "Castrati are highly prized in the great city. If the boy can sing, he will fetch a high price. Sell him to me instead. It seems a waste to cast him overboard."

"I will not remove my trousers," Alexis said.

"Yes, you will." The captain pulled a sword from the scabbard at his waist. "The pants." He held the sword's point beneath the boy's nose. "If you try to run, you will do so without one of your ears."

"There's no place to run," Alexis said. He jerked his arm away from Faiq and pulled off his trousers. "You're going to mutilate me with that sword. But you might as well kill me, for I will come back when I am a man. And I will kill you, and kill your wife, and kill all your children."

"I have no plans to castrate you," Faiq said, "although such a punishment would fit your crimes. Hold out your hand."

Alexis looked at the captain's sword, then held out his hand.

"Smart to the last," Faiq said. "Holding out your left hand. Smart. But not smart enough." Faiq held a tube over the boy's hand and squirted something into it.

"What's that?" Papusza asked.

Tejmur stifled a laugh and whispered, "Superglue. Faiq watched me stitch his sword wounds with it."

"Quick," Faiq said, "grab your balls and hold on."

Alexis did as he was told. "When can I let go?" he asked.

"Never. Your dirty thieving hand is now married to the nastiest part of you."

"Witchcraft," the boy said, and for a moment he looked terrified as he tried to release himself.

"Why did you do that?" Papusza asked Faiq.

"So if he makes it to Constantinople, people will see what a nasty boy he is and not fall victim to his schemes. Instead, everyone will laugh. I did it to protect the innocent of the city and to punish this rogue. What better punishment is there than laughter?"

"Lower him overboard," Captain Bruto told the oarsman beside him. "Give him the log to cling to, so he has a chance to live. Boy, count yourself lucky. You have one free hand to cling to a float, so you will not die today."

"My pants," Alexis said.

"No," Faiq said, and "Yes!" Papusza said.

"Let him have the trousers," Tejmur said. "It is enough to cast him into the Bosporus with his hand glued to his private parts."

Alexis struggled into his trousers. "I'll live today. And tomorrow I'll find a powerful witch to remove the spell, and I will one day make all of you sorry. All of you."

The fierceness on the boy's face sent a shiver up Tejmur's back.

As the boy, clinging to the small log, floated away from the boat, Papusza said, "He is a brutal, feral child. But we should have offered him kindness, not more brutality. All we did was show him that we, too, are brutes. Perhaps with kindness we could have helped him to change his ways."

"Only death will change his ways," Faiq said.

"Enough of the treacherous boy," Tejmur said. "We have the entire city of Constantinople before us, and a new life to begin. The beauty and the glory of this place will surely give us a grand adventure."

"Where do we dock?" Masud asked the captain.

"Close to the Hagia Sophia, along the wall just before we get to the Sea of Marmara. The city keeps a heavy chain in the waters to prevent raiders from entering the Bosporus. My guess is that the chain is in place today, and high. So we must dock before we get there, on the top edge of the Golden Horn."

"The largest marketplace in the world is there," Faiq said, his voice trembling with excitement. "It lies just above the city wall where we will dock. With our load of silk, and my merchant's heart, we will soon be rich beyond our wildest dreams. Think of it, my master!"

"Lodging first," Papusza said to Faiq, "riches later. We must keep Tejmur still while his shoulder mends." She turned back to Tejmur. "We will explore the city together, Tejmur, once you have healed. Promise that you will allow me to nurse you until your wound has healed completely, and that we will seek lodging and rest before anything else."

"I promise. While I recover, Faiq and the rest of you can explore the city. But only with armed guards. Lodging first, armed guards second, riches third. Perhaps Captain Bruto can help us locate guards that we can trust."

"Of course," the captain said. "I will introduce you to a man who can help you, both with lodging and with a suitable escort."

As the *Santa Barbara* nosed into the dock beneath the great walls, Tejmur suddenly felt tired. *Lodging* and *rest* were indeed fine words, he thought. Especially at the beginning of a new life in the most beautiful city of Medieval Europe, with Papusza. It would be a happy life, he promised himself. A loving and peaceful life—much better than the cold, gray, and windy Baku of the twentieth century.

Tejmur climbed the steps to the dock where Papusza turned to him, her eyes shining with joy to be standing beside him there beneath the magnificent dome of Saint Sophia's Cathedral. As he held Papusza in a brief embrace, he glanced back at the *Santa Barbara* with its rows of shields lining the sides above the oar locks.

Then he turned to enter the city with Papusza at his side.

Medieval Trebizond on the south shore of the Black Sea, important in the silk trade